C000184049

Lorna Cook is the author of

Forgotten Village. It was her debut novel and the recipient of the Romantic Novelists' Association Joan Hessayon Award for New Writers as well as the winner of the Katie Fforde Debut Romantic Novel of the Year Award. Lorna lives in coastal South East England with her husband and two daughters.

Also by Lorna Cook

The Forgotten Village
The Forbidden Promise
The Girl from the Island
The Dressmaker's Secret
The Hidden Letters

The
Lost
Memories

LORNA COOK

avon.

Published by AVON
A division of HarperCollins*Publishers*
1 London Bridge Street
London SE1 9GF

www.harpercollins.co.uk

HarperCollins*Publishers*
Macken House
39/40 Mayor Street Upper
Dublin 1
D01 C9W8
Ireland

A Paperback Original 2024

1

First published in Great Britain by HarperCollins*Publishers* 2024

Typeset in Sabon LT Std by Palimpsest Book Production Limited,
Falkirk, Stirlingshire

Printed and bound in the UK using 100% Renewable Electricity
by CPI Group (UK) Ltd

This book contains FSC™ certified paper and other controlled
sources to ensure responsible forest management.

For more information visit: www.harpercollins.co.uk/green

For my dad.
Because you're the best dad a girl could ever
wish for and I'm so lucky to have you.

CHAPTER 1

Suffolk, England
Summer, 1944

Panic rose. The worry, pilling up over the past few weeks, threatened to overwhelm her as she stood at the line where the sunburned grass of the farmhouse garden drifted seamlessly into the yellow wheat field stretching in front of her.

The wheat was at its highest at this time of year – before the harvest; its buttery hue stretched into the distance to meet the glaring rays of the summer sun. She barely noticed its roughness as she ran her hand through it or registered the small tractor-drawn combine harvester as it started scalping the landscape. She stared through all of it towards the tree line of the woods further away, listening, waiting. This was the last chance, the last chance for him to come back to her. After that, it would all be decided – her fate would be unquestionable.

And then an exhale of relief as there it was, finally, the noise she'd been waiting for, for hours – ever since she'd heard them take off in the early hours of the morning. Far in the distance the drone of a b-17 bomber sounded in the clear blue sky as the Americans returned from another daylight raid over occupied Europe. The din of the planes was such a regular occurrence that it hardly registered with most people in the village now.

But to her it was everything.

Every time the usual thirty-six planes in the squadron formation took off, she counted them out with fear, and then counted them back in with dread, hoping that the number returning matched the number that had taken off.

Once in a while, they all returned home safely.

She shielded her eyes against the sunshine, waiting for the hulking grey planes to tail each other minutes apart over the Suffolk countryside.

One appeared in view.

And then two.

And then no more. *Please let him return. Please let him return.*

In the distance, yellow dust smoked the air as the tractor began to cull the pale crop. By the end of the day the field would be harvested. And all the men in the B-17 bombers would have returned safely.

Because they had to.

Because she needed them to.

She needed one in particular to return home safely, to her. Because that was how it was supposed to be. It couldn't be any other way. Not now.

Overhead, the engine roar deafened her thoughts, the landing gear lowered and the plane overhead made its lumbering descent towards the runway. The draught created from the speed of the aircraft made her hair fly in her face as she looked at it.

They all had to return. They all had to return. Far in the

distance, a third plane appeared in the sky and then behind that, a small dot indicated the fourth. She kept her eyes trained on the sky. Thirty-two remained to count in.

Please let him come back to me. Please let him come back to me. She took a deep breath and then continued counting the planes back in.

CHAPTER 2

Suffolk, England
Summer, 2011

Amy was racing through lanes she knew like the back of her hand in order to make it home in time for her own birthday dinner. She'd just delivered and set up a three-tier wedding cake for a couple who'd married at Hintlesham Hall this afternoon and had been invited to toast as the happy couple celebrated with friends and family. It would have been rude to say no. This was only her second wedding cake commission and if she was going to get most of her major work through recommendation then she'd need to make sure people remembered who she was.

As she entered the village of narrow streets – mostly unchanged since medieval times barring the odd Tudor addition – she wanted nothing more than to climb the stairs into her flat above her timber-framed tearoom, close the door and sleep. But sleep wasn't an option. Instead she had to rush down to the road to meet her family.

She parked her catering van outside her tearoom, its sign reading Amy's Tearooms swinging in the gentle breeze above the door. The blinds were pulled down over the windows, her sister and co-worker Caroline having locked up for the day. Amy still felt the usual flicker of disbelief and excitement that she owned her own tearoom in such a beautiful location and smiled as the last of the evening sunshine filtered down among the tourists and locals. She unlocked the door and let herself in, going up to her flat above – her own space. She hoped she'd always feel like this about being her own boss and doing something she genuinely loved. Her tearoom sparked joy but buying it three years ago had come about by complete accident. Back then she'd only known how to waitress and make the most basic of cakes when waitressing there. But even she could see its dreary decor and meagre portions were leading to a lack of customers. Just as she'd been about to suggest some changes, one of the two elderly sisters who owned it had passed away and the remaining owner suggested Amy might like to buy it. And she had. She could see its potential.

Once she'd got over the fear of applying for a loan and her tendency to over-order supplies, her sister Caroline had joined the business part-time, which had swiftly turned into full-time, and it had become a family affair. She'd worked so hard to build the tearoom – she couldn't remember the last time she'd had a holiday or a full weekend off.

Amy unlocked the internal door and climbed the stairs to her flat above, rushing around, tidying up her makeup and hair, hopping into a wrap dress and some flat ankle boots and then rushing straight back down the stairs and practically running down the road towards the Duck Hotel, where her family were waiting for her.

She'd sent a quick text to her sister after leaving the wedding late but she winced, hating keeping them all waiting, especially because her gran had said tonight she wanted to treat them all to this meal.

Amy sped through the hotel's ornate wooden front door. But just as she crossed the threshold she crashed into a man.

'I'm so sorry,' Amy said quickly and instinctively.

The man looked down at his shirt – wet with his own spilled beer.

'I'm so, *so* sorry,' Amy said, realising what she'd done. The man wasn't speaking, just carrying on the act of looking down in abject confusion at his shirt. She stepped towards him.

'I'm really sorry,' she repeated in a quieter voice.

He raised his head to look at her. She took in his dark hair, dark eyes and look of total horror as the beer soaked through his shirt. His pint glass was completely empty.

'Did *all* of that go on you?' Amy asked tentatively.

'It's fine,' he said stiffly but politely, his accent American. 'Don't worry about it.'

A customer tried to bustle past them muttering *excuse me* and the drenched man moved out of the doorway and into the street. Amy wasn't sure what to do. Leaving him to it was rude so she reluctantly followed him out into the warm summer evening and tried apologising again.

'Can I . . . What can I do? Can I buy you another beer?' she offered helplessly.

'No.' He drew his words out slowly. 'It's okay,' he said. 'You can buy me another shirt instead.' He threw her a mock-challenging look.

Amy looked distractedly through the open door to see if she could spot her family inside. She was now ridiculously late. She glanced at the shirt in question, hideous and covered in flowers.

'Listen, don't worry about it.' He looked down at his wet shirt. 'It was awful anyway.'

'The shirt or the beer?' Amy dared. 'Because the shirt is . . . unique.'

The man laughed, holding his wet shirt away from his chest. He had a nice laugh and his face lit up when he smiled.

'The beer,' he replied. 'How do you drink it so warm?'

'I don't really drink it,' she confessed. 'I'm sorry about the shirt again,' she said, angling to leave.

'The shirt will live to fight another day. It was a present from my father. I felt I should wear it in his company,' he said. 'I do not normally wear Hawaiian shirts. I just wanted to make that clear.'

She stifled a smile. 'Is that so? I can . . . wash it for you if you're staying here,' she said, desperately trying to make amends. 'I only live down the road. I could run it back to you tomorrow or . . .' She glanced at her watch.

A faint smile appeared at the corner of his mouth as he tried to wring the beer out of the wet material. 'No, it's fine. Thank you.'

'Oh you're here.' Amy's sister Caroline appeared at the door holding a Champagne flute. 'I was just popping outside to see if your van was parked up yet. I was going to start ringing you.'

Amy looked at Caroline's near-empty glass. 'Hi. Phew, you've started without me.'

'We did. We've been on the bubbles while we've been waiting for you. Gran bought a bottle and we've polished it off. There's none left for you, birthday girl, unless we buy another one, which I strongly suggest we do. Who's this then?' Caroline's eyes swivelled to the American who looked a bit stunned at having suddenly found himself stuck in a new conversation between two women he didn't know.

'Jack,' the man introduced himself under the gunfire of Caroline's enthusiasm. 'Pleased to meet you.'

'I'm Caroline. Amy's slightly older but very single sister.' Caroline held out her hand to shake Jack's. 'You're dripping in beer, Jack. Did you know?'

'I had no clue. Thank you for alerting me.' Jack glanced at Amy and they exchanged a smile.

'We should eat,' Amy suggested, watching her sister wobble gently.

'Nice to meet you, Jack,' Caroline trilled as she turned to go back inside.

'Bye,' he said to Caroline with laughter in his eyes. He turned his attention to Amy. 'And happy birthday.'

'Thanks. And I really am sorry about the shirt,' she said as she walked back through the doors. 'And the beer.'

'Don't worry about it,' he said genuinely.

She threw him a final apologetic smile and turned, quickly walking into the hotel and locating the room called the Airmen's Bar. She spotted her mother and grandmother in the far corner sat on comfortable brown leather sofas and gave them a wave and an apologetic look. An empty Champagne bottle was upturned inside an ice bucket and Caroline's smile was wicked as she asked Amy, 'What was *that* all about?'

CHAPTER 3

As Amy blew out the candles on her birthday cake after they'd eaten dinner in the main restaurant, she stared at the pink 3-0 candles that let everyone know exactly how old she was. Although everyone knew everyone in the village, so they all knew anyway. Their waiter appeared carrying a second bottle of Champagne and an ice bucket. 'May I take this all through to the bar for you?' He gestured towards the cake, the candles still smoking.

Amy turned to the waiter and pointed towards the Champagne. 'We didn't order this.'

'A gift from a gentleman at the bar,' he replied, picking up the cake and heading off as the women rose from their seats to let the restaurant have the table back.

'Wasn't American by any chance, was he?' Caroline asked the retreating waiter, glancing towards her sister.

Amy looked towards the bar to see who had sent it over. But there was no one there. She'd ask the waiter again in a quieter moment when her sister wasn't there to potentially make jibes. Although, if it was the American, she had no

9

idea why he'd done that. What a lovely gesture. If anything, it was *she* who owed *him* a drink.

She turned around to check if her grandmother was following or if she needed an arm for support but was taken aback to see she was some way behind, lingering near the doorway that divided the restaurant from the bar. Gran often became nostalgic when they came to The Duck; she had grown up in this pub – had been born in a little flat upstairs before it had all been turned into boutique hotel accommodation and had lived here until she was a grown woman, pulling pints for farmers and airmen alike. Usually she would tell Amy and Caroline stories about their great-grandparents and Great-Aunty Janie who'd moved to America when the war had ended to marry her sweetheart. But now Gran was standing still, in the pub where she used to live during the war, looking at the list of American pilots, their names written on the wall nearly seventy years previously when they'd been stationed at the airfield nearby. They had scrawled their names on the pub wall along with marking the time it had taken them to drink a yard of ale. Amy watched her gran focus on a particular place, a particular name, then reach out to put her fingers to it. Almost immediately, she withdrew her hand, turned and continued following her family towards the bar.

The bags under Amy's green eyes were huge the next morning. Her sleep had been frenetic at best. She and her sister had merrily worked their way through the mysterious gift of Champagne before moving on to cocktails while their mother and grandmother each nursed their one glass of fizz. And now Amy was feeling the effects of excess. Drinks in The Duck were a rare occurrence. Drinks *anywhere* were a rare occurrence these days, so focused was she on the tearoom. The business consumed her, especially now she had started offering celebration and wedding cakes to cater offsite. But she couldn't slow down, not yet.

She rubbed concealer into the blackish skin under her eyes and applied mascara to open them up. She would spend the day in the kitchen. She'd bake and handle the lunch and afternoon tea orders, while trying not to throw up the contents of her stomach; her sister and second-in-command Caroline could do the public-facing bit. Caroline always handled hangovers much better than she did.

Not wanting to see people went against the grain of owning a tearoom. Normally she loved socialising with customers and chatting to the tourists about what they'd done during the day and where they were planning to visit the next day – the timber-framed Guildhall or a National Trust house, a jaunt along the coast to Southwold or Aldeburgh. But today she'd skulk in the back, wishing the day away. She remembered with trepidation that before she could hide away she had a bulk order for the hotel to fulfil. The Duck had placed a huge order for what they simply called 'lots of traditional English things'. They were expecting an influx of Americans for the Second World War Heritage Day celebrating the rather un-catchy sounding 'Friendly Invasion of Americans to the East of England' during the war. The Duck had played a part, as the American airmen of nearby airbases had used it as their local watering hole.

Yesterday afternoon she'd made various fruit and cheese scones and this morning she only had to cream and jam the Victoria sponges and put the finishing touches to the lemon drizzle cakes then deliver them to the hotel.

She hoped this was what they were after. David, the hotel

manager, had been confident leaving Amy to it and if he wanted something a bit more 'wartime' it was too late now.

She put the boxes down in the tearoom and lifted the floral blinds in the front windows. They matched the tablecloths and Amy had recently spent a fortune on Liberty fabric making the place look just right. The tea sets she used were vintage fine bone china. While she couldn't afford to buy new tables and chairs yet, the linens and crockery were one of a few steps Amy had been able to make to spruce the place up a bit and make it less 'nursing home' and more 'vintage tearoom'. She was proud of what she'd achieved so far. But there was still so much more she wanted to do. There just weren't enough hours in the day.

The day was hot and Amy pulled the door closed but didn't bother to lock it behind her. Caroline would be along any minute and the crime rate was almost zero in the village – something else she loved about living here. She rushed down the street, lined with a mishmash of sloping medieval houses and narrow, higgledy-piggledy beamed shops and galleries towards The Duck. Amy loved this village. It was a picture-postcard brought to life. And she counted her lucky stars she lived somewhere so beautiful. It had everything she'd ever needed and wanted. She had good friends here, a thriving business and the chocolate-box village was one of the most beautiful places she'd ever known, even in winter. Especially in winter, when the snow fell and the light from the stained-glass windows of the church at the top of the road glowed brightly as a welcoming beacon to all who passed it.

'Morning, Amy,' David, the manager hailed her brightly as she entered The Duck.

Amy dodged the low beams and wondered if David ever

12

had a bad day and didn't smile. Recently moved up from London, he'd not been living in the village long enough for her to work it out yet. She greeted him and opened a couple of boxes for him to look at. The smell of cakes and scones emanated into the ornate space. He made an appreciative noise before helping Amy close the boxes back up.

'Do you have your invoice for me? Think we still owe you for last week,' he asked.

'You do.' She presented him with the paperwork. David disappeared into his office.

'Might be able to give you cash if you can run a receipt up to me,' he called.

'Sure,' Amy called back. She looked around the empty low-beamed lobby and rubbed her tired eyes, forgetting she was wearing mascara. She walked over to the fireplace and looked in the mirror above it to check whether she'd smudged her makeup. As she looked into the glass, a reflection from the furthest corner of the room made her swing round.

'Oh,' Amy said as she caught sight of the man from last night sitting on the sofa.

'Good morning.' He folded his newspaper up and put it on the coffee table. 'How was your birthday dinner?'

Amy rubbed under her eyes self-consciously as she took in how immaculate he looked – his jeans and white T-shirt neat, dark hair perfectly in place and his brown eyes friendly.

'It was delicious, thank you.' Why couldn't she remember his name? She'd drunk so much last night she was surprised she could remember her own name.

'The food here's pretty incredible,' he agreed. 'We've only been staying here a couple of nights but we ate in the restaurant the first night and it was great.'

She didn't miss his use of the word *we*. She stole a glance at his left hand. No wedding ring.

'What did you have?' Amy tried to cover the pause.

'Fish with a white sauce that was to die for.'

'That wasn't the answer I was expecting,' she blurted

He frowned. 'Really? What did you think I was going to say.'

She looked him up and down for effect and narrowed her eyes. 'You look like a steak man.'

He looked at her hard for a few seconds. 'Aren't all men steak men really?' He smiled.

Amy wasn't sure how to answer.

He leaned forward confidentially. 'I was so jetlagged I didn't know which way was up. When I got to my room after dinner I was still *so* hungry I ordered a cheese burger and fries from room service.' He grinned. 'Is that more what you were expecting?'

Amy's gaze fell to his arm as he leaned forward to drink the last of his coffee. The cotton of his shirt stretched tightly over his muscles as he flexed his fingers round his coffee cup.

'That's more like it,' she agreed while staring at his arms. She flicked her eyes away, connecting back to his gaze, but he obviously hadn't missed where she'd been looking. Amy glanced back to find David standing behind the reception desk. He waved a white envelope at her.

'Nice to see you again.' Amy waved briefly. 'Enjoy your day.'

'I will. Thank you.' The American raised his hand to wave in return and she collected her money from David before dashing out the door and over the road to the tearoom.

Amy hated that the American had noticed her admiring

his arms. She hadn't lusted after a man in . . . God, she had no idea how long. Years. And she'd surprised herself that she'd been even vaguely interested in him.

Amy found Caroline in the kitchen, prepping ingredients. Radio 1 was playing and her sister was singing at the top of her voice. Amy's head thudded and she turned it down. 'Do you mind?' she asked with a wince.

Caroline looked mock-offended. 'Is my singing that bad?'

'No. Your singing is delightful as always,' Amy lied. 'But I'm currently nursing a hangover and need a bit of quiet. And coffee. I need more coffee. How are you not hungover?'

'I'll make the coffee. That Champagne was probably what finished you off. Do you think it was that gorgeous American who sent it over?'

Amy looked at Caroline in horror. 'Oh no,' she said, closing her eyes, realising she'd forgotten to thank him for the bottle of Champagne. And what on earth was his name?

Amy took her cup of fresh coffee and inhaled the aroma as she stood at the window. She couldn't exactly go running back over to the hotel to say thanks, after making a dash for it only minutes ago. She'd look mad. She'd pop back later with the receipt for David and see if the man was there. She'd thank him then. Or leave him a note. Or something. But what if it wasn't him who'd gifted her the bubbles? Then she'd look even more like an idiot. Her brain wasn't engaged enough for this. Maybe after another coffee.

She looked out of the window and towards The Duck as she sipped. The coffee was nectar, slowly dousing her hangover. In the distance she could see the American leaving the low-slung black-and-white-timber-framed hotel, narrowly avoiding hitting his head on a series of pretty geranium-filled

15

hanging baskets that adorned the building. Amy stood up straight and watched him walk round the side of the hotel and out of view. A few minutes later a car rounded and the American, behind the wheel, drove along the wrong side of the road. Amy gave a short chuckle as the car lurched suddenly to the correct side of the road and then parked outside the hotel. He got out and went back inside the hotel's entrance. He'd obviously not had much experience driving in England yet.

She was curious to see who he was going back inside to fetch and if it might be a woman. She held the cup halfway to her lips in anticipation and waited.

'Want me to make a start on the coffee and walnut?' Caroline shouted from the kitchen. Amy jumped, narrowly avoiding spilling her coffee.

'No, it's okay. Enjoy the quiet for a minute or two. I'll do that one in a bit,' she replied, still staring out the window.

Down the road, the American and another man appeared. He was older, in his late fifties. Was this the dad who had bought the infamous Hawaiian shirt? As they drove slowly away on the correct side of the road this time, Amy turned and went into the kitchen to start on the cakes.

As the day wore on, more Americans arrived in the village in preparation for the Heritage Day. Slowly they filtered in and out of Amy's tearoom as she worked in the kitchen. Every time she heard a vaguely youngish American male voice she found herself peering out to look until she finally realised why she was doing it and gave herself a strong talking to.

Amy glanced at her phone as it started to ring. She turned off the tap and quickly dried her hands as she saw her grandmother's landline flash up on the screen. 'Gran!' Amy cried.

'Hello, my darling. Did you sleep well?'

'Not really, no.'

'That'll be the drink, poppet.'

'Hey!' Amy laughed.

'Well you girls did go a little bit heavy. The cocktails looked delicious though. Especially that pink one with the naughty name.'

Amy thought she might be sick if she thought about those martinis.

'Listen darling. I wanted to invite you round tomorrow. I'd like to give you your birthday present. It was too big to bring to the restaurant last night.'

'Gran you didn't have to get me anything. You paid for dinner last night. That was so expensive. I'm not expecting a gift as well.'

'Well you've got one. I'm rather proud of it. It's Sunday tomorrow. Come for a roast lunch. It'll just be the two of us. We've not spent a Sunday together in a long time. Two o'clock?'

Amy felt a rush of happiness as she readily agreed. A home-cooked roast dinner at her gran's house was just what was needed.

CHAPTER 4

For all of its historic medieval beauty and mishmash quaint buildings, Amy's favourite house in the village had always been her grandmother's traditional grey brick farmhouse. Situated on the very edge of the village, its lush green gardens sprawled down to the edge of the wheat field. In the distance, the end of the old disused airfield could just about be seen through the tree line. The house and its acres of land held so many happy memories for Amy. She and Caroline had played here as children, running from room to room in noisy games of hide and seek while Gran cooked dinner. There were too many rooms to hide in and so the game came to a natural conclusion when neither girl could find the other. After four or five minutes of looking, which felt like an eternity when they were small, Caroline would always eventually find Amy in the library looking at all the leather-bound volumes. *The Wind in the Willows* had been Amy's favourite back then. In part, she blamed Mole, Ratty and the gang for cementing her enduring love of the countryside.

Sunday was the only day that Amy didn't feel fully guilty about taking off even though there was always something to be done in the tearoom. The guilt was self-inflicted while she built the business and could only afford Caroline to share duties with, operating on rotation with her on precious weekends. Caroline had started out as a waitress but that role had swiftly grown and now Amy couldn't do without her sister as she shared front of house and back-office duties with a willing Caroline so Amy could focus on expanding the catering side. But while she loved her work, even Amy couldn't argue with taking Sundays off every now and again when she was forced to.

Her car crunched over the comforting sounds of her gran's gravel driveway and Amy parked and climbed out, greeted by a mouth-watering smell of roast beef from the open kitchen window. She'd skipped breakfast this morning knowing she was going to get the feeding of her life. Gran's roast dinners were the stuff of legend.

The flowers Amy bought had survived the short drive on the front seat – the long-stemmed lilies huge and just starting to open. The farmhouse's back door creaked reassuringly as Amy pushed it open. For as long as she could remember everyone used the back door into the large kitchen.

'Come in, come in,' Kitty called as she threw a tea towel over her shoulder. She was still as sprightly as ever and was wearing an old apron that instructed the reader to give the chef a glass of wine. It had faded over the years, and Amy remembered having given that to her gran for her birthday about a decade ago.

She nodded to it as she kissed her gran on the cheek. 'I brought flowers, not wine today I'm afraid.'

'Probably a good idea given your hangover.' Her gran smiled at Amy and stirred the gravy.

'I'm over that now, thank you very much.' Amy popped a piece of beef into her mouth, closed her eyes and made an appreciative noise. 'Is there anything I can do?'

Her gran leaned over to smell the lilies. 'Could you pop those in water, please? We're almost ready. They smell divine. Thank you for buying them for me.'

After she'd filled a vase and placed the flowers inside, Amy cleared the scrubbed pine table of newspapers and letters and started to lay place settings, glasses and crockery.

Her gran served and they chatted for a few minutes. There was something about a home-cooked roast made by her gran that Amy had always looked forward to, ever since she was a child. It was grounding, settling, reaffirmed how much she loved and needed to be close to her family.

As Amy put her knife and fork together at the end of the meal, she noticed her grandmother looking intently at her. 'Darling, I'm not one to beat about the bush. You look very tired.'

Amy sat up straight in her chair.

'You're working too hard.'

Amy nodded. 'Yes. But . . .'

'No *buts*. You're working too hard, too late, too long. You're wearing yourself down. You were late to your own birthday dinner. You must try to slow down.'

There was nothing Amy could do but pay her gran lip service. 'I'll try,' she said, in a non-committal way.

There was silence as Gran was clearly working out how to make the same point in a different way. Amy looked at the tablecloth she'd laid. It was the same one that had been placed on the table for family dinners for as long as she could remember. The edges were slightly frayed and the odd red wine stain was visible if you looked hard enough, but her gran had always said that added to its history.

'I know it's different for you young folk. I know times are harder and things cost more. But you don't have to work yourself into the ground. Let your sister help. Let your mother help. Let me help.'

'You? Gran. I'm not having you waiting tables.'

'That's not *quite* what I meant,' she said. 'But I know how to bake the odd cake or two. You don't have to take *everything* on your own shoulders, you know?'

'I know,' Amy said reluctantly.

'And with you working all hours in that little kitchen all day every day . . . there can't be many opportunities for romance.'

'Romance?' Amy queried at the sudden turn in conversation. 'No. Not really. Quite hard to meet fit, kind, solvent men while at work. They don't tend to just stroll into the kitchen looking for love, sadly.'

'More's the pity,' her gran sighed.

Amy laughed.

'Perhaps one of those dating websites that your sister's on?'

'No thanks,' Amy baulked. 'I'm not quite sure it's my thing. I'm not really sure it's Caroline's thing but she's persevering regardless. And I'm not looking for a boyfriend at the moment. Perhaps in a few years when the tearoom and the catering business have taken off a bit more.'

'A few *years*?' It was her gran's turn to baulk. 'I'd been married for over a decade by your age.'

'People don't really marry that young anymore, Gran.'

'Yes, I think I might have been a bit worried if you'd

announced you were marrying when you weren't even twenty so I do realise times have changed. Let's leave the romance question to the side for now then. I just worry for your health, predominantly. I worry you're working too hard and you have been for the last few years. I just want you to know it's been noted and I wonder if you might think about a way to address it. That's all. I'm not nagging. I just care. We all do.'

Her gran reached across and took Amy's hand in hers, reaching her conclusion. 'Darling. You are young.'

'I'm thirty now.'

'Exactly. You are still young,' she reiterated. 'I don't want you to miss out on life, stuck in that kitchen, day in day out. You only get one life.' Her eyes took on a serious look. 'This is not the dress rehearsal for the next one. Take it from me. I know.'

The lost look in her gran's eyes was quickly replaced with a happy smile. But it was too late. Amy had seen the expression that had passed over her face.

'I know, Gran. I promise I'll try to live a bit more and maybe try to work a bit less.' But as the words left Amy's mouth she knew it was a fib.

'That's all I'm asking,' her gran said, appeased.

A quiet descended in the kitchen and Amy stared at the gravy streaks on her empty plate. She nodded.

Her gran leaned forward, squeezed her granddaughter's hand and let go.

'Now,' she said after a few moments. 'Let's have a moment between courses and let me give you your present. You're going to have to come with me into the drawing room though because it's a bit awkward for me to carry on my own. Your mother helped me sort this so some of the praise must go to her. It involved the internet.' Her gran almost whispered the last word as if the internet was a magical beast one must not speak of. Amy pressed her lips together to stifle a smile. For all her grandmother's modernity there were some things that simply stumped her.

Positioned in front of the large but simple stone fireplace with its flagstone hearth was what looked suspiciously like a large, framed picture. It was wrapped elegantly in pale pink paper with a white ribbon tied in a neat bow.

Amy whooped. 'Oh, I love presents.'

'I thought you said you didn't want a gift.' Gran laughed.

'I lied. And I know I'll love whatever it is because you've put thought into choosing something for me.' Amy sat on the thick light blue Chinese rug and pulled at one end of the ribbon to release the silky threads while Kitty sat on one of the sumptuous cream sofas.

Amy pulled the pink paper off and scrunched it into a ball. The picture was facing the wrong way and so she turned the frame and looked. What she saw made her exclaim with joy. It was a black and white photograph of the back of a little girl, clutching the arm of a teddy bear and standing at an old oak tree, looking up into the branches. A vague memory flitted at the edge of her mind but she couldn't quite place it. 'Is that me?'

Gran nodded. 'It is you, yes. You were four, I think. Or thereabouts.'

As she stood, Amy positioned the picture against one side of the fireplace and stood back to admire the photograph. The girl in the photo didn't feel like her. Or rather, Amy couldn't really remember it. Not really. Unsurprising given whoever had taken it had done so when Amy was facing the other way.

23

'Your grandfather took it. I was going through the attic. I've been having a bit of a clear-out. It's time to put some old ghosts to rest.'

Amy turned her head. 'Such as?'

But Gran sidestepped the question. 'I found all your grandfather's old photo albums from when you and Caroline were little. Some from when your mother was small as well. Your grandfather was the photographer of the family. It was his first passion.'

'And you,' Amy suggested, remembering her mum's stories about Amy's grandfather and how in love he had been with her.

Gran smiled. 'And me . . . I was so lucky,' she breathed. Amy looked at her grandmother but her gaze was far away. What was she remembering? How she and Amy's grandfather had been so happy? How they had first got together? It was towards the end of the war. And shortly after they'd married, Amy's mum had been born. That much Amy did know. Gran had been a young bride and a young mother. It was all so normal back then, people marrying at the drop of a hat in wartime when the hours were precious and life intensely lived.

'So lucky,' Gran repeated. 'He was a good man, the best of men, a wonderful father and grandfather.'

'He was,' Amy replied thinking fondly of her grandfather. She had a vague recollection of him pushing both her and her sister simultaneously on the swings in the park, his walking stick propped up against the metal frame of the nearby slide.

'Indeed. He loved you girls. The way he looked at your mum when she was first born. I knew then. I knew how lucky I'd been.'

Amy wanted that love, that luck, eventually. She'd had relationships at college and at university and in the years prior to taking over the tearoom. But the tearoom purchase was three years ago. Time had flown. How long before that had she last been on a date? She couldn't remember. Was she as sad and overworked as her gran was making out? Did Amy actually have no life other than working and living here and seeing her family?

Amy looked at her grandmother. 'Gran . . . are you lonely?'

She paused and then said warmly, 'No, I have all my lovely girls.'

'I mean without Grandad.'

Gran smiled. 'A little. But It's the way of the world isn't it . . . the way it's supposed to be. No one lives forever. I'm sure I won't be far behind him.'

'Gran!' Amy chastised.

In the later years since her grandad's death, Amy thought Gran had always coped so well on her own. Amy had been in primary school when he'd passed away. Such a long time ago. She looked back at the photograph of her pre-school self by the old oak tree. Carvings on the tree – where young lovers of years gone by had etched their initials – were present in the photo then and were probably still there now, albeit having moved slightly higher on the trunk as it grew over the years. It had been such a long time since she'd been on the other side of the field by the oak tree. Why did she never go there anymore? She used to find such comfort underneath its boughs. 'The photo's beautiful. Thanks, Gran.'

She kissed Gran on the cheek and as she did so she noticed that her eyes were wet. When Amy fell in love she wanted it to be the kind of love that could do that to a person in later life. She wanted it to be all encompassing, the kind of love that held her in its grip and never let her go . . . even long after the person she loved had passed away. She wanted love, both to give it wholeheartedly and to receive it. She just wanted that person to enter her life in five years' time when her catering business was flourishing and she wasn't working all the hours God sent.

Later, as she washed up the roasting tin, Amy stared out the window above the Belfast sink and into the distance where the grass border met the start of the wheat field. The day was stifling and the wheat was at a perfect standstill without a breeze to ruffle the crop.

Gran, at the dining table, had stopped pouring coffee from the cafetière. Instead she too was looking absently out of the window and had that faraway look back in her eyes, as if she'd gone somewhere else.

CHAPTER 5

1944

Despite the latticed windows being open all day it was still roasting inside the pub. Kitty's blonde hair was sticking to the nape of her neck so she unbolted the door of The Duck from the inside and let the faint summer breeze flow over her warm face and sticky neck. She'd just heard, and loved, Bing Crosby's latest, 'Swinging on a Star', on the wireless in the flat upstairs as she contemplated her future, but now she had a good hour to get a few chores done behind the bar before they opened and were legally allowed to serve. Soon the pub would be heaving with Americans from the base and she and her father wouldn't have a moment to themselves until closing time when she'd tidy, help the pot boy wash up and then crawl towards bed. In truth, it had surprised her that the Americans were still here and in such great number. With the Allied invasion of France having only taken place only two months before, and having watched what must have surely been every single plane in the land take off over what had been dubbed D-Day and the days that followed, she'd expected them all to be gone. That the American flyboys had returned and in such great number had come as something as a surprise to her, although she knew the foot-soldier GIs were now long gone, making their way towards . . . who knew where? Berlin, she reasoned. Wasn't that the end goal? Berlin, Hitler and the eventual end. She had a look at the newspaper, left out on the bar for anyone who wanted it, to see if she could glean any further information about events in Europe. But other than an uprising in Warsaw taking place in a bid to oust the Nazis from Poland . . . she was none the wiser. How did any of this affect her out in her little corner of Suffolk countryside, anyway? Her world was so far removed, although war work was her eventual goal and she was so close to it, so close.

As Kitty turned to go inside, mentally ticking off the tasks she'd already completed, the noise of footsteps thudding on the path made her glance up. A young man in an olive-coloured flight uniform was heading her way at speed, not quite running, but not quite walking either. Kitty rolled her eyes. It was far too early. She hated having to turn away the American bomber boys who, arriving in England, had no idea about the pub's legal opening times. She braced herself and adopted what she hoped was her usual friendly smile and prepared the small speech she kept handy for these occasions.

He stopped in front of her and looked up. It was as if he'd not been aware of her presence until he realised the door was barred by a human. He stared through her.

'Excuse me,' the American muttered.

'I'm sorry, we aren't open yet.'

He dragged his eyes from the direction of the bar with its rows of bottles and locked his gaze onto her face. 'What?' he snapped.

'We aren't open yet,' Kitty repeated. She looked at his face, slightly grubby as if he'd just torn his flight mask off and hadn't bothered to wash. Against his brown eyes it made him look almost Heathcliff-like. His brown hair was messy, bits of it sticking out and up at interesting angles.

'I just need a beer.' He ran his teeth over his bottom lip. He looked almost nervous.

'I'm not allowed to serve—'

Kitty was cut off. 'Listen, sweetheart . . .'

Kitty opened her eyes wide at his patronising tone. But the man was speaking so fast she couldn't get a word in.

'If you'd seen the things I'd just seen . . .' He trailed off, clenched his jaw then continued quietly. 'You'd be in there drinking the goddamn bar dry. Now just give me one beer and I'll be out of your hair.' He looked so hard at Kitty with a gaze so penetrating she didn't know what else to do, so she dumbly stepped aside and let him past. Her father would be livid if she served him. Kitty looked down the street to see if any other Americans looked to be staging a protest about pub opening hours and then followed the pilot inside.

He was already seated at the bar on a stool, his legs moving up and down rhythmically as Kitty stepped behind the wooden bar. She listened out for movements in the flat above, praying her father wouldn't come downstairs. Hopefully this dishevelled man would drink his beer and leave before he got her into all sorts of trouble.

She stared at the man's head, which was hanging down, hiding his face. His elbows were now on the bar, his head in his hands, and he kneaded his grubby fingers in and out of his messy hair. His hands were shaking. Thoughts of asking him to drink quickly and leave disappeared as she looked at the state he was in.

'Would you like something to eat?' she asked gently. She would reluctantly be able to whip up a quick spam sandwich if need be, but the young man didn't reply, wiping his eyes of what Kitty suspected might be tears. She pulled him a glass of beer and watched his hands continue to shake. God knew what he'd just been through. She placed his drink on the bar and glanced towards the staircase. *Stay upstairs, stay upstairs,* she silently begged of her father. The pilot didn't look up, his hands still worrying at his hair. She coughed pointedly and moved the glass towards him. It was the sound of the glass scraping over the wooden bar that roused his attention and he lifted it, drained it, placed it on the bar and went back to putting his hands in his hair.

'Kitty?' her father called from the top of the stairs. 'Is that lamp still playing up down there?'

Panicked, Kitty ran to the bottom of the stairs and called up. 'I don't know. Give me a minute and I'll check.'

She turned towards the bar to usher the pilot out but he had already gone. She stopped and stared at the place where he'd been sitting and then at the door. He'd left so quickly, so silently and without a word. Also, he'd not paid for his drink.

'Lamp's fine now, Dad,' Kitty called up after flicking it on and off a few times and then she ran over to the bar, removed the airman's glass and washed it up quickly, putting it back in place on the shelf above the bar. It was a good job her father hadn't seen any of this. She hurried round and pushed the pilot's barstool back in, wondering what on earth had happened to him that had rendered him a shaking mess.

Although she felt useless helping in the pub, she knew it wasn't forever. While women weren't being conscripted under the age of nineteen, they were being encouraged, and she'd been hoping to join the Women's Land Army for fresh air and the outdoors rather than being cooped up behind the bar. But her father had, so far, put a stop to that, citing that he needed her to help him in the pub as long as possible. He *wasn't getting any younger*, or so he kept saying, and the guilt of leaving him didn't bear thinking about. There was such a lot for a man of his age to do, even with the pot boy for assistance. She couldn't leave him voluntarily, not when he'd looked so desperately concerned when she'd originally suggested it.

But she'd turned nineteen last week and, it being conscription age for unmarried women, she knew she'd be officially called up to aid the war effort within weeks if not days. So she'd got her act together and had enrolled in the Women's Land Army before her birthday. If she hadn't been quick about it she might have ended up being drafted into a munitions factory and that was categorically *not* what she wanted to end up doing. This time last year the War Cabinet had temporarily disbanded recruitment into the Land Army due to its popularity and the fact the factories weren't seeing their fair share of women workers. When Kitty had read that she could have sworn she'd stopped breathing for a full minute. But five months later women were required to fight in the fields once again and recruitment had reopened. Now, after being told she'd passed both the formal interview and medical assessment, Kitty would be posted to a neighbouring farm that served as a training ground for the Women's Land Army, most likely. And then, a few months later, if the farmer didn't need her, she'd be posted on somewhere else in Britain. *It could be anywhere*, she thought joyfully. How she'd then have *that* conversation with her father didn't bear thinking about.

Kitty loved living in the countryside. She knew nothing else and was desperate to get out into the fresh air and help the war effort . . . *truly* help the war effort and not just serve thirsty pilots beer. She thought of the young pilot who'd barged his way in to the pub and hoped that she'd done some good today just by serving him a drink. Although she suspected not.

And then she listened as the ever-present roar of aeroplanes sounded again today – American bombers once again flying over the village, headed for the airbase after another mission. She wondered how far into Europe they'd been and what they'd been bombing and how many of their number they had tragically lost. She wondered how many of their own men on the ground they were flying over each day, all making headway across Europe, she hoped. She thought of what those American boys had to face day after day flying over occupied Europe. And with a sense of perspective about her upcoming work predicament, Kitty raised her eyes heavenward and thanked God she wasn't a man.

The evening shift was busy, noisy as usual and airmen filtered in and out, desperate to enjoy time off the base. There had been a new wave of recruits, eager young men with a confident swagger that Kitty had come to know all too well over the past few months until the swagger gently eased away as life and the war took its toll on them. These new airmen weren't yet as deflated or worldly wise as those who were a few missions deeper into their tour. Newly formed crews bonded with each other in what they were unofficially now naming the Airmen's Bar. They'd set themselves drinking challenges on evenings when they knew they wouldn't be flying the next day and it was causing a boom in business that Kitty's father was delighted with. The extra money would help pay for her sister Janie's wedding to Bobby, the American ground crewman that Janie had met less than two months ago.

Kitty secretly wondered if Janie might be pregnant. If not, what was the urgency? Although on reflection, he was very attractive and so perhaps Janie's hurry to take him off the market was down to that. Janie also considered it a touch of fate that she'd fallen in love with a ground crewman, rather than a pilot. With so many planes *not* returning to the base, having Bobby safely on the ground felt like everything. Although as an ARP warden in Ipswich, Janie had recently seen the horrors of being killed while considered safely on the ground as the V1 rockets – doodlebugs – rained indiscriminately down around the nation. Janie was starting to reconsider what constituted safe, and the stories she told when she returned some nights had rather put Kitty off joining up for Civil Defence.

Kitty couldn't understand why anyone would want to do anything other than war work and being a Land Girl in particular. Posters of jolly, smiling girls in green jumpers, rosy cheeked and enjoying the outdoors, filled her mind. She'd been desperate to be one of them and had cut out every picture from the magazines she could get her hands on over the past few years – often pointedly carrying out this task over the breakfast table so her father could see she wasn't going to drop the idea so easily.

And now she'd received her precious Land Girl badge, stealing a glance at it whenever she could. She was one of them. In name only if not in practice while she desperately waited to find out where she'd be sent. She wasn't eager to leave the village especially. But a change of scene could hardly be considered a bad thing. She kept the badge hidden in her undergarments drawer, knowing it would be the last place her father would ever look for anything. She would tell him, she would. She just had to find the right moment.

Kitty pulled glasses of beer, made conversation and merry chit chat with the men, deflected a few nosy enquiries as to whether she had a sweetheart, whether she'd like to accept one of them as her sweetheart, and glanced at the clock above the bar – counting down the final hour until she and her father could close the pub, clean up and head to their beds for a long and well-earned sleep. Kitty rolled her head around, easing the stiffness that was settling in along her neck and spine. Would now be a good time to alert her father that on receipt of her instructions she probably wouldn't have too much time to prepare and that she'd be leaving? There was no good time but she inhaled, prepared.

'Can you clear those glasses?' her father asked as he took an airman's order.

Kitty nodded, deflated at having to continue keeping her secret and started collecting glasses from a table of uniformed men who all looked heavily intoxicated. One sat back as she approached, widened his legs and adopted a confident stance that made Kitty smile. Let them have their few moments of bravado, she thought. It was probably what they needed. Who knew what awaited them in the skies over Europe?

'Did you hurt yourself when you fell from the heavens?' the man started.

Kitty laughed.

The man's face fell. 'I was just being nice,'

'I know. I wasn't laughing *at you*,' Kitty placated. 'Only . . .' She adopted a confiding tone, 'I have heard that one a few times and was rather hoping for something fresh.' The young man missed the playful tone entirely and took offence.

'Look lady, we're out here, busting a gut for you and your country and all you got is—' The man was cut off as another American voice sounded from directly behind Kitty.

'Cliff, leave her alone.'

She spun round and looked up into the face of the dishevelled, shaking man from earlier. Only now he was neither shaking nor dishevelled. He was groomed, out of his flight clothes and wearing a neatly pressed uniform. He looked like a completely different man. Less like a gypsy and more like a shining example of an all-American film star. His brown hair was neat and his dark eyes didn't have the dull, vacant look from earlier on. And what's more, he was so close.

Realising this, he stepped back a pace. 'I'm sorry,' he said as he looked at her with concern.

Kitty had no idea if he was apologising for his friend's behaviour, for surprising her just then or for their encounter earlier in the day. It took a second or two for words to form. 'It's fine.'

She remembered how shaken he'd been earlier and delivered her next sentence softly. 'It wasn't a problem. Honestly.' Whatever he was apologising for, she felt that covered all eventualities.

The American looked as if he was about to speak and Kitty waited. But he glanced over her shoulder and waved to someone in the furthest corner of the bar. He glanced back down at Kitty, nodded at her politely and walked past her to greet his friends.

As the night wore on and customers started leaving – the bomber boys back to the airbase and the villagers to their homes nearby – Kitty was struggling to stay awake. She'd been working in the pub in the evenings for months, ever since the young man who'd helped her father behind the bar had received his call-up papers. There was only the pot boy left now and he was what Janie called 'not quite the ticket.'

The few remaining Americans looked as if they were finally ready to be coerced out the door. Her father was collecting glasses and Kitty was busy drying them while simultaneously trying to read a newspaper that had been left open on the piano. She stifled a yawn. It was far past Kitty's bedtime and if her mother had still been alive she'd have chastised her youngest daughter for the ill effects the lack of sleep would have on her skin.

Kitty smiled thinking about her mother. If she'd seen what her death would have done to Kitty's father she might have clung on to life a bit longer. He'd completely closed down, clinging to his daughters like a life raft. Cancer. She wished she hadn't started thinking about it and closed her eyes to shut out the memories but all she saw was her mother, kind, smiling. This wasn't helping. When she opened her eyes she was shocked to find the American pilot from earlier in the day standing in front of the bar looking directly at her. His friends had gone ahead of him. He looked pointedly at Kitty's father, who was paying no attention, then the American gestured with his eyes towards the door.

Kitty looked blankly at him. He glanced again quickly at Kitty's father and then nodded his head towards the door again. She understood, or at least thought she did but a part of her worried. Should she follow him outside the pub? If anything untoward happened, at least her father was within shouting distance. As the young man left the pub, the last to leave, Kitty counted to ten and then said, 'Dad, leave that and go to bed. I'll finish here and then lock up.'

'Really? Oh you are a love. Thanks. Don't be too long. You need your rest too, you know.'

'I know.'

'You are a good girl. You know that, don't you?'

'I know, Dad,' Kitty agreed. 'Now go to bed. Before I change my mind and make you tidy up.'

'I'm going. I'm going.' He placed the cloth he'd been using onto the polished wooden counter. 'Don't be too long. I mean it.'

The top stair creaked as her father went upstairs and Kitty made her way to the front door of the pub, opened it and quickly and quietly closed it behind her to ensure the blackout stayed as intact as possible. It took her eyes a few moments to adjust to the pitch black of the road. The Tudor and medieval timber-framed shops and houses opposite had all faded to nothingness in the blackout. She suddenly felt very vulnerable, alone in the street. There wasn't a sound and Kitty kept her hand on the old, oversized brass door handle, ready to click it open and step back inside. He'd gone. For some reason she couldn't fathom, Kitty was disappointed. And then his voice in the darkness broke the night silence.

CHAPTER 6

'I'm sorry, I didn't mean to startle you,' he said as Kitty jumped.

'You didn't,' Kitty lied into the darkness. She kept her hand on the door handle – apprehensively.

The pilot stepped towards her. Her eyes still hadn't adjusted to the pitch black and he was shrouded in darkness. She had no idea what to say. She wanted to know what he wanted, why he'd summoned her outside, specifically away from her father. She tried the question out in her head and it sounded so rude that she kept quiet and waited. She heard the rustle of his uniform as he stepped closer and she could finally see him properly.

'I just wanted to say thank you,' he said. His voice was deep and he sounded exactly like every American movie star she'd ever seen at the pictures.

'For what?' Kitty breathed.

'For today,' he replied. 'You made everything okay when it had all gone so bad.'

'I just gave you a glass of beer,' she reasoned.

'That was all I needed.'

'What happened?' Kitty asked.

He skirted her question. 'I owe you an apology.'

'Actually you owe me money.'

'Oh no. I do, don't I?' He laughed. 'I stole a drink.' He paused, rubbed his hand across his mouth and then, 'I don't think I've ever stolen something before.'

He put his hand in his pocket and pulled out a pile of coins. 'You're going to have to help me in the dark I'm afraid. I've no idea what's what, even when it's daylight.'

'It's alright,' Kitty said. 'Really. It's my treat. Or rather, my father's treat on this occasion, as long as we don't tell him. I'm sure you'll spend enough in the bar to compensate.'

She could just about make out his smile as he put his change away. 'Then thank you,' he said. 'It's generous of you. Especially as I was so rude to you earlier.'

He'd been shaking earlier in the day, distressed. 'Not at all,' she said.

'What's your name?' he asked.

Kitty told him. He put his hand out and she unfurled her fingers from the door handle to return his handshake.

'Nice to meet you Kitty, I'm Charlie,' he told her.

'Charlie,' she said. She preferred the way he said his own name – the r more pronounced. The way she said it sounded so short and clipped, so English. 'It's very nice to meet you.'

'Likewise.' His grip was gentle as he held her hand within his, and in the silence of the night where neither of them spoke for a few seconds, all Kitty could hear was her heart thumping all the way up to her ears.

'Do you smoke?' he asked, letting go of her hand.

'Sometimes,' she replied.

'Would you like a packet of cigarettes?'

'A whole packet?' She laughed.

'What's so funny?' She could hear the uncertain laughter in his voice.

'I wasn't expecting you to offer me an entire packet. You caught me by surprise, that's all. It'll take me about a month to smoke that many.'

'Then . . . can I give them to you for your father? A trade for the stolen drink perhaps – only maybe let's not tell him about that bit.'

Kitty wasn't sure. How would she explain where they came from? What would her father say if he saw her out here with this man? He was being ever so protective of Kitty ever since Janie took up with Bobby. He didn't want to lose another daughter to an American flyboy.

'I think it's best I don't accept them, actually. If that's alright? I don't mean to offend.'

'Sure,' he said. 'I'm not offended.' He opened the soft packet and put one between his lips. He struck his match, lighting up his face as he leaned into the flame, his lips parted, his dark eyes lowered. Kitty watched, fascinated.

He breathed smoke out and waved his match to put it out. 'If you're not much of a smoker, do you want to share this one with me or would you like one for yourself?'

'We can share.' She gestured towards the other side of the road. 'There's a bench over there.'

He followed her, passing her the cigarette as they sat down. Kitty inhaled deeply. 'Oh that *is* good.'

'But you don't smoke much?' he queried with a laugh.

Kitty shook her head. 'I can take them or leave them.' She inhaled and then passed the cigarette back to him.

'I can't. I need them. And beer, obviously. Used to be whisky but you guys don't have too much of that anymore thanks to Hitler. So I've adapted my tastes.' The smile dropped from his face and she looked at him alongside her on the bench. His gaze looked blank and he was staring into the distance. She wouldn't ask him again what had happened to make him so sad. He clearly didn't want to talk about it.

'I'm sorry about my friend,' he said eventually. 'He was rude to you.'

'It seems the day for it,' Kitty teased as he handed her the cigarette. 'But thank you for intervening.'

'My pleasure. He's new here. He'll get the hang of your British sense of humour soon enough, I'm sure.'

'You're not new then?' Kitty enquired.

Charlie shook his head. 'Not new to England. But I'm new round here. I've been transferred down from a base in Norfolk. I'm an old-timer now,' he joked. 'I'm on my second tour.'

'Your *second*?' Kitty hadn't meant her tone to sound like that of a fishwife. She spoke more gently. 'Why on earth are you on your second tour? You boys usually go home after your twenty-fifth mission, or so I keep hearing. If you . . .' She was going to say *if you live that long* but stopped herself just in time. She wondered why in God's name he was inviting death into the ring for another twenty-five rounds. The man must be stark, raving mad. She inched away from him slightly on the bench.

He turned and looked at her and then looked away quickly. 'It's late,' he said softly. 'Perhaps it's a story for another day.'

Kitty looked back from the doors as they said goodbye, Charlie watching for her to step inside. She gave him a brief wave, which he returned before moving off in the direction of the base. She closed the door as quietly as she could so as not to wake her father and Janie.

In the pub, Kitty eyed the spilled beer that the airmen had left on some of the tables and grabbed the cloth from the countertop. She cleaned quickly and righted the chairs, bolted the doors and finished the washing up. Upstairs, she cleaned her face, applied cold cream and climbed into her nightdress. On catching sight of her reflection in the mirror, she stopped in surprise. For the first time in what felt like ages, Kitty was smiling.

In the graveyard the following day, the evening sunshine was brighter than it had been yesterday. Kitty stood up from her mother's grave and dusted off the tell-tale grass stains on her knees. While other village girls were either wearing stockings provided by the Americans, who had an endless source, Kitty's supply had dwindled to none given that her father had decreed she wasn't allowed to accept gifts *like some sort of floozie*. She felt like a fraud painting a wobbly line of boot polish up the back of her leg to emulate nylons. After having watched the post master's dog lick the gravy browning off a horrified Janie's legs, she wasn't about to resort to that either. So she was bare-legged but the summer sun had browned her a little so hopefully no one would notice.

Kitty admired the poppies and daisies she'd picked from a patch of grass that morning and had now placed at her mother's grave. The lanes around the village were filled with beautiful wildflowers and they provided a free source of beauty.

Her father rarely visited the grave anymore, despite the church being a stone's throw from the pub and their home above. He maintained a stoic expression whenever Kitty mentioned her late mother but she could tell he was pained by thoughts of her, even after all these years.

'I miss you, Mum,' she whispered to the granite headstone.

A cough behind her made her jump and she spun round to find Charlie standing on the gravel path by the church. Kitty reddened, feeling silly for talking to a gravestone. He raised his hand in greeting.

'Fancy meeting you again so soon,' he said as Kitty walked towards him.

'It's a small village,' she said. 'It's bound to happen. I see plenty of your lot roaming the streets in search of something to do.'

As if to illustrate the point two Americans cycled past the low stone wall that divided the church from the lane. Kitty pointed towards them. 'See?' she said.

Charlie smiled.

They stood for a few seconds, neither knowing quite what to say. Kitty took the time to work out how old he was. He only looked a few years older than her.

'I'm playing tourist today,' he said. 'Care to join me? Unless you're busy?'

Kitty looked back down the road towards the pub where she knew her father would be. She had planned to talk to him today about her enrolment into the Land Army. Time was running short and she'd be expected to report for duty soon when her instructions arrived, but cowardice was getting the better of her. She *had* to tell her father today but right now, for a reason she couldn't fathom, she'd rather be here. She glanced back towards Charlie. 'I'd love to.'

'Great,' he said instantly. 'You're at the controls then. I've no idea what there is to see and I've just been wandering aimlessly. I've been past the church twice today already. I thought maybe this time I should actually look inside.'

'Wandering aimlessly is the best way to sightsee. I'll show you inside the church if you like, while we're here, and then the Guildhall in the main part of the village?' Kitty furrowed her brow. 'I'm rather afraid we'll be finished within the hour.'

'Let's go slow then,' he advised as they walked towards the church door.

'It's a beautiful village,' he said. 'I've never been anywhere like this. You're lucky to live here.'

Kitty pushed the church's wooden door open. It creaked loudly. 'I am lucky,' she agreed as they stepped inside.

Inside the church, all was quiet. The baker's elderly mother was sat at the front, worshipping alone, and she glanced around as Charlie and Kitty entered. Kitty mouthed apologies to her for their chatter.

They wandered silently along the aisle to the font. Kitty knew every detail of the ancient stone church inside and out and so she found her mind wandering, hoping the baker's mother wouldn't report in to her father how she'd been seen with an airman in the church.

Charlie stopped to read and admire the memorials on the flagstones and plaques on the walls. They reached the front and stood by a wood and gilt statue of a woman with a memorial plaque in front of her. The wood was chipped through age but someone had obviously seen fit to attempt a ham-fisted restoration. Bright paints in varying colours and lashings of gilt adorned almost every part of the statue.

Kitty was familiar with the plaque that paid tribute from a man to his wife in the seventeenth century. The woman looked so serene with her hands clasped and her face cast towards the heavens.

'This is probably one of the most beautiful things I've ever seen,' Charlie whispered. 'So romantic.'

Kitty glanced at Charlie to check he wasn't joking but he looked deadly serious.

'Really?' Kitty angled her head to one side, wandering what she was missing.

He nodded. 'It's so old. And beautiful. The lady's husband is paying tribute to the woman he loved by installing an effigy of her. It shows he cared. It shows he loved her. It shows he was moved by her loss enough to make this grand gesture.'

Kitty made a face.

Charlie turned to her. 'You don't like it?'

'Not really, no. Sorry. It's very . . . gold.'

Charlie laughed. 'It is very gold, yes.'

'It's a bit gaudy actually,' Kitty ventured. 'I can't find the beauty in anything quite so . . . obvious.'

They were silent for a moment and Kitty stole a glance up at Charlie who was looking at her, a smile playing on his lips.

'You have to remember,' Charlie said, 'that this was commissioned by a man and we aren't often noted for showing how we feel. This might have been the only way he knew how to show the world how much he loved her.'

Kitty tried looking at the effigy through fresh eyes and smiled slowly as she repeated Charlie's words in her head.

'Or,' he continued, 'he had to offload a heck of a lot of tax money very quickly and this was the only way.'

Kitty snorted with laughter. Her hand flew to her mouth.

Charlie held his ribs as he laughed. 'What was that noise you just made?'

Kitty tried to control her laughter but the damage had

been done and the woman in the front pew stared angrily at them.

'Come on,' Charlie said between laughs. 'Let's get out of here.'

Kitty dabbed at her eyes with her handkerchief as Charlie held the door open for her. He closed it behind and they sat outside on the bench facing the gravestones.

They were both smiling until Charlie eventually asked, 'What do you do for fun around here?'

'Oh, there's not much I'm afraid.' Kitty sighed. 'The Women's Institute run the odd tea dance at the village hall. Or there's the pictures in Ipswich. Have you been yet?'

Charlie shook his head. 'What else?'

She thought. 'Sadly, that's about it.'

'Do you have someone special who takes you to these tea dances or to the movie theatre?' Charlie asked.

'What a forward question. No. No one special.'

'Is it a forward question?' Charlie asked. 'I'm sorry. A guy's gotta know if it's worth taking a chance.'

'Does he now?' Kitty teased, glancing at her watch in order to look nonchalant. Then she noticed the time. 'My father will probably start wondering where I am,' she said rising from the bench. 'I should be getting back. Can I leave you to look at the Guildhall by yourself if I point you in the right direction? It's just in Market Place. It's easy to find.'

Charlie nodded, rising from the bench. 'Can I see you again?'

Kitty looked at him and smiled but he wasn't smiling back. He was watching her, waiting for her answer.

'You can see me in the pub,' Kitty tried.

He shook his head. 'That's not what I mean. Can I take you out somewhere?'

'I'm not sure,' she said. 'I . . .'

'Would you like to go on a picnic? Day after tomorrow?' His face was eager. 'I don't really know that many people here yet. Can you take pity on a sad, lonely American pilot who may die any day and let him take you out for a feast?'

Kitty laughed at the twinkle in his eyes. 'Using your potential demise to get me to go out with you is a bit low.'

He laughed. 'I know. Is it working?'

'Maybe,' she said, unable to stop smiling. 'I think we'll struggle to cobble together a feast though,' she said. 'Rationing's a bit of a killjoy when it comes to picnics these days.'

He glanced down at her as they started walking. 'Leave it to me.'

CHAPTER 7

Kitty had a spring in her step as she walked back towards The Duck. Charlie's charming smile and ability to suddenly make her laugh had made Kitty's melancholy trip to her mother's grave somewhat remarkable. She hugged herself as she entered the upstairs kitchen.

'You look happy.' Her father looked up from his newspaper. 'Where have you been today? I was wondering where you'd got to.'

'Just the church. Mum's grave.' Kitty filled the kettle and placed it on the stove to make them both a cup of tea. She stole a glance over her shoulder to see if her father wanted more information but he was studying his newspaper.

'That's nice,' he said.

'I put fresh flowers down.' Kitty put tealeaves in the little pot, opening and shutting the freestanding dark wood cabinets and drawers that only served to make the room feel small and dreary.

'Janie's in. Use the big pot. I'm sure she'll want some tea.'

Her sister was probably beautifying herself for her date

with Bobby. It was galling that Janie was allowed to step out with Bobby but her father had put a stop to any notion of Kitty seeing an American, citing Kitty's age as the main reason. *You're too young. And your sister's not too young,* which was ridiculous because Janie was only two years older. Kitty would have to keep the picnic with Charlie a secret, for now. She didn't want a row with her father and there were already too many secrets. She wondered if now was a good time to talk to her father about joining the WLA, while all was calm in the kitchen.

The brass knocker on the front door sounded loudly.

Kitty sighed. 'I'll go.'

But Kitty didn't have time to move as Janie suddenly ran past on her way to get the heavy front door of the medieval building. 'It'll be for me,' Janie called.

'That'll be her over-fed, over-paid American,' Kitty's dad said into his newspaper before looking up and giving Kitty a knowing glance. He licked the tip of his pencil as he started the crossword.

Kitty continued with her tea-making and Janie dashed past the kitchen towards her bedroom.

'It's for you,' Janie said, heading back to her room. Both Kitty and her father stopped what they were doing and looked at the kitchen doorway to see who the visitor was.

'Hello?' a female voice called from the corridor.

'Susan,' Kitty called to her friend and moved to welcome her as the young woman appeared in the doorway.

'Did Janie just leave you in the corridor?' Kitty asked incredulously.

Susan laughed. 'She left me by the front door actually but don't worry. It's not a bother.'

'She's in her own world, that girl,' Kitty's father said.

'She's in love,' Kitty volunteered. 'Love makes people silly, or so I've heard.'

'I wouldn't know,' Susan said.

'Neither would I,' Kitty agreed.

'And that's the way it stays,' Kitty's father muttered. Kitty rolled her eyes at her friend.

The doorknocker sounded again and Janie rushed past. 'I'll be back by ten.'

Their father opened his mouth to protest and then closed it again and looked down at his crossword.

Kitty finished the tea, gave her father a cup and then left him to his newspaper. She signalled to Susan to leave the kitchen. She'd not seen her friend in weeks and so much had happened since then.

'Is Janie still stepping out with Bobby?' Susan asked, following Kitty into the sitting room.

'They're engaged.' Kitty winced as Janie slammed the front door on her way out. 'And he makes her happy, which is the main thing.'

'They're engaged? How did I miss that?' Susan asked and the girls chattered as they sat on the faded red velvet settee. Like most of the rooms above the pub, the sitting room was small and oak beamed, whereas the kitchen was dark and cramped, with a surplus of furniture. The sitting room had been her mother's special room. Table lamps and pot plants gave the room a cosy feel and Kitty loved it. It reminded her of her mother, although she would have baulked at its faded glory now. The arm of the settee was almost threadbare and her father wouldn't hear of throwing anything out that his wife had chosen when they'd married. Not that they could throw anything out with these wartime shortages. No, thought Kitty, that settee would outlive them all.

She was vaguely aware of her friend talking. 'So are you?' Susan asked.

'Am I what?

'Free, the day after tomorrow? I've been invited to the pictures by a divine-looking navigator and he asked if I'd bring a friend for one of his crew.'

'Oh I don't know,' Kitty said uncertainly. 'You know what Dad's like. And besides, I meet enough of them in the bar and . . .' She shrugged dismissively.

'Oh, don't be like that.' Susan laughed. 'One of these days you'll meet someone you really like and then you'll be utterly helpless.'

For some reason Charlie's face, creased with laughter in the church flashed into Kitty's mind. She smiled and played with the thread on the settee before quickly stopping. No wonder it was going threadbare.

After a pause Susan said, 'I think he's lonely,'

'Who?' Kitty's head shot up.

'My American's friend.'

'Oh.' Kitty relaxed. 'Aren't they all? So far from home with no female company. Some of them are so young, you almost feel they need a mother not a sweetheart.'

The two women talked and Kitty refreshed the teapot, making sure her father got a decent measure in the kitchen as he finished his crossword. Kitty returned to the sitting room and poured fresh cups.

Susan broke the silence of the moment. 'I can't hold it in any longer, I've got to tell you.'

'What? What's wrong?'

'I've been accepted into the Wrens,' Susan said with glee.

'Oh you have! Oh I'm so happy for you. I know how much you wanted the Wrens. The navy-blue uniform is the best of all the services,' Kitty enthused with a wicked smile.

'I've not joined just for that, obviously.'

'Obviously,' Kitty agreed with mock-seriousness.

Susan continued with a wide smile. 'I got my papers this morning. Alongside the beautiful uniform I'll get to travel a bit, I hope. Even if it's only England it'll be marvellous to get out of here and do something a bit different. And useful.'

'That's brilliant,' Kitty said, 'I'm so pleased for you.' Then she glanced around at the door to check her father wasn't lurking. 'What would you say if I told you I'd done the same thing.'

'The Wrens?' Susan said in loud disbelief. 'The Navy? You love being landlocked though.'

'Sssh,' Kitty said, quietening her friend. 'Of course not the Wrens. The Land Army. I've been going on about it long enough.'

'You have,' Susan agreed. 'And I wondered if you were going to get on with it or if you might miss your chance and then end up on an aircraft production line or in a factory making bullets or some such horror. I was going to ask at your birthday tea only I couldn't take you to one side and mention it when your dad was right there. You've been absolutely desperate.'

Kitty glanced towards the door again. 'I still am. I passed the interview stage and I'm waiting for my letter of instruction. I knew it was likely to take some time, placing me on a suitable farm, but I do hope my information's not gone missing.' Kitty frowned thoughtfully. 'It's been weeks.'

'Is your dad still that upset about it we need to whisper?'

Kitty made a face. 'He doesn't know yet. But he knows

it's coming. It's join up or be conscripted. I'll end up somewhere. I'm just putting off the inevitable – risking upsetting him again. He doesn't want me to go away, be posted God knows where. But I had to do something. He wants me to work in civil defence like Janie and be posted in Ipswich where I can come home every night. But I just can't. I need to do something *more* or I'll go mad. I'm so cooped up in this pub. I need some fresh air. Regularly.'

Susan nodded. 'You never know. The war may drag on another decade and you might regret your decision to be a Land Girl in the depths of midwinter when you're up to your neck in snow.'

Kitty smiled. 'I can't wait. And it's doubtful the war will drag on much longer now we've got back into mainland Europe again. It'll all be over any day now. I probably won't get the chance to be a Land Girl for more than five minutes at this rate.'

The next day was a slow one in The Duck. The Americans that were out on raids were either gone too early or back too late to make the pub anything other than a quiet and fairly sombre place to be with only a few elderly village regulars reading a newspaper or playing chess. All the young men who normally lived in the village were long gone, off to war.

Kitty was glad of the peace and went to bed a bit earlier than usual, sleeping soundly until the bang of her wardrobe doors woke her the next morning with a start. Her eyes opened and she shot up into a seated position in her narrow single bed just as the second wardrobe door slammed.

'You've got nothing decent either,' Janie said to the closed wardrobe doors.

Kitty blinked and waited for her heart to slow back to its normal pace. 'I'm sorry?' she said through rapid breathing.

'Shoes.' Janie turned towards her younger sister.

'Nothing fancy. Not these days, no.' Kitty watched her sister as Janie's eyes roved around Kitty's room, taking in the faded wallpaper and the photographs of their mother holding Kitty when she was a baby.

Janie looked away and back at her sister. 'I'm catching the bus into Ipswich for some shopping before I go on duty. I might just have enough clothing coupons. Want to come?'

Kitty's eyes widened. If it was shoes Janie was after she'd be out of luck most probably, even with coupons.

Kitty sighed. 'I can't. I've got to stock take and sort the order out with the brewery this morning.'

'That's a shame,' Janie said. 'I was *hoping* you might lend me a bit of money and maybe a clothing coupon just in case I don't quite have enough after all?'

'Is that why you invited me?' Kitty teased.

'No.' The corner of Janie's mouth twitched.

'Fine. There's a few shillings in my purse on the dressing table. It's yours if you let me go back to sleep.' She lay back down under the blanket.

'Thank you! You're the best sister a girl could ever have.'

'I know,' Kitty said, her eyes already closing.

'I've found the perfect material for my wedding dress,' Janie announced suddenly.

'Where from?' Kitty was impressed and sat back up again. Fabric, especially wedding-dress-worthy material was almost impossible to get hold of.

'One of Mum's old lace tablecloths. It's still white. Sort of. I'm going to sew it over some cream cotton to make a skirt and bodice. No one will know.'

54

Kitty's hand flew to her mouth. 'Mum's tablecloth?' she said from behind her hand. 'You can't.'

'I have to. I've got nothing else,' Janie wailed. 'I've been waiting for Bobby to produce an illicit silk parachute from the airbase but they aren't as easy to get hold of as I'd been led to believe. I need something to get married in.'

'But Mum's—'

'If Mum was here she'd let me use it, you know she would.'

'I suppose she would,' Kitty agreed sadly.

Janie stood in the doorway, eager to be on her way. 'What else are you doing today? Other than the brewery order?'

Kitty opened her mouth and paused, thinking about Charlie and the picnic. She didn't need her talkative sister accidentally letting slip to their father where she was going. Whatever this friendly picnic was with Charlie, her father would have something to say against it. 'Nothing much else. Just the usual shifts downstairs.'

Janie made a face. 'Ugh, enjoy.'

'I will, enjoy looking out for enemy bombers and guiding people to shelters.'

'And shoe shopping,' Janie said with excitement and bounced from the room.

Charlie had asked to meet Kitty by the Guildhall. Streams of children were making their way inside. Charlie looked at them with a friendly but puzzled expression. Kitty waved at him from across the street as she walked towards him and he raised his hand, giving her a wide smile. In his other hand was a wicker hamper.

'Who are all of those?' Charlie gestured towards the children.

'Evacuees. The Guildhall's become a sort of temporary home for them.'

'We aren't the only newcomers then.'

'Everyone's welcome. There's a war on,' she teased.

He looked at her and angled his head to one side as if he was looking at her for the first time. 'Thank you for coming,' he said softly. 'It means a lot that you did.'

She liked his warm, genuine smile. She liked *him*, she realised. He was easy to like. Too easy to like. She looked away. 'Well, thank you so much for inviting me.' She'd lapsed into awkwardly stiff formality and had no idea why or how.

She recovered by giving him a brief history lesson about the village and telling him about the Guildhall, describing its origins as the centre for the town's once-thriving wool trade before it had eventually become a workhouse. He listened intently, his gaze roving from the building to her and back again. Every time his eyes met hers she felt herself grow warm, heat racing up her neck.

As they walked out of the village, Kitty looked around for her father, just in case or for anyone who might mention it to her father. She was hiding so much from him this week. Charlie adjusted the wicker picnic hamper from one hand to the other.

'What's in there?' Kitty asked, unable to contain her excitement over the prospect of foreign food. She'd been hearing about all the delicious American goods courtesy of Bobby and now she might actually get to taste some of it.

Charlie tapped the side of his nose and smiled. 'Wait and see. You okay to choose the picnic location? I'm not really sure where we should go, I'm afraid.'

Kitty nodded. 'Alright.'

'What did you do yesterday?' he asked as they continued on.

'Too boring to tell I'm afraid. Work mostly. What did you do?'

Charlie looked thoughtful. 'Work too.'

'Your work's a *little* bit different to mine though.'

'True. But yesterday was a good day,' he said.

'Really? Why?' she asked.

Charlie winked. 'Because we all came back alive.'

Kitty drew in a sharp intake of air. 'Gosh, don't say that,' she begged. 'That just sent chills through me.'

He laughed. 'I'm sorry. I didn't mean to shock you.'

'It didn't shock me. Not really. It's more that it . . . scared me.'

Charlie looked serious. 'I'm sorry,' he said again.

Kitty wondered what she was doing with this handsome pilot, picnicking with him, getting to know him. She'd enjoyed their chance encounter at the church and here he was on this day when even he had no idea if he'd be alive the next. A cold feeling descended on her as she looked up at his face as they walked. She must not get too invested – just enjoy it for what it was, spending time with a handsome, kind pilot and no more. Nothing more. Because if this all ended in tears she'd only have herself to blame. And besides, if her instructions from the Women's Land Army came through, who knew where she'd be sent? Far away from here, surely. No, there really was no point becoming too invested with this pilot, regardless of how attractive and friendly he was.

His face brightened. 'Where are we going?'

She tapped the side of her nose as he had done a few minutes earlier and repeated his line, 'Wait and see.'

CHAPTER 8

The wheat in the field was knee-height, its blades of yellow almost a blanket of gold that stretched as far as the eye could see. It was a shame that in a few days the harvest would begin and the scenery would be gone, scalped. But it was necessarily the way of things, Kitty appreciated. It would be harvested, and in the autumn the land would be ploughed, seeded soon after and then the circle would begin again.

Charlie let out a long whistle. 'This is pretty. Reminds me of home.'

'Really?' Kitty negotiated the crops and started leading Charlie through the field towards the patch of grass where the old oak tree sat nestled at the start of the woodland. The tree was at the edge of the farm, marking the boundary between private land and the woods. 'Where's home?' she asked.

'Iowa.'

When Kitty was silent, Charlie continued, 'Know where that is?'

'No,' Kitty admitted. 'Sorry.'

'Midwest,' he said as they walked. 'It's pretty. Lots of farmland. I grew up on a farm not too dissimilar to this as it happens.'

Kitty looked up at him and as they arrived at the oak tree, Charlie took off his uniform jacket and laid it on the ground. 'I forgot a blanket. I'm sorry.'

'It's more fun like this.' She sat on one half of the jacket and left room for him on the other half. 'Do you miss home?'

'I do. I miss it so much. I miss my mother most of all. She's not too well. When I finish this tour I'm going home.' He had a determined look in his eyes.

'I'm so sorry. What's wrong with her if you don't mind my asking?'

'I don't mind you asking. Leukaemia.' He went quiet and then, 'Shall we break into the picnic?'

Kitty looked at him, at the sadness in his eyes. He lifted the lid of the hamper but Kitty suddenly wasn't hungry. 'I'm so sorry about your mother,' she said. 'I lost mine when I was little.' She wasn't sure why but she felt it was important to tell him.

'That's awful, I'm sorry also.' And then after a beat, 'Is that whose grave you were laying flowers by?'

Kitty nodded and hated herself that tears had formed in her eyes. She blinked them away. Charlie let the hamper lid close and laid a hand on hers. She liked it, that feeling.

'Do you remember her well?' he asked.

'Sort of,' she said, wiping her eyes. 'The little things really, like when she plaited my hair or buckled my shoes. I wish I could remember the bigger things.' Kitty looked down at Charlie's hand, resting comfortably on top of hers. It felt nice. His gaze followed hers and he slowly removed his hand.

'The little things are important too,' he offered.

'I know,' Kitty said quietly. 'Can't you go home to see your mum now?' she asked. 'Get some kind of special dispensation or something like that?'

'I wish. I'll have to wait until the end of this tour and then I'll go. I'm just over halfway through.' He paused. 'I only found out last week that she was sick. She was going to wait until I came home to tell me face to face. But I wrote her, told her I'd signed up for another tour and so she wrote me back, telling me as gently as she could.' His face fell and he closed his eyes. 'I feel awful,' he sighed. 'I'm the worst son. I shouldn't have stayed here. I shoulda gone home. Especially given she's all by herself.'

'Where's your father?'

'He died in the Great War, joined up the minute the US entered the fray. Never came home. I was born a few months after he died so I never knew him. So now my mom's lost another of her family to the war. Although I intend to survive. I'm doing some good, I hope, but I feel guilty for her all at the same time.'

It was Kitty's turn to reach for his hand. She clutched it meaningfully. 'It's not your fault,' she said emphatically, squeezing his hand for good measure. 'You couldn't possibly have known and you're here for such a good reason.'

'No. I know. But . . . still.'

'You mustn't feel guilty for doing something good for the war.'

He looked at her softly. Kitty wasn't sure what she was feeling. It was something that she couldn't put her finger on. It was such an honest conversation with someone she hardly knew.

'Why on earth did you stay?' she asked gently. 'Why a second tour when you'd survived the first?'

He shrugged. 'It's not just your war, you know? Here in Europe. It's all our war. It felt wrong to just go home at the end. All that flight training. To go home and do what with it? Nothing. I feel like I'm supposed to be here. We got through a complete tour together, the crew and me. We were like brothers. And we survived. It felt like a sign. That if I did it again, it would all be okay like it was the first time. Like I could get another crew through alive.'

'I thought you might be half mad,' Kitty said. 'Now I'm absolutely *convinced* of it.'

Charlie laughed.

'It's very honourable,' Kitty pointed out.

He shrugged and looked out across the field. 'I try.'

'Did all your crew stay for a second tour?'

'God, no.' He laughed. 'They wised up. They all went home.' He looked intently at the ground and started picking blades of grass.

'All of them?'

Charlie nodded. 'Clever boys. I got a new crew now. Well, not that new. We're halfway through this tour. After which, I will encourage the ones that are left standing to go home – be with their families.'

'The ones that are left standing?' Kitty didn't understand.

His gaze was still on the ground. 'I mean the ones that are left alive. The other day, when I practically fell to my knees and begged you for a drink?'

Kitty nodded.

'We'd just lost our tail gunner.'

'How?' Kitty asked quietly.

He exhaled slowly. 'The usual way. Sometimes we're just sitting ducks up there.'

Kitty was quiet and waited for him to continue.

61

'There's this point, it's just maybe thirty to forty seconds, which passes in the blink of an eye in real life. But when you're up there . . .' He signalled skyward. 'It feels like forever, when the bombardier is waiting to drop the bombs, and training his sights on the target, when I only have one job – to keep her steady and level. And the guns are going off below us. If the bombardier doesn't get the target in sight, well, we have to go around again and repeat the process. So we try and get it right first time, y'know?'

Kitty nodded once more. But she didn't know. Not at all.

'That day, we'd had to go around and be sitting ducks for a second time. That's when our tail gunner got hit. Just a kid. Not even old enough to vote.'

Kitty didn't know what to say. She clutched his hand tighter. 'Some days,' he continued, 'you have such a run of luck you feel invincible. And then you lose a friend, a crewmember and you realise you're just flesh and bone after all.' He looked from the grass to her and Kitty saw his eyes were starting to dampen. She nodded, feeling his heartache. He pulled his hand away gently, wiped at his eyes and then stood up, making an exhausted noise at himself as if angry he'd allowed himself to cry.

'How old's this fella?' He changed the subject, tipping his head up to look up at the vast expanse of green leaves that formed a canopy above them on the oak tree.

'I'm not sure. Two hundred, maybe three hundred years old?' Kitty looked up at the tree, wincing at the bright sunshine filtering through the leaves.

'The things it must have seen.' Charlie's voice was wistful and Kitty smiled. 'You have a beautiful smile,' he said.

She felt her stomach flip over and her cheeks redden

with heat. She thanked him so quietly she was almost whispering.

Charlie looked back at the tree. 'Have you seen these?' He pointed to something on the tree trunk.

Kitty climbed to her feet to see what he was pointing at. She stood next to him and saw two small carvings of hearts with initials inside; made by two different couples.

'We're not the only people who sit under this tree. These lovers have been busy.' Charlie was about a foot taller than Kitty. He glanced down at her and Kitty was standing close enough to smell his cologne. He smelled wonderful and as she looked up at him she was vaguely aware her breath had slowed. His gaze drifted slowly from her eyes down to her mouth and she exhaled. Something had shifted suddenly. Or maybe it wasn't sudden at all.

As it dawned on her that Charlie might be about to kiss her, a movement by the farmhouse in the distance caught her eye. Without meaning to, Kitty glanced over Charlie's shoulder suddenly and saw a young man waving at her from the other side of the field.

Charlie looked. 'Do you know who that is?'

'Christopher Frampton,' Kitty said as she lifted her arm to wave back to the man.

'Friend of yours?' Charlie questioned as he too lifted his hand to give a quick but polite acknowledging wave to the man who was walking round the side of the house and out of sight.

'Sort of.' Aware the moment between them had passed, Kitty left Charlie's side and sat back on his jacket. 'We used to play together as children. He's a little bit older than me. I don't see much of him now.'

'Why not?' Charlie frowned and looked at the large and

rambling stone farmhouse in the distance as he lay down on his jacket. 'Class divide?' he joked. 'Of which I hear about lots but don't fully understand.'

'Well, yes actually. I suppose so.' Kitty frowned. 'We used to enjoy each other's company when he was home from boarding school in the holidays. And then we grew up and found different friends. He was going into law but when war broke out and his father died he had no choice but to stay here to run the farm. I hardly see him these days. He never comes into the pub.'

Charlie's eyebrows shot up. 'He's here permanently? He didn't want to fight?'

Kitty shrugged. 'I don't think it was a case of *didn't want to*. More that he's in a reserved occupation. His father died recently in an air raid when he was in London and there's only Christopher able to farm now. If he doesn't do it, the business will go to wrack and ruin.'

'That's something I know lots about,' he said wryly. 'I left my mom to run the farm but she was always kinda hands-on, in charge, and we have farmhands who she can rely on. But his mother couldn't help?'

Kitty's mouth twitched as she thought of the haughty and unapproachable Mrs Frampton helping with the harvest. Currently it was up to Christopher and Nancy, the Land Girl who worked with him and who Kitty had seen in the village. More Land Girls would arrive soon in time for the harvest. 'Oh my word, no. Christopher's mother doesn't lift a finger on that farm. She thinks she's far too good for actual work. She doesn't know what she's missing. She's so lucky having all that land. Those animals.'

Charlie stretched out on the grass and lay on his side, looking up at her. 'You sound envious.'

'I suppose I am in a way. But all that's going to change,' she confided quietly.

'How?'

She regretted saying it now. She'd only told Susan, not even her father or Janie yet but there was just something so honest about Charlie and she wanted to talk to him about it – wanted to tell him.

'I've joined the Women's Land Army.'

'Have you?' He nodded his approval. 'I saw those girls in their uniforms up in Norfolk, working as hard as anything. When are you going?'

'Imminently, I'd imagine. A four-week training programme on a farm, usually, and then who knows where I'll be sent after that. I'm just waiting to be told where to go.'

'You want to work on a farm?' He looked interested.

'Yes. Always have done, really. Perhaps it's because I feel cooped up in the pub. Perhaps it's because my mother was a farmer's daughter . . . She used to tell such stories. I know it'll be hard work but . . .' She shrugged, feeling silly.

He had a twinkle in his eye. 'You don't like working in the pub.' It wasn't a question.

Kitty looked at him, wondering how much she could tell this man she'd only known a few days. She shook her head. 'Not really, no.'

'Your father makes you?'

'No.' Kitty laughed loudly. 'It's not like that. Since my mum died, it's just been the three of us. My sister Janie's getting married soon, to one of your lot. I imagine she'll be off to America at some point and then it'll just be Dad and me. I hate the idea of leaving him. But I think for the duration of the war . . . if I'm to live a bit and do something I enjoy – really enjoy – and help the war effort, then now is the time, while Janie is still here. And then I can return home and be with Dad.'

'And work in the pub until you die?' Charlie asked.

'Yes. Hang on . . . no,' Kitty said, giving him a look.

'I'm only teasing,' he replied. 'I'm sorry. It sounds like a good idea. Seize the day.'

'Yes. I suppose so. I've waited a long time because my father didn't want me going off until conscription age. But I've reached that and if I don't do what I *want* to do then I'll only be conscripted into some sort of factory,' she said. 'And no disrespect to factory girls but . . .' She made a face again. 'It's not for me. To escape being cooped up by being cooped up again. No thank you. So . . . I've enrolled.'

'Instead you'll be in the freezing cold English countryside smothered in pigswill?' He laughed. 'That's better?'

'It is to me and don't tease.'

'Hey, I'm a farm boy . . . I also love being covered in pigswill.'

Kitty laughed. 'What made you want to leave?'

'Adventure,' Charlie offered. 'The opportunity to help right a wrong, to fight for freedom. The farm will still be there when all this is over. I'll go home eventually. I was sad to leave my mom, especially now . . .' He trailed off.

'I'll be sad to leave Dad,' she confided. 'But wherever I'm posted it won't be the thousands of miles you've covered.'

Charlie waved his hand as if batting a fly. 'He's a grown man. He'll get over it. He'll find help from elsewhere.'

Kitty narrowed her eyes. 'Maybe. And I'll come back whenever I'm allowed and I'll be back properly when the war's over,' she said, more to reassure herself, 'which can't be long now.'

'No you won't,' he said. 'You'll be snapped up by a handsome farmer and your father won't see you for dust.'

'Be quiet,' she said, thumping him playfully on the arm.

'Ow,' he said, laughing. 'Okay, now for a serious question.'

'Another one?' she asked in mock exasperation.

'Kitty?' he asked with pretend seriousness, holding her gaze.

'Charlie,' she replied in the same tone, holding his gaze in return.

'Would you care to join me for a picnic now?'

'That's your serious question?'

'That's my serious question. I'm a man. I'm *always* serious about food.'

How easily he made her laugh. 'Yes please.'

CHAPTER 9

Summer, 2011

Overnight, the village had become inundated with pensioners. Amy's tearoom was full to bursting with war veterans, some in wheelchairs with younger companions; many with wives or husbands. It astonished Amy that even the older generation of Americans all had perfect teeth. They were all so friendly and charming that she couldn't help but have a spring in her step, despite the fact neither she nor Caroline had stopped all day.

When she'd helped the final elderly gentleman down the tricky front step and pointed him in the direction of The Duck, Amy joined Caroline at one of the tables she was cleaning.

'Today has been ridiculous,' Caroline said. 'I don't think I stopped once and I've not eaten anything all day.'

'Me neither,' Amy said as her stomach chose that moment to groan in hunger. 'Do you know I didn't even think about it?'

'I did.' Caroline moved towards the cake domes and lifted the last hefty slice of Victoria sponge into her mouth, taking a bite. 'Going all day without eating . . . I'm sure there's some kind of workers' rights violation going on here,' she joked.

'Probably,' Amy agreed. 'But if you sue me, we'll both be out of jobs.'

'Fair enough. I'll take a glass of wine in The Duck instead?'

Amy perked up. 'What a good idea.' They locked up and headed into the early evening sunshine.

'Thanks for today,' Amy said as they made their way across the road to the hotel's bar. 'You really are a lifesaver.'

'I know,' Caroline replied with an air of mock-seriousness. 'But it is my job too, remember. I'll get a table, you get the wine. And crisps. Lots of crisps. Oh . . .'

The sisters stopped. The Duck was heaving with tourists. All the tables had been taken and there was barely any space at the long wooden bar.

At the other end of the bar Amy spotted the American, Jack – she'd finally remembered his name – with the man she'd seen him in the street with yesterday. He was engrossed in conversation and was halfway through a pint. She toyed with the idea of going over and saying hello but stopped as David sidled his way through the bar towards them.

'I've got your receipt,' she told him, digging in her bag to retrieve it. 'Any room for us?'

'Thanks,' he said, taking the paperwork. 'We're a bit busy tonight I'm afraid. Standing room only. We're fully booked for dinner and rooms for the next week,' David said proudly.

'You're always fully booked,' Amy countered.

'Is there any chance you could get us each a glass of cold white wine?' Caroline begged. 'We can't get to the bar?'

David gave Caroline an engaging smile. 'Leave it with me.' He disappeared into the throng. The women moved to

69

a space near the far wall by the restaurant entrance, tucking themselves out the way. The many tourists in the room were looking contemplatively at the wood panelling on the walls, at the names of the men who'd been stationed nearby during the war written on them.

Amy and Caroline were shuffled out of the way numerous times by those who wanted to look at the names.

David beckoned to Caroline as he held up two large glasses of wine. 'Oh phew,' Caroline said. 'I'll see if I can beg some crisps as well.'

While Caroline moved off, Amy found her gaze wandering towards Jack. He and the man he was with turned, catching sight of her. Jack said something to the older man and they both headed towards her, cutting through the throng.

'Hey, how are you?' Jack gave Amy a broad smile as he approached.

Amy returned Jack's infectious smile. 'Tired. In need of wine. We've been flat out all day.'

'Allow me. White or red?' Jack started towards the bar.

Amy put her hand on his arm to stall him. 'No need,' she said, spying Caroline returning with two bags of crisps gripped in her teeth and a glass of white wine in each hand.

Caroline thrust her a packet of crisps and her drink, said a quick hello to Jack and then made herself scarce, joining some of their friends in the corner.

'Amy, this is my dad, Emmett. Dad, this is Amy.' Amy juggled shaking hands while holding her wine in one hand and crisps in the other. Jack gently took the crisps from her and opened the pack, holding it out so she could eat. She smiled her gratitude to him.

'How are you enjoying it here?' Amy asked before popping a crisp in her mouth.

'It's beautiful.' Emmett smiled. He was a carbon copy of Jack, only older. 'My dad was stationed here in the war and he used to explain it to me as being like a village lost in time. But I wasn't sure whether to believe him or not.'

'He was right though,' Jack chimed in. 'Are you going to the Heritage Day at the old airfield?'

Amy nodded. 'Caroline and I are running the tearoom in the marquee,' she said. It was hard not to sound nervous. It was her first foray into full-on event catering and she wondered if she'd bitten off more than she could chew. Wedding cakes were one thing but setting up for hundreds of people was something else entirely.

'Have you ever been there before?' Emmett asked. 'To the old airfield I mean?'

'I hadn't since I was a kid but I went to have a meeting with the organisers and take a quick look the other week to work out where we were going to park – how far to carry all the food, electrics . . . that kind of thing,' Amy replied. 'The control tower is still there but the rest of it is all just fields. The other buildings were long gone before I was born: hangars, sleeping quarters. It'll be good to see it open again at the Heritage Day. Have you been to take a look yet?'

'Not yet,' Emmett said. 'Jack and I have been busy sightseeing some of the places I'd heard mentioned to me so many times when I was a kid. When you're young you don't pay attention to what your elders tell you. I wish I had though.' He looked remorseful. 'Still, not much of the airfield is left from what you say but it'll be nice to see

71

inside the control tower though.' He yawned. 'Sorry. Jetlag is still getting to me. If you kids'll excuse me I think I'll head off to my room for a nap before dinner. Jack, see you down here at eight?'

Jack nodded.

'So,' Jack said when he and Amy were alone, 'event catering at the Heritage Day?'

'For my sins.' Amy gave a frightened look. 'I'm actually looking forward to it in a mad sort of way. I've got a few days to knuckle down and prep and we're already so busy as it is. Caroline's on at me about workers' rights so she's going to get a shock this week. We've got a *lot* to get through.'

'Well, if you need an extra pair of hands, I can bake. Kind of. I have to watch the cake through the oven door though. I don't trust the oven not to burn it.'

She laughed. 'I'm trying to imagine you in a pinafore, sat in front of the oven watching a sponge cake rise.'

'Many times,' he said, chuckling. 'Many times.' He looked at his empty glass. 'I'd better go freshen up for dinner. I guess I'll see you around?'

'Sure,' Amy replied. She was still smiling.

He gave her a wave and turned. Suddenly Amy remembered something.

'Jack?'

He turned back.

'Thank you for the Champagne. The other day. For my birthday.'

He looked at her blankly.

'It was you, wasn't it?' she asked desperately.

A slight smile played at the corners of his mouth. 'I've no idea what you're talking about.' He gave her a small

72

wink, turned and left to take the stairs to the rooms above.

Amy watched him go thoughtfully and then let her smile spread even wider across her face.

CHAPTER 10

The oven timer beeped, pulling Amy out of a tired daze the next evening after the tearoom had closed. She looked at the fresh batch of cupcakes and wondered if she had too many? Or maybe not enough? She'd keep them stored and ice them the day before the Heritage Day with edible printed paper covered in pin-up girls from wartime cinema and old B-17 planes to place on top of the buttercream.

Glancing at her checklist, Amy allowed her shoulders to unstiffen, rolling them back and forth. So far, everything was going according to plan. The two stand mixers had been going for so long, with different mixtures for varying cakes, that it was a marvel the motors hadn't burned out.

An hour or two more in the kitchen should do it. She could get another few cakes mixed and baked in that. Who knew how many would turn up for tea and cake at the marquee in a few days? Best to over-cater.

A faint tapping sounded on the glass in the shopfront and Amy looked round the kitchen doorway to see who it was, forgetting the blinds were down. She wiped her hands on a tea towel, dusting flour off her fingers, and switched the mixers off before heading to the front door. The bell above it jingled as she opened it.

'Hi.' Jack raised his hand to greet her and gave her a broad smile.

'Hi,' she returned a bit too loudly, surprised to see him.

'My dad took himself off to Thomas Gainsborough's house in Sudbury. Again. And then for an evening walk,' Jack said. 'And while it was great the first time I'm not sure I need to see Gainsborough's house a second time. So . . . I'm at a loose end, if you need a hand?' He shuffled on his feet.

'That's really kind. Um . . . how are your cake-mixing skills?' Amy said after a beat.

'Mid to fair.'

'That'll do.' She laughed. 'Come in.'

Jack looked around the tearoom as he wiped his feet on the mat. 'This is pretty.'

'Thanks.' Amy blushed. 'I'm quite proud of it. There's so much more I want to do, but for now . . .'

'Looks good enough to me.' Jack followed Amy through to the kitchen.

'That's because you're a man.'

Jack raised an eyebrow. 'So?'

Amy laughed. 'Never mind.'

'No, go on.'

'Well . . . when it comes to customers, the women choose where to eat . . . It's where looks prettiest, busiest, nicest. The men go where they're told.'

'Huh.' He looked thoughtful. 'Probably true.'

'Aesthetics are everything.'

'Well, that's me told,' he said, his dark eyes creasing as his mouth lifted into a smile.

His smile was infectious.

'Would you like a pretty apron?' she teased.

'I would *love* a pretty apron. And then put me to work.'

Amy looked around the tiny kitchen. 'You could spoon that mixture into that cake tin and then I'll get the next batch ready.'

They chatted amicably while they worked together. 'How long are you on holiday for?' she asked as he put the first batch in the oven and Amy mixed the next.

'A couple more weeks. My dad and I have worked our way round London. We did it in a few days, which I couldn't believe. Dad goes at a pace that puts me to shame. We're getting a lot of the energetic stuff in before we tour all the bases he wants to see.' Jack moved to the sink to wash up. 'And he's desperate to see as many as he can.'

'Not really your cup of tea?' Amy asked.

Jack chuckled. 'I love that English phrase. Not really my cup of tea, no. But I'm a dutiful son so I go, keep him company.'

'What do you do when you're not visiting England's finest tourist attractions?' She put the second tray of cakes into the other oven.

'I'm a photographer.'

'*Are* you?'

'You sound surprised,' he said as he spooned mixture into cake tins.

'I suppose I am a bit. What kind of photographer? What do you mostly photograph?'

'Portraits, mainly.'

She stopped what she was doing and looked at him. 'Of who?' she asked, even more interested now.

'All kinds of people. Although I've accidentally ended up

photographing mainly models for fashion shoots or beauty commercials. It's good for the travel perks.'

'Sounds amazing,' she said.

He made a non-committal noise. 'Not really.'

'Taking pictures of models all day while travelling? My heart bleeds.'

'I know, I know,' he said, laughing as he moved the mixing bowl towards her. 'Maybe I've just done it too long. I'm ready for a change.'

Amy leaned against the counter and watched him. 'What would you like to do instead?'

'I still want to take photographs.' He looked like he was thinking. 'But I want to capture something that's more *real* in some way. And landscapes. Nature. I don't know,' he said, brushing off his dreams.

Amy waited for more.

'Landscapes don't show up late or get angry if the coffee isn't decaf,' he reasoned.

'Oh I *see*. People can be hard work,' she said.

'They really can be.' Then his attitude brightened. 'You've some beautiful scenery around here,' he said. 'The fields are pretty and the light is glorious. Your Suffolk summers seem pretty special. Sometimes I really miss the country. You're real lucky to live here.'

Amy smiled warmly. She *was* lucky.

Jack folded a tea towel. 'Anything else I can do?'

'No thanks. I'm just going to wait for all this lot.' Amy gestured at the ovens. 'And then that's me done.'

Jack leaned against the counter and put his hands in the pockets of his jeans. Everything about him was casual, easy.

'You know,' Amy said thoughtfully, 'my grandmother has

a beautiful farmhouse with a huge, glorious garden and at the end of it, the grass stretches out and merges into a wheat field. It's beautiful at this time of year. Like a sea of yellow. Until the combine harvesters arrive in a week or two.'

Jack nodded.

'I mean,' Amy clarified. 'It would probably make a lovely image. If you wanted to take some pictures of the Suffolk countryside you could do worse than start there.'

'It sounds great. I'd love to. I'm actually free tomorrow for a little bit.'

'Lovely,' she said.

'Are you going to come with me? If not, you'll have to give me directions.'

'That's a good point. Um . . . sure. I guess I should probably phone my gran and see if she's available. If not, she won't mind us going around by ourselves.'

'Great.' Jack pushed himself away from the counter. 'I'll stop by and pick you up? What time works for you?'

Amy tapped her fingers on the counter as she thought. This plan had formed fast. She was so busy prepping for the Heritage Day that she didn't really have time to be gallivanting with Jack but she found that she really wanted to. 'I suppose I could sneak out of here around three o'clock for an hour or two before I carry on with this lot. We'll be a bit quieter after the lunch rush.'

'Alright then.' Jack walked through the tearoom and opened the door to the street as Amy followed and called after him teasingly.

'Jack, if you like the apron that much you only had to ask me for it.'

He looked down and laughed, untying it and handing it back. 'Ha. Sorry. Pink's not really my colour.'

'Thank you for helping,' she said, taking the apron from him.

'It was my pleasure. I didn't do much. But I enjoyed it. See you tomorrow. Three o'clock.' As he walked a few paces down the street he turned and smiled at her.

Amy looked at his retreating figure and wondered again if he was single. Why was she no good at asking the important questions?

CHAPTER 11

They could have walked to her grandmother's farm from the village in about fifteen minutes but Amy was always so busy trying to fit work and life into her busy days that she was used to hopping in the car to get to Kitty's. Now though, she was regretting it.

'I'm new at this.' Jack looked apologetic as he pulled away and crunched the gears of his rental car from first to second.

Amy adopted a polite smile but clutched the edge of the passenger seat. 'New at what?' She dug her fingers into the seat harder as he swerved suddenly. 'Driving?'

The gear crunched from second to third. 'No.' He winced at the noise. 'Driving a stick shift. On the wrong side of the road.'

Jack had brought the car to the shop at exactly three o'clock the next day and Amy hadn't been in the slightest bit ready. She was sure she had flour on her face and looked in the mirror on the car's sun visor to check. She had, but Jack was obviously too polite to say. She wiped her cheek quickly.

On the short journey through the countryside – the disused airfield's old grey control tower visible across the lane's hedges – Amy remembered she hadn't even had time to ask her grandmother if it was alright if she brought a visitor. It wouldn't be a problem, surely. Gran was always easy-going and loved company, and if she wasn't home, Amy was sure it would be fine to let Jack in and make a pot of tea.

They parked in the gravel driveway and it was all Amy could do not to breathe a sigh of relief as they arrived safely. He really was a terrible driver. Jack killed the engine and looked at her.

'It's been a while since I last drove, you know, properly. I just get cabs around the city back home.' Jack gave her a sideways smile and looked up at the grey brick farmhouse as they walked towards it. 'Beautiful house. You lived here?'

'No. It's always been my gran's. And my grandad's, when he was alive.'

'Where *do* you live?' he asked as they climbed out of the car and he opened the boot to retrieve his professional camera.

'Above the tearoom. But as a kid, we were on the outskirts of the village. My mum was an only child and she left for London when she was eighteen. And when my dad left us, she moved back to a newbuild house on the outskirts. We lived there. Just the three of us.

'Do you still see your father?' Jack asked as Amy led him towards the kitchen door.

'No. I never knew him really. He was gone by the time I was a toddler.'

'You can't miss what you never had?' Jack suggested.

'Exactly.' Amy smiled and opened the kitchen door, calling loudly for her gran. There was no reply. 'She might be out in the garden or gone to visit a friend.'

Jack frowned. 'If she's out, she just leaves the door unlocked?'

Amy gave Jack a knowing look. 'It's not that kind of place. I often leave the door unlocked if I'm nipping to the shop or whatever.'

He shook his head. 'That's refreshing. You can't do that where I live in New York.'

'No, you probably can't leave your door unlocked in New York and expect your possessions to still be there when you get back. Shall we head to the garden and I can show you what I mean about the field looking so magical?'

Jack nodded and held up his camera to indicate he was ready. He glanced around and Amy saw the house through Jack's eyes as they moved through. Ramshackle, old, in need of a lick of paint, but full to the brim with antiques. It was beautiful, he was right. And homely too. Amy loved it.

There was no sign of Kitty round the side of the house either or in the garden. Jack smiled as he looked down the lush green grass and towards the field.

'See?' Amy asked. She really wanted Jack to see it as she did.

'Wow,' he said. They were viewing it on a particularly sunny day. In the distance the rays of sun caught the wheat in such a way as to make it glint like honey-coloured glass, while the grass directly in front of them was lush and manicured. The field was the only bit of farmland Kitty still owned and it was only still part of the property because Kitty refused to hand over her view to someone who might build another housing estate on it. Instead, the farmer who'd purchased the old airfield managed Kitty's remaining land for her. Amy suddenly remembered padding barefoot on the soft grass and running into the field as a child. She smiled to herself. Where had that

82

memory come from? She'd been small. Had she been carrying her teddy bear? She wondered if that was the day her grandfather had come looking for her and photographed her at the oak tree. Jack looked as if he was in the zone and so Amy kept quiet. He hooked his thumb in the back pocket of his jeans and held the camera down low with his other hand. He looked as if he was assessing something. Perhaps the light?

She wondered if she should pull up a rattan garden chair and make herself comfortable. The cushions had been put out and a cup of tea was on the glass table. Amy wrapped her hands around it. Still warm. Her grandmother must be here somewhere.

Jack was looking at her. 'You coming?' he asked, indicating the field.

'Sure.' Amy walked towards him and they moved to the edge of the boundary where the lawn met the field. As they moved through, Amy bent down and plucked a small handful of wheat. It wasn't quite yet high enough to harvest. It would be in a few weeks and then the whole filed would look completely different.

'Hoodlum,' Jack said as she pulled the crop from the ground.

Amy laughed and as she turned back to give him a guilty look the breeze caught her hair and whipped it behind her. Jack pressed a button, his camera already raised to take a picture of the field. Amy had been caught in the photographic crossfire. She tucked a lock of hair behind her ear and gave a nervous laugh. 'I'll bet I looked windswept?'

Jack clicked a few buttons on the camera and looked at the picture on the screen. Amy, a few paces away, didn't want to dash over, looking vain and staring at a picture of herself.

Jack glanced at the screen and then back to Amy and smiled. 'Beautiful. Even if I do say so myself.'

Amy felt her cheeks go red. 'Can I see some of the other pictures you've taken?'

He walked over and Amy and he stood in the field with the wheat swaying around them as Jack scrolled through the other images slowly.

'These are so good,' Amy said. 'I don't know anything about photography but . . .'

'But you know what you like?' Jack suggested.

Amy nodded. 'They're wonderful. Really.' Among the shots were those of the Guildhall, now run by the National Trust and the River Deben, the summer sun blasting the varying landscapes with an array of hazes and sheens. He'd even managed to make the churchyard look like a desirable location for an afternoon outing.

She glanced up at him. His photos *were* good. The kind that would look wonderful gracing the walls of homes or in interiors magazines. A thought struck her.

'I could sell these,' Amy suddenly said. 'In the tearoom.' Jack gave her a puzzled look. 'Really?'

Enthusiasm took over. 'Yes, really.' She scrolled back to an image of a sprawling mulberry tree. 'Where's this?' she asked.

'It's the garden at the Gainsborough House Museum.'

'Tourists will love this,' Amy said as she scrolled. 'With photos as beautiful as these, you'll make an absolute killing. The walls of my tearoom have only got generic canvases. If we get some of these framed, I'll happily put them up and see if I can sell them for you.'

'You'd do that?' Jack asked, looking at her.

'You'd be doing me a favour.' Amy shrugged. 'Beautiful

art for the tearoom and it's good for both of us if I do sell some.'

'Okay. You've got yourself a deal.' Jack laughed and held out his hand.

Amy shook it. Was it she or he who held it a fraction of a second longer than was strictly necessary? Amy slowly pulled away and their fingers brushed as they parted, sending a jolt of elation through her.

Jack gestured where the field ended and the woodland began. 'Can we take a look at that oak tree over there?'

Amy was grateful for the distraction. As they arrived at the tree, Jack turned and looked back at the sprawling farmhouse in the distance. 'This place is magical,' he said.

Amy quietly watched him focus and then take a series of photographs of the field towards the house. She leaned against the oak tree for a while and closed her eyes, enjoying the sun's rays as they filtered onto her through the branches. She didn't notice Jack move next to her until he was close. She looked up at him and took a sharp breath, but his gaze was towards the tree trunk and he hadn't noticed.

'Do you see those? Up there?' Jack asked.

Amy spun and looked up to where Jack was pointing. Above them were a series of heart-shaped carvings made by lovers from years gone by. Inside each were different initials.

They looked on respectfully, silently, neither of them speaking. Amy read the initials; some were dated during the war but most of the markings simply had initials emblazoned.

After a while Jack pointed to one, 'C&K 1944,' he said. 'Lovers from a simpler time.'

'Or a more complicated one,' Amy added. 'Might be my grandparents. These are their initials and they married in the war.'

Jack nodded and took a photograph of the carvings and then slowly turned towards her. Amy felt her pulse quicken as Jack's smiling eyes looked down into hers.

'What?' she asked softly. She wondered if she still had flour on her face.

He shook his head. 'Nothing.' And then, 'I'm having a nice time.'

'Me too,' she replied. A gust of summer breeze rippled the wheat in the field and Amy's eyes were drawn past Jack. Over by the farmhouse, she could see Kitty watching them intently.

Amy raised her hand to wave and Kitty responded similarly. Jack glanced over his shoulder and waved politely.

'Your grandmother?' he enquired.

Amy nodded. 'Come on. Let's go and make a pot of tea.'

Kitty was back inside the farmhouse kitchen by the time they arrived. The scrubbed wooden table held a few box files and a large photo album.

Amy looked at them. 'These aren't from the loft, are they? You haven't been up there? On your own? What if you fell down the ladder?'

Kitty ignored her. 'And this young man is . . .?'

Jack introduced himself, shaking hands with Kitty. 'Your granddaughter invited me to photograph the land around your house. I hope you don't mind.'

'Not at all,' Kitty said kindly.

'You're very lucky to live here. I think I got some fantastic shots. Landscapes like this are thin on the ground in New York.'

'May I see?' Kitty looked at the images Jack showed on his screen while Amy busied herself making tea. Amy smiled, listening to Jack and Kitty talk about photography and the beautiful Suffolk light.

'We used to have a lot more land than this.' Kitty's voice sounded far away and she looked at the screen as Jack scrolled through the images. 'But we sold it long ago. The farm wasn't profitable. Broke my husband's heart the day we sold it. Some of it is still farmland but most of it's a housing estate now. It all used to be part of the old airfield during the war.'

'How do you end up owning an airfield?' Jack asked. He mouthed a thank you as Amy handed him a cup of tea and then placed milk and sugar on the table.

'A huge portion of the farmland was given over to the American Air Force when they arrived and at the end of the war it was handed back to the farm, runway and hangars still in situ. The old hangars were turned into a rough sort of cowshed for the dairy farm eventually. But they started to decay and we couldn't afford the upkeep of the whole farm. It made sense to sell it and just keep what was manageable. Some of the airfield is still there though, on the other side of the housing estate,' Kitty continued. 'The landing strip can just about be seen through the grass but the tarmac has crumbled away a lot now. And the control tower is there of course, preserved. It's all on a fraction of the land it used to be. A farmer owns all that now and keeps the original control tower intact.'

Jack looked out of the kitchen window in the direction Kitty was pointing. But, unable to see much over the line of trees on the far side of the field, he turned back. 'Are you going to the Heritage Day at the old airfield?' Jack pulled out a chair for Kitty as they sat down. 'I believe they're unveiling a memorial to the bomb group stationed there.'

'Thank you.' Kitty stirred the tea Amy had placed on the kitchen table in front of her. 'I may do. I'm not sure yet. It might be too much for me.'

Amy flashed her grandmother a look. Kitty had just been careering her way up and down the loft stairs. Why on earth would a memorial unveiling be too hard?

Amy nodded towards the dusty files on the table. 'What are all these, Gran?'

'Some of your mother's school reports. One of her photo albums. There are some dreadful ones in there of me with bouffant hair in the sixties. Have a look. It's a giggle. You know,' Kitty continued, 'Amy's grandfather was an excellent photographer. His albums are packed safely away in the loft. You should take a look, Jack. And if you're feeling strong you two could be angels and bring them down.'

CHAPTER 12

Amy clutched the cold metal loft ladder as it swayed dangerously underfoot. She was furious that her grandmother was going up and down such a rickety ladder. She had a good mind to tell Kitty she was banned from going up here from now on. But she knew her grandmother wouldn't listen and would carry on regardless.

Jack gave Amy a look that also conveyed his alarm that someone of Kitty's age had negotiated the ladder as his head appeared through the loft hatch.

Above them the bulb shone dimly. Old trunks and box files were packed haphazardly around each other on the dusty floorboards. Amy stamped on the boards to check their strength. Not even a creak from the attic floor, bringing relief. Heights weren't her favourite thing. At the end of the apex roof a small window scraped stiffly when she opened it, providing much needed air to the otherwise stuffy space. Jack's face said it all as they assessed the jumble.

'I know,' Amy agreed as she looked around at the rammed

loft. 'I don't know what possessed her to sort all this now. What a mess.'

Kitty had cleared a small area so they started there first. They dug through boxes of old photographs and mementos, finding records, school report cards, theatre programmes and crumpled postcards dated just after the Second World War to and from various family members. They looked at each in turn, marvelling at an era neither of them knew much about. Each box held a treasure trove of wartime lives once lived, long ago.

Eventually in a battered leather trunk they found what they were really looking for: Amy's grandfather's photographs. Whoever had put them in albums had done so diligently. Each of the red leather-bound volumes was dated by year. Inside the albums was an array of well-composed photos: some of Kitty, some of Amy's mother Alison as a child. A few less professional-looking ones were of Amy's grandfather as a young man. Amy assumed Kitty must have taken them as he had been captured in a rare moment in front of the camera, instead of having been behind the lens. The landscape images he'd taken were interspersed between the family photos, stuck in with browning sticky tape over each of the corners onto the thick, textured album pages. Jack turned the pages slowly. 'Beautiful composition,' he murmured.

He was clearly engrossed in the artistry. They were mainly photographs of the farmhouse and surrounding fields but whenever the family had been on holiday to various beaches or other near-flung locations, Amy's grandfather had documented it all in wonderful black, white, sepia. There were even some of the airfield, back in the day, crawling with American Air Force men, although their faces couldn't be seen. They were running in many of the shots and Amy's grandfather had captured the frenetic energy of an active bomber station.

'These are stunning,' Amy agreed. She was proud of the grandfather she'd only known a short time.

Jack agreed. 'Forget selling mine. You should sell these.'

'No.' Amy opened another album. 'They aren't mine to sell and you want to make a living from yours.'

'I'll start carrying some of these down to your grandmother,' Jack said. As he removed some of the remaining albums, underneath Amy spotted something shining in a ray of sunlight. She picked it up, a small silver St Christopher pendant, dusty and tarnished with age. She held it up; there was no inscription, nothing to show it was important or special. It looked as if it had been discarded casually in the box. Amy pocketed it to show her gran and then she picked up what looked like a series of notebooks, laid at the bottom of the heavy trunk. She peered at the book covers in the dim light before reaching in to pull one out.

Behind her, Jack went slowly down the rickety ladder. But Amy was only dimly aware that he'd disappeared from the attic as she flicked through a few dusty pages. Within seconds Amy had been transported to another time, another place. Kitty's young ramblings were endearing. Amy's heart went out to her grandmother as she read descriptions of loneliness at the loss of Kitty's mother – Amy's great-grandmother who she'd never known. A few pages later Kitty had written passages expressing her frustration at working in the pub, her anxiety at not feeling useful when all around her seemed to be wrapped up in the war. Even Kitty's father had joined the Home Guard. From the scrawls it was clear Kitty just wanted to dig for victory.

She glanced from the pages to look around the large

farmhouse attic and towards the window where the view stretched over fields and trees. Her grandmother had achieved her heart's desire. She'd ended up running a farm and, as far as Amy was aware, had lived a happy life doing what she loved.

Amy closed the book, dust motes circling the air, and tried to push away the sudden onset of guilt at having invaded her grandmother's privacy, reading her diaries from almost seventy years ago. Amy gathered the books into her arms to take to her gran as Jack appeared at the loft hatch.

He offered to take her armload. Between them they carried the remaining photo albums and Kitty's diaries downstairs. Perhaps Kitty would enjoy looking back down memory lane. After all, she said she'd wanted to lay old ghosts to rest.

CHAPTER 13

Kitty browsed through their haul at the table as Jack made himself useful in the kitchen, refilling the kettle and spooning tealeaves into the pot. Amy stifled a laugh as she watched Jack make a complete mess of the tea task.

Tealeaves were flying everywhere as he scraped the spoon against the side of the caddy. Seconds later he was holding the tea strainer out in front of him, not quite sure what to do with it.

'Do you even drink tea?' Amy giggled as Jack frowned at the tea strainer.

He glanced at Kitty, who was fully engrossed in the pages of her diaries. 'Not really. We don't even have kettles, much. I'm a coffee man but I didn't like to say. What do you do with this?' He gestured to the strainer.

Amy explained its purpose and together they tidied up the spilt leaves. She stood next to Jack while he poured the water into the teapot and then he peered inside it and smiled as the leaves swirled.

'Even though I don't really drink it, there is something calming about tea.'

Amy put her fingers around the warm pot to lift it. 'I'll be mother.'

'What does *that* mean?' Jack asked.

'I'm not sure, actually.' Amy smiled. 'I got it from Gran.' Amy raised her voice an octave so Kitty would hear. 'Perhaps it's just a thing elderly people say.' She waited for her grandmother to playfully scold her for suggesting Kitty was old.

Amy and Jack looked expectantly at Kitty with conspiratorial smiles on their faces but Kitty didn't reply. She was miles away, reading her diaries from almost seventy years ago.

As Amy brought a cup of tea to Kitty and glanced at the writing over her grandmother's shoulder, she paused at what she saw. The words 'I'm frightened' stared legibly out of the page. Amy moved away and stole a glance at Kitty's face. It was unreadable. If anything it looked . . . not remorseful but simply as if she was remembering. Whatever had Kitty found frightening back then?

An early evening breeze had started up, traversing across the field, ruffling the honeyed crop and forcing Amy to pull her cardigan tighter around her as she and Kitty stood in the drive and waved Jack off. Amy wanted to spend some time with her gran and would walk back to the village later on. Jack's car took a juddered turn out of the wide gate and lurched into the road. Kitty's hand stalled mid wave as he disappeared out of sight.

'Does he know what he's doing in that thing?' Kitty asked with wide eyes and a serious tone.

Amy laughed. 'Possibly not, no.' She linked her arm through her grandmother's as they turned back to the house. Watching Jack lurch out of view made her now feel guilty that she wasn't there to co-pilot him through the narrow lanes. He clearly wasn't getting the hang of driving in England whatsoever.

Once inside Kitty resumed reading her old diaries. After Amy tidied away the tea things and washed up, she sat down, joining her grandmother, and spun one of the photo albums round to look at.

Every now and again Amy glanced up at her grandmother. For a while Kitty's face had been still, her eyes unmoving, as if she was looking through the pages and into the past. Amy's gaze rested on Kitty, wondering what age her gran had been in those pages and whether the diaries were simply wartime moans about rationing or the noise of planes or the excited chatter of discovering American airmen were stationed nearby. And then of course, that phrase, *I'm frightened*.

Suddenly Kitty scraped her chair back over the kitchen tiles and Amy jumped at the sudden movement.

'Excuse me for a moment,' Kitty mumbled as she stood up and stepped into the hallway. The sound of Kitty's slippered feet grew softer as she walked down the hall.

'Gran?' Amy uttered but there was no reply. She frowned as she looked at the empty doorway. Slowly her gaze drifted across the table and to the diary. Upside down it was impossible to read the inked writing and Amy wasn't entirely sure she wanted to invade her privacy again. Something in it had obviously brought back memories and upset Kitty.

The longer Amy sat there, waiting for her gran to return, the more curiosity took hold. She stalled, chewed her nails for a few seconds and then made a decision. She only meant to get a quick feel for the circumstance and then wander off in search of her grandmother to see if she was okay. She wanted to know what, in the pages of that diary, had upset her grandmother so much? She spun the diary round and started reading.

CHAPTER 14

1944

A few days later, the large farmhouse came into view as Kitty gave a few final pushes on her bicycle pedals. The war had been getting Kitty down. It was getting them all down. It felt as if it would never end. But in a dark corner of her mind she half wanted it to go on just a little bit longer so she could actually experience being a Land Girl. Pouring drinks in the pub for tired American flyboys wasn't exactly what she'd had in mind for the entirety of the war and now even her best friend Susan was leaving the village for pastures new. Janie would soon be married and when the war ended she'd be living on the other side of the Atlantic. Kitty just wanted at least a month or two of doing something vaguely helpful before Churchill led them all to a storming victory. And this was it. Because finally, *finally,* this morning she'd received her instructions, albeit with mixed feelings.

Although she'd not been *totally* desperate to leave, this posting wasn't what she'd imagined at all. In fact, if she'd wanted to work where they were sending her, she could have just walked five minutes down the road and asked the farmer herself. She'd been waiting all this time to be posted just moments away. Actually, now she thought about it, her feelings weren't mixed at all. It was a strange sense of disappointment she was feeling, although she couldn't have said why, especially as she'd be able to live at home still. Perhaps it was the lack of adventure that she was now having to reconcile herself with. She took a deep breath, steeled herself and forced herself to recognise that she would be doing something useful, something good for the war *and* she'd still be able to stay at home with her father, which would help keep things on an even keel. Perhaps that would ease the burden of not being quite as available in the pub to help work as he'd have liked her.

'Honestly, Kitty,' she chastised herself. 'Just go and get on with it.'

'Talking to yourself?' A man's voice came from behind her. Kitty wobbled on the bike as she turned her head to see Christopher Frampton walking towards her from the direction of the side gate.

'A little bit, yes. Giving myself a talking to as it happens.'

'What about?' he asked, his warm smile the same as it had always been. He stopped in front of her. Flakes of wheat dust coated his trousers as if he'd stormed his way through the field and he looked as hot and bothered as Kitty now felt.

'All sorts of things,' she said. The last time they'd seen each other to talk to properly was years ago, despite the fact he'd been in and out of the village quietly every so often, church on Sunday and then back to the farm.

'Good to see you, Kitty,' he replied genuinely, in his voice that was just that little bit more upper crust than she remembered it. He'd definitely picked that up at his expensive school. He walked round the front of the bike and held the handlebars steady as Kitty climbed off and smoothed her skirt down.

'It's been a long time,' she said.

'Not really.' Christopher smiled. 'I saw you with your . . . with a man by the oak tree the other day, remember?'

'Oh yes, I mean . . . I meant it's been a long time since I saw you *properly*.' Kitty suddenly felt stiff. 'I never see you anymore,' she continued. Now she was standing in front of him it was almost as it had always been when they'd been children. She'd missed Christopher.

'I'm just busy,' Christopher sighed. 'What I wouldn't give for a drink in The Duck but I just don't seem to ever be able to stop work here.' He looked towards the farmhouse and then back towards the field as if he hated them both then wiped his hot brow with the back of his hand.

'Then the timing of this couldn't be better,' she said. She reached into her pocket and handed him her letter of instruction. Christopher read it aloud.

'*Dear Madam, it has been arranged for you to start work at Frampton Farm . . .*' He laughed aloud. 'Is this real?'

Kitty laughed too. 'Of course it's real. You should have received a copy too, I hope?'

'Probably on the doormat. I've been out since the crack of dawn. Not been back to look.'

He shook his head in disbelief, read on. '*Your starting wage will be thirty-two shillings per week and . . .*' He scanned on quickly. '*On receipt of this letter please write without delay to Mr Christopher Frampton, the farmer, saying what time you will arrive.*'

He looked up with good humour and returned the letter

to her. 'Well, fancy that.' He looked at her anew. 'You're one of the new Land Girls I've been so desperate for.'

'Looks that way,' she agreed, starting to feel more positive. Christopher had always had this ability to cheer her up.

He gave a short laugh of disbelief. 'You have no idea how happy that makes me.'

'Me too,' she said warmly, consoled that this might actually not be so bad after all.

'He says with it being harvest season he's been desperate for more Land Girls. There's five in total including me, and he can do with all the help he can get. He's been begging the Women's Land Army if they could spare another worker for weeks,' she told Susan at the front door to her friend's cottage in the village on her way home, her bike propped against the cottage wall. 'I just have to square it with Dad now but he can hardly undo an official order.'

Overhead, the drone of an American bomber sounded as it made its way back to the airbase. Both women looked up. Kitty wondered where Charlie was right now. If he might be inside that very plane or elsewhere in Europe, fighting his way through anti-aircraft flak on another daylight raid.

She was excited at the thought of telling Charlie that the first step on her new adventure had finally begun – that her days would no longer be about helping the pot boy and washing up glasses. Although she'd have to help a bit still, she was sure – if she had any energy left after a day of farm work. She'd be doing something useful, finally. Her father could hardly argue with her being so close to home. And also, if Charlie wanted to see her again and if she wanted to see him, then Kitty would be remaining here after all, at least until Christopher didn't need her and she was posted on somewhere else. And if that happened then it only added to the sense of adventure she was missing out on here. It was almost too perfect.

'These bloody Yanks,' Kitty's father mumbled discreetly into her ear with a half smile.

Kitty's head shot up from washing glasses as the end of her shift drew nearer. Her father had just uttered something brave considering the pub was full to the rafters with Americans, all of whom were responsible for keeping the pub afloat now most of the young village men had long-since gone to fight.

'What do you mean?' she returned, equally as quietly.

'There'll be no young women left for our boys, when they come home, at this rate. Just look at that.'

Kitty gave him a puzzled look and turned.

'First your sister and now Helena Ancross.' Kitty looked in the direction of her father's gaze. Dolled up to the nines and proudly sporting a bit of brass on her engagement finger was a girl Kitty had been to school with and knew well. Helena Ancross looked very different to how she'd looked a few weeks ago. For a start she was wearing a proud victory-red lipstick and, Kitty noticed enviously, a pair of brand new stockings. This was all a bit far removed from how most of the village women were looking these days. Helena looked like a new, shiny version of herself.

'Her young man will have given her that glamorous new look, no doubt.' Her father harrumphed.

Kitty opened her mouth to continue the gentle ribbing he was giving Helena but she had no chance to speak.

'What is it they say about those Yanks? Overpaid and over here. And the other.'

Kitty's mouth formed a surprised O at her father's words as he swung round and plastered a merry smile on his face as he started serving again. As if she knew she was being talked about, Helena looked up at Kitty and smiled. Kitty quickly smiled back.

Good luck to her, she thought. Helena looked happy enough. The man at her side beamed a dazzling white smile and held Helena tightly around her waist. There was love there, wasn't there? Kitty took a closer look. Hadn't that young man been giving Kitty the glad eye only a few weeks ago? She shook the uneasy thought away as quickly as it had come. Were they really out for only one thing?

The door opened and banged shut quickly and a dripping wet Charlie stood at the door. With the pub in blackout, Kitty hadn't realised it was raining. He took off his cap and banged it against his leg to bash the water out. Water had caught the ends of his eyelashes and his dashingly wet look was heart-stopping. He stamped his feet on the doormat and caught her eye as he did so, giving her a wide smile.

Kitty returned it and just for a moment it was, to her, as if there was no one else in the room. The look that Charlie gave her was one of intense joy, his smile making his eyes crinkle, as if he hadn't expected to see her, despite the fact he must know she would be there at this time; exactly as she was most evenings.

Except, with her work due to start on the Frampton farm the day after tomorrow she wouldn't be here all that much anymore. The door opened behind Charlie and he moved further inside the pub to let his fellow airmen in as they tumbled in behind him ready to drown their day in glasses of warm beer. As the chatter got louder Charlie turned away and joined his friends. Kitty was grateful he wasn't coming over to her, forcing her to have to explain her friendship with Charlie to her father. With her father's growing distrust of the American pilots' motives in England, she didn't want to face an inquisition. Two awkward conversations in one night was a thing of dread. She could feel herself frowning.

Eventually Charlie wandered over innocently, placing his order for a round of drinks. 'How are ya?' Charlie asked.

She smiled at his slang. 'I'm fine. In fact I'm more than fine. I've got my instructions to start farm work,' she whispered.

He smiled back sadly. 'You'll be leaving then – congratulations.'

'Yes. No. I mean . . . I'm going but I'm staying. It's a funny story,' she said.

'Okay,' he drew out the word, uncertainly. 'That's wonderful news then I guess. Are you happy?'

'Yes, I think so. Yes, I am. After I have an awkward conversation with my dad, I know I will be. I've been putting it off.'

'When do you start?' he asked.

'The day after tomorrow,' Kitty said guiltily, casting a look at her father.

'Then I'm happy for you, Kitty.'

Kitty glanced around and noticed her father watching her curiously. 'We have to stop talking for a bit.'

'Can I see you tomorrow?' Charlie whispered.

'It'll have to be the morning I'm afraid.'

'Can you get down to the base?'

'Yes, I have a bicycle. Nine o'clock?' Kitty whispered

103

quickly and turned as Charlie nodded. She moved away hastily and served other customers.

'I didn't ask you how you were yesterday,' Kitty said to Charlie after she'd dismounted her bicycle. A few moments earlier they'd met by the gates to the base and Charlie had told her he had an idea, then politely requested she climb off the saddle and climbed on in her place.

She tried for the third time to hoist herself on to the handlebars while he held it steady.

'How do the other girls do this?' Kitty asked. 'They make it look so easy.'

'Do you mind if I . . .?' From behind, Charlie's hands held Kitty round the waist and he lifted her on to the bars. 'There. I couldn't watch you carry on like that any longer,' he said with a hint of laughter.

'Oh,' Kitty replied, having rather enjoyed the feel of Charlie's firm hands around her waist, if only for a second. 'Thank you.' Kitty tried impossibly to recover some form of ladylike composure now she was perched awkwardly on the handlebars. The moment Charlie had seen her bicycle he had eyed it appreciatively, having confessed the pushbike he'd commandeered on the base had been run over by a Jeep after he left it somewhere stupid.

Charlie suggested they ride through the countryside lanes. Or rather, he would ride and Kitty would wobble indelicately in front of him. She placed her feet on the fender, and after a few eye-widening moments where Charlie forgot which side of the road he was supposed to be on, they were gliding through the country lanes, Charlie peddling while standing up so he could see over the top of her head. Even though he was doing all the work, Kitty's part was harder than it looked. She'd seen countless village girls doing this with plenty of airmen. They all looked as if they were enjoying themselves immensely. Kitty suspected they were putting it on as she stayed stock still, not daring to move a muscle in case she tipped them both over either one way or another.

Charlie pulled the brakes suddenly and Kitty lurched so hard that she started to fly through the air, but instead of landing on the ground, she found Charlie's arm hooked around her waist, dragging her back onto him and to safety. It took her a few seconds to catch her breath as he stood, stabilising them both and holding onto her as she leaned against his chest. She turned, looking up at him. His expression mirrored hers: serious, shocked he'd nearly sent her over the handlebars. She opened her mouth to exclaim but found she couldn't as his expression turned swiftly to mirth. His shoulders shook as he held her and she found herself laughing alongside him, despite the fact she was in the least elegant position of her life.

'I am so, so sorry,' he said when they'd both finished laughing at their situation.

'Did you forget how to brake?' Kitty asked between laughs as Charlie adjusted her awkward position for her and landed her neatly on the ground. 'Feet first, how novel,' she uttered with a smile.

'I just pulled the one brake,' he said, shaking his head in disbelief at his own actions. It's an old habit. I usually ride one-handed, my left hand's normally carrying something, a drink or a book or something. I never pull the back brake on a bike. But then I've never been going fast enough to need both, usually. I can't believe I just did that. I'm so sorry,' he reiterated.

'It's quite alright,' she said mock-primly, making them

both issue a quick chuckle as Charlie dismounted the bike and walked it a few moments along the lane with her. 'What was the urgency?' she asked. The shock had made her legs feel wobbly.

'This,' he said as they came by a gap in the hedge. 'I spied it on my way up to you and couldn't remember where it was. I thought on the way how it's the perfect place to sit and how we wouldn't have to climb awkwardly through brambles. But now I realise brambles might have been less traumatic than what I just did to you.'

'Trust me,' she replied. 'Being trapped in brambles is much worse.'

'I'll take your word for it,' he said, ushering the pushbike through the gap and checking Kitty was following through the gap in the brambles safely.

'This okay for somewhere to sit?' he asked as he eyed up the field. It was grassland and where it would have been lush and green a few months ago, the intense summer heat had dried the grass a little. 'I thought it looked kinda perfect,' he said, 'but up close I guess we'll have to sit on my jacket as it's a little tough.'

'It is perfect,' Kitty said, meaning it. 'Sitting anywhere but on those handlebars is perfect.'

'Why are you finding it so difficult, just to sit there?' he teased, laying his jacket on the ground. He sat, holding out his hand to help Kitty alongside him. 'You can ride back if you like, I'll run alongside you. It's *got* to be easier than that.'

She swatted his arm playfully as she dropped onto the ground next to him. 'No, we're going to perfect this on the return journey,' she declared. 'I'm not the kind to give up and I suspect neither are you.'

He sighed by way of agreement as he pulled two bottles of ginger beer from the saddlebag. He opened them with his pocketknife, handing her one.

'How do you know?' he asked between mouthfuls.

'Pardon?'

'That I'm not a quitter?'

'I'm not sure, really.' Kitty looked thoughtfully across the field. 'Perhaps it's everything I've learned about you so far. You signed up for a second tour for one thing.' She turned to look at him. 'And you have a look, in your eyes that says you don't give up easily.'

'Is that so?' He gave her a knowing look and then Kitty watched his Adam's apple move as he tipped his head back to drink from the bottle.

His skin was freshly shaved and in the quiet of the field she took time to gaze at his jawline. As he brought his head back down, he glanced down at her with a slight smile. Kitty returned it, but slowly the smile on his face was replaced with a look that Kitty couldn't read at all. He reached over and swept a lock of her blonde hair off her face that must have fallen down from her rolls, a casualty from the perilous ride. He tucked it behind her ear for want of anywhere else to put it and then gently stroked her face with his thumb as he brought his hand back.

A slight gasp sounded at his touch and Kitty was horrified to realise it had come from her. But Charlie wasn't laughing at her, as she'd feared. Instead he had turned to her, a serious look in his eyes as he scanned her face. As if he was trying to work out what she was thinking.

She was holding in a breath, although she had no idea that she was. Exhaling, she could feel the drumbeat in her chest quickening as he leaned in and kissed her. His kiss was delicious, warm, deep and she felt she might pass out, grateful she was sitting or else her legs might have buckled. She reciprocated, closing her eyes, yearning coursing through her. He brought his hand back to the side of her face and lifted his lips from hers.

After a few seconds, when she didn't speak, he scanned her gaze. 'Was that okay?'

Kitty blinked in the sunlight. She could only nod. She couldn't speak. She had never been kissed like that before. She had never been kissed at all and her mind was whirring. She felt heady and wanted and then suddenly she felt dizzy. Charlie reached down to take one of her hands, which had been in her lap throughout – Kitty having not known what to do with them.

Finally she found her voice. 'It was more than . . . okay' She tried the American slang out, wondering if Charlie would laugh at her for using it. But he squeezed her hand, not seeming to notice. The morning sun rose higher in the sky and he looked at his watch.

'I have to get back soon,' he said quietly. 'Which means only one thing. And we'll have to be real quick.' He gave her a sly smile.

Panic rose in Kitty's stomach. He couldn't mean what she thought he meant, could he?

'You'll have to sit back on those handlebars, I'm afraid. And I'll have to pedal real fast.'

She laughed with relief and Charlie pulled her to her feet.

'I'm glad I got to see you today,' he said as they rushed through the lanes. 'I'm going to be busy for the next few days and I'm not sure when I can get out again so you may not see me for a while. If you want to keep seeing me, that is?'

'I do,' Kitty confessed as the wind whipped her hair and she endeavoured to keep her skirt down.

'But don't worry,' he said as Kitty immediately started worrying. 'I'll be fine. Like I always am.'

She nodded, fearful of doing anything else on the bike as she clung on at an awkward angle. He pulled up in front of the gates to the base and climbed off the bike, turning it round so she could get back on and ride back to The Duck.

Kitty shook her head. 'You keep it safe for me,' she said. 'Just watch out for errant Jeeps.'

'No, it's yours,' he said. 'You need it.'

'You need it more than me,' she pleaded. 'You can get into the village quicker to see me this way.'

'I'll guard it with my life.' He stepped forward, leaned across the bike and kissed her. The same strands of longing threaded themselves through her body.

They pulled apart reluctantly. 'There's a dance soon,' Charlie said. 'Here, in one of the hangars. Would you like to go with me?' He gave her the day and the time. 'I can pick you up on your very own bicycle and then drop you home later.'

She thought of her father. There was still so much she had to tell him and now there was Charlie. If he turned up at the pub on her bike she'd have even more to explain.

'Perhaps I should walk down,' Kitty suggested. 'I could bring my friend Susan in that case. I doubt my father would let me go alone anyway.'

'Okay, if you're sure? I'll see you at the dance then?'

She nodded.

'Are you gonna be okay walking back home now?'

'Of course. I've been walking through this landscape my entire life,' she said.

He smiled. 'Keep yourself safe, Kitty.'

'And you,' she replied softly as she watched him cycle through the manned sentry-gate. He stopped and turned around to give her a wave before disappearing among the throng of vehicles and American personnel.

As Kitty walked back to the pub, she touched the place on her lips where Charlie had kissed her. If she squeezed her eyes shut she could still feel his lips on hers. Her heart beat to its own fast tune just thinking about it. She hadn't been looking for romance at all. And then funny, kind, handsome Charlie had arrived. Kitty almost skipped home.

CHAPTER 15

She couldn't stop thinking about Charlie for the rest of the day. He engulfed almost all her thoughts. Heavens knew where he'd gone and for how long. Kitty wondered how he was and how he was feeling, each mission – each day more terrifying than the last, more gruelling. How often did he let his guard down, show how traumatized he was? Just that one time, the first time she'd met him? Or did he sit alone, out of sight, processing his emotions regularly? She'd learn all this about him, over time, as they got to know each other, surely.

While it gave her father comfort to know that the Americans were finally pulling their weight in the war, it gave Kitty shivers. She couldn't stop imagining Charlie and his crew being blown up or shot down in flames. Before, she'd half-heartedly counted the planes out and counted them back in. And when the number had been short on the return as it often was, she'd sigh, wonder for a moment or two where they'd been shot down, mourn the loss of the young ten-man crew and then go about her day. The final number returning hardly ever matched the number flying out. But now this thought made her nauseous. Now she knew what lovesickness felt like. Susan had told her one day she'd come to know that feeling. And Kitty didn't like the thought of it one bit.

With the pub so quiet, Kitty steeled herself in the bar. She breathed in, breathed out. 'Dad?'

'Mmm?' he said, stacking glasses.

She inhaled again and when she didn't reply he turned, looked at her. 'You alright?'

'Dad, I need to tell you something.'

'Go on.'

'I don't want you to be angry.'

'Oh no, what is it?

'I've enrolled as a Land Girl,' she said quickly, bravely, suddenly. Best not beat about the bush.

His face was expressionless. 'Have you now.'

'I'm going to get conscripted anyway, Dad. You know that,' she pre-empted.

He nodded reluctantly. 'I know,' he said quietly.

'It's out in the fresh air or it's cooped up in a factory,' she continued making her case.

'I know that too,' he said after a beat. 'I just thought I'd have a bit more time with my little girl.'

'I'm not little anymore, Dad,' she said. 'I'm nineteen. Not a girl anymore.'

'Don't I know it. Bloody Americans sniffing around both my grown up daughters. Gives me the frights.'

'We can talk about that in a minute too if you like.'

He studied her. 'I'm not sure I want to, actually.'

'There is good news,' Kitty continued.

'Is there?' he asked dejectedly.

In the corner of the pub an elderly man spilled his glass of beer and Kitty rushed over, helped mop it up and then returned to her dad. 'I'm not actually going anywhere. So your wish has come true not to entirely lose me to the war effort.'

He gave her a puzzled expression.

'I start tomorrow up at the Frampton farm.'

'The Framptons? You've been sent there?'

'Christopher's needed an extra Land Girl for a while, he says, especially now it's harvest season. And so that's where I'll be learning the ropes, and I believe I'll be staying on afterwards too but it's not confirmed. Sometimes they send you off to train for a month, but Christopher's is a training farm so I'll be working there and then I'll be back here each night,' she babbled. 'I've been putting off telling you, even though I applied for it ages ago, because I knew how sad you'd be. I just didn't want to tell you until I knew something concrete had come of it.' *And then it'd be too late for you to stop me,* she thought. 'But you'll still get to see me every day and I'll still be sleeping here each night so it's not that bad really.' She looked at her father with concern when he didn't speak.

'Are you angry with me?' she asked tentatively.

Her father sighed. 'No, I'm not angry with you. I'm sad you felt you had to go behind my back though. I don't like secrets.'

'Neither do I,' she said, rushing towards him. 'I didn't go behind your back to hurt you. I wanted to make sure that if this war drags on and on forever that I'd be doing something useful that I might actually enjoy.'

'And you're sure the Women's Land Army will satisfy that? It's manual labour. A *lot* of manual labour. Although

113

I know you've never shied away from hard work, but this will be *very* hard work from what I've read. I suppose it's too late to ask this if you've already signed up but are you *sure* you want to do this?'

'I'm sure, Dad. I stand behind this wooden bar all day and all evening and I need something different, something useful for the war. Some fresh air and growing veg for the nation or whatever it is Christopher will have me doing . . . It's what I want.'

Her dad nodded. 'There's no point me trying to talk you out of it then. You've clearly got your heart set on standing in a field all day. I suppose I could have a discreet word with Christopher, see if he'll go easy on you.'

'No, Dad,' Kitty said, louder and sharper than she intended. The elderly man in the corner looked up at them briefly. 'Please don't do that. I can fight my own battles. Although there's no battle to be fought. Christopher's a friend and, regardless, he won't rag me to death.'

'There was a time I thought he might be sweet on you,' her dad said.

'No, of course not. We were children. We're just friends. I haven't seen him properly in forever. He sounds ever so posh now.'

'Always did, I thought,' he said absently. 'And friends or not, you're a pretty girl and he'd be mad not to be keen on you so keep watch for that.'

'Dad . . .' she sighed.

'I worry about you. You're not as worldly wise as you like to think. Your sister's got a hold over her Bobby – has done from the start. He's proposed, quick as a flash. Just be mindful *you* don't say yes to the first American who comes along.'

114

'I'll be careful, Dad,' Kitty sighed. 'And remember, you can still keep an eye on me because I'll be here a lot still, and probably still able to help some evenings if I'm not bone tired,' she said, changing the subject on purpose.

'I wouldn't expect that of you,' her dad said. 'And I suppose it's time I got proper help anyway.'

Kitty put her hands on her hips in mock annoyance. 'Charming. What have I been this whole time?'

'I mean staff,' he clarified. 'Someone who hasn't been called up. After the war I had an idea that I'd open all those closed storage rooms above as accommodation. They aren't in any habitable state now. Got to get those floorboards fixed, sort the roof and tart it all up a bit. You never know, people might want to travel out to our little corner of Suffolk. If anyone's got any money. And if we aren't bombed out or invaded with Nazis,' he joked.

'Don't say that,' Kitty begged. 'That won't happen. People like Char— The Americans are here doing so much. What with them and our RAF boys, the navy and the army, we're being looked after.'

'And the Women's Land Army,' her dad said with a smile.

'Exactly,' Kitty said proudly.

CHAPTER 16

Kitty appraised herself, moving her head this way and that as she looked at herself in a mirror in a guest bedroom in the Frampton farmhouse, where her uniform had been sent. It didn't fit as well as she'd like and she tied her own belt she'd been wearing tighter around her dungarees to at least make her waist not look like a potato sack. She'd seen another new Land Girl arrive this morning rolling up her trousers to form makeshift – if somewhat bulky – shorts as the sun rose in the sky, bringing a start to the day's heat.

Brown corduroy trousers and a beige blouse were straight out of all the photos she'd ever seen in the pictorial magazines. The bottle-green pullover was far too hot to wear today but it would come in handy for the winter months. She'd always thought the light brown dungarees were a bit of a silly colour. They'd be impractically muddy soon enough. And then she tied a headscarf on to keep her hair out of her eyes. She pulled on her regulation leather gumboots and considered herself as complete as she was ever going to be.

The roar of planes sounded closer here than it did in the village, the airfield being just out of reach beyond the tree line of the Frampton farm. Was Charlie among those flying out this morning? She wasn't often one to pray, just on Sundays in church when she closed her eyes and sat quietly listening to the vicar. But today she closed her eyes briefly in front of the mirror and prayed specifically for Charlie's safe return. As each engine sounded, she counted them out one by one as she put the finishing touches to her outfit.

She'd been ages, so excited had she been to finally wear her very own WLA outfit. She pinned her treasured badge onto her blouse and checked it was on tightly. She didn't want to risk losing it so soon and then having to pay the sixpence for a replacement. Finally, she was a real Land Girl.

'Are you alright?' Christopher asked through the closed guest room door. 'Do you need . . . um . . . a hand?'

'No, I'm fine. Thank you,' she rushed. 'I'll only be a few more seconds.'

'No hurry,' he said politely. Although of course there was a hurry. There was a war on. 'Most days I'll need you here at about eight or nine o'clock so not too early,' he called through the door. 'And you'll work until about four or five, give or take, depending on what's needed each day, with a break for your midday meal. But it'll all vary as we go. I promise I'm not a slave driver.'

Kitty knew all this, making sounds of agreement through the door. Her working week on the farm was supposed to be fifty hours in summer and a bit less in winter but she suspected Christopher was filling the silence with easy chatter for chatter's sake.

'Well don't you look a picture,' he said when she emerged.

117

'A good picture?' she asked uncertainly.

'As if you could be anything else.'

She didn't like to encourage and wondered if what her dad had said about Christopher once having been sweet on her was true.

She'd think about that later. But for now, 'Put me to work.'

He smiled broadly. 'How do you feel about meeting the other Land Girls and then later you can help me fix the tractor? I'll instruct you what to do and you can carry out the task. If that's alright?'

She almost jumped for joy. 'Yes please.'

'You've got to tuck your trousers into your socks,' one of the Land Girls – Nancy, a girl from East London – told Kitty knowingly when they were discussing the upcoming harvest. 'It's hot work, but last year when I was on a training farm up north, a rat shot out of the crop and up my leg and I nearly died of fright. Never again. We're poisoning them but there's always a few that manage to outlive our efforts.'

Kitty nodded soberly. 'I won't forget.'

'I'll be there to remind you,' Nancy said. 'I'd only just joined the Land Army as well and no one thought to tell me. Probably thought it was funny but I screamed that loud.'

'You've been a Land Girl for a year?' Kitty asked, awed.

Nancy nodded. 'I feel I've been one forever but this is only my second harvest. Thought I wouldn't see another one, thought we might have won by now what with the Yanks being over here, but here we go again. Anything to avoid going back to working at the fish and chip shop.'

'Fish and chips? Sounds heavenly.'

'You can have too much of a good thing,' Nancy said knowingly.

'When do we start the harvest?' Kitty asked.

'We should be ready in the next couple of weeks. I think we're going to be late though. Bloody tractor keeps breaking down. We'll be scything it all by hand at this rate. Then in September we plough, sew and start again. At least I can show you the ropes so you won't be so green.'

By the end of the first few days on the farm Kitty thought she'd collapse with exhaustion, crawling gratefully into her bed above the pub every night. Christopher had brought out plenty of hot cups of tea each day and they'd made time to stop as he showed her the ropes. Kitty was relieved to have made a new friend and to willingly take instruction from Nancy, the more experienced Land Girl who was originally from somewhere called Wandsworth, which Kitty had never heard of but was assured was 'in London and getting bombed to buggery.'

Kitty pulled her weight, making sure she went above and beyond. Every now and again she'd notice Christopher watching her. Kitty suspected Christopher was worried she was going to scarper in fear so she was making sure to make positive remarks about how useful she felt, how she'd be happy taking on more arduous jobs. But even as she said it, her back ached and her head simply thumped. And the exhaustion. Oh, the exhaustion.

Kitty was in the stable yard mucking out the horse stalls. She was in the process of putting down fresh straw and with dust motes in the air was trying not to sneeze when she heard the words, 'Well don't you look wonderful.'

119

Kitty turned to see Charlie propping the bicycle up against one of the closed stable doors. The smell of the manure had been so overpowering it was all she could do not to be sick, but she didn't like to show it, or to complain, and she fervently hoped she didn't smell of horse muck.

'Oh *there* you are,' she burst out in relief. She'd been so worried about him over the last few days, not knowing if he was alive or dead, not knowing when she'd see him again. She knew she was becoming too invested in this man. But she liked him. She liked Charlie, she really did.

'And there *you* are,' he said in reply, walking across the cobbled stable yard. 'Looking incredible in that get up, might I add.'

She looked down uncertainly at her dungarees and gum-boots. 'Really?' He nodded emphatically as she stepped towards him and he scooped her into his arms, kissing her. She held her body willingly against his, wishing they were anywhere but in the stable yard.

'God, I've really missed you,' he said, pulling back, still holding her and looking down into her face. 'Is that mad to say? I mean, we've not known each other long but . . .'

She pulled back to look at him. 'It's not mad. I've missed you too and I've been so incredibly worried about you,' she blurted.

He touched her cheek and she noticed dark circles under his eyes.

'Are you alright?' she asked.

'Yeah,' he said quietly, slowly, uncertainly. 'Although I know how I look tells a very different story.'

She narrowed her eyes. 'You look like you've not slept in about a year.'

'Well thank you very much.' He laughed. 'I take back everything I just said about how damn fine you look.'

But Kitty didn't laugh with him. He looked truly awful now she looked at him properly. 'Where have you been?' she asked. She wasn't sure she wanted to know the answer.

'I've seen some very beautiful European cities from above. Only now they're rubble.' He put it so simply.

She put her head against his chest, closing her eyes, allowing the feel of his uniform to comfort her, although surely it was he who needed comforting. Her heart hurt thinking about the awful job he had to do, dropping bombs from a great height – and of the fate of those who were unfortunate enough to be on the receiving end.

'The guidebooks of Europe are going to read a little differently after this war's over,' he said despondently. He issued a thin smile. 'If it ever ends. I can't imagine what it's like down on the ground when they see or hear those bombs coming. I can't imagine,' he repeated. 'All those people.' He sounded far away.

'Don't think about it,' she said, looking up at him into his brown eyes. 'You can't think about it. You have no choice. It's war. And . . . they're doing the same to us,' she said – her heart not really in it.

'I know,' he said quietly. 'It doesn't make it any easier though. Or any more correct.' Charlie glanced around the stable yard. 'I don't think anybody saw me arrive here but . . . now I think about it . . . am I allowed to be here?'

'Probably not,' Kitty agreed.

'I thought as much. I should go. I don't want to get you into trouble.'

'I don't think Christopher would mind but I don't want to rub his mother up the wrong way, although I never see

121

her. She's a bit reclusive but I've caught her looking out of the window at us girls every now and again.'

'In that case,' he said, kissing her quickly and letting go of her waist. 'I'll make myself scarce. I just . . . I just needed to see you.'

'And now you have,' she teased.

'And now I have.'

He turned the bike, began wheeling it and then looked back to her. 'Do you have a dress for tomorrow?'

'What's tomorrow?'

'The dance? Did you forget?' he asked with a knowing smile.

She had forgotten. Kitty couldn't imagine dancing after a long day working on the farm. Her body was worn down and it had only been a few days. Perhaps she would get used to the tiredness, the nausea from some of the more . . . fragrant jobs. Perhaps any day now she would be able to return from her work and help around the pub a bit more, help cook supper rather than just trying not to fall asleep at the dinner table while Janie served them all.

'Hey, if you're not up to it, it's fine,' Charlie said, 'honestly.'

The creases around the edges of his eyes were deepening and she worried that his job was having a terrible effect on him, ageing him prematurely. Maybe he needed to dance, to forget. He looked like he needed it. 'I still want to,' she replied. 'And yes, I have a dress.'

'Great. I'll meet you at the gates at seven o'clock.' He smiled but he looked tired, so tired.

'Promise me something,' she asked him before he left.

'Anything,' he said without hesitation.

'Promise me that you're looking after yourself,' she begged. 'That you aren't doing anything . . . stupid.'

'Everything I do is stupid,' he said. 'But it's all because I'm told to.'

'Charlie,' she chastised.

He laughed involuntarily. 'I promise.'

'I mean it. I care about you,' she said bravely. She did care about him – more than she wanted to admit.

'Do you? Really?' He turned fully to face her.

She avoided his gaze. 'A bit, yes.'

He laughed again. 'A bit? I don't believe you. I think you're falling for me as hard as I'm falling for you.'

She drew a breath deep inside her lungs. 'I . . .' She had no idea what to say. And then she did. 'You Yanks are so bloody confident.'

He roared with laughter. 'And don't we know it.'

Charlie raised his hand in farewell and rode her bike out of the stable yard. Kitty watched him until he turned the corner and all the while she knew he was right. She was falling for him. And he was falling for her.

CHAPTER 17

The dog-tired feeling was hard to ignore. By the time she'd had a hot bath in her regulation five inches of water, Kitty wanted nothing more than to curl up in bed and sleep for a million years. But there was the dance to think of. She pulled her cornflower-yellow summer dress with the white collar from the wardrobe and eyed it suspiciously. When was the last time she'd had occasion to wear something this nice? She wriggled exhaustedly into it, pulling it this way and that until it sat neatly. She wished she could buy something new but rationing was a killjoy. It just about did the job.

A slick of red lipstick made her mouth look full and she'd lifted her hair nicely and smoothed it into victory rolls. She turned her face in the mirror and for the first time in a very long time thought she looked rather presentable – if it wasn't for the slightly faded dress. Kitty thought about changing into something else but time was knocking on and she was already late. She shouldn't have spent so long in the bath, but her muscles hurt so much and she was so tired it was a wonder she hadn't fallen asleep in the rationed, soapy water. Charlie would be waiting at the gates to the base. Despite their growing seriousness, she was aware things between them were moving ever so swiftly.

I think you're falling for me as much as I'm falling for you. His words buoyed her almost out of her tiredness. He was right. She had fallen for him. She had. And he'd fallen for her. Did that mean love? Did he love her? Already? Surely not. But she was falling in love with him. How quick and seamless was the motion of *falling* to having *fallen*? It had never happened to her before. There was love there. The thought made her feel so warm, so cared for. It all felt too perfect – so perfect that she felt sick. Lovesick.

Kitty descended the stairs and found her father in the storage room.

'Well don't you look a picture. Where are you off to?'

'The dance,' Kitty said tentatively. 'Remember, I mentioned it? I'm going with Susan,' she reminded quickly to appease.

'Of course,' he replied. 'I don't know how you've got the energy after a day on the farm.'

'I don't,' Kitty said, forcing a laugh. 'But I'm meeting someone there,' she said even more tentatively.

Her dad turned, warily, giving her his full attention. 'Are you? Who?'

She steeled herself, yet again for an awkward conversation with her father, who she loved so much and who she didn't want to hurt. But she had to live. She had to make her own mistakes. 'He's called Charlie and he's the loveliest man I've ever met.'

'You've not met many,' he said quickly, with a tone Kitty knew all too well.

'I know,' she acquiesced. 'But I've met him and he's kind

and genuine, he's gentle and he likes me. He wants to spend time with me and I want to spend time with him. He sought me out at the farm just to see me, just to hold me. He's a pilot and he's going through the mill a bit and he's on his second tour—'

'Second?' Her father cut in. 'He's either brave or a lunatic.'

'It's the first one. He's a good man. It's early days but I think you'd really like him, Dad. I really like him.'

Her dad thought. 'Fine,' he said sharply. 'I'll meet him. I'll see what he's like.'

'Oh,' Kitty said. 'Well . . . I hadn't . . .'

'Problem?' her father asked.

'No,' Kitty said quickly. 'I'm just nervous now. What if you don't like him?'

'You just said I would,' he countered.

'You're getting me flustered on purpose,' she said with a pointed expression.

Her dad smiled. 'What time is he coming to pick you up? I can meet him now.'

'Susan and I are walking down together. I'm meeting Charlie there.'

'That's convenient, isn't it?' her father replied with a sideways smile. 'And why aren't you riding your bicycles down to the base?'

'I let Charlie borrow it briefly and Susan said she'd walk with me. Dad, you'll like him. I know you will.'

'Kitty,' her dad said. 'I love you. And I only want the best for you. You're young and these pilots . . . they don't always come back. You know the risks of this don't you? Trust me, losing your mother . . . Grief . . . It's the hardest thing I've ever had to live with. I don't ever want that for you.'

Kitty stepped forward, held her father in a warm embrace.

'I know. I know it's probably not forever. I know there are risks to falling for a bomber pilot in the middle of a war. I know that. But . . . I can't help it. I can't stop.'

Her father hugged her back warmly. 'Love is incredible,' he agreed. 'It's also bloody awful.'

Kitty laughed against her father's chest and he released her, holding her at arm's length and looking into her eyes. 'Go and have fun at the dance. Enjoy yourself. Just take care.'

'I will. Thanks, Dad.'

'And Kitty?'

'Yes?'

'Find some time soon to introduce us.'

Kitty made a nervous face that her dad didn't miss.

'Because you're not getting out of it that easy young lady,' he said, turning back to the shelf he was tidying.

On their walk down to the base, Susan and Kitty discussed Kitty's father's reaction to news of Charlie. Susan also felt very put out her friend hadn't told her about Charlie.

'There hadn't been too much to tell. Not really,' Kitty defended.

'Promise me when there is something to tell, that you will tell me?'

'I promise,' Kitty said.

'Even if you have to do it by post?'

'By post?'

'I've been given notice to go to the Royal Naval College in Greenwich soon, report in and start training.'

'Oh, Susan, I'm so pleased for you. You'll look so glamorous in your Wren's outfit. I might be quite jealous of that lovely blue.'

'Don't be. You're out in the sunshine all day long with Christopher Frampton. It's me who's jealous of you. How is it you've got two men after you and I'm struggling to keep any interested?'

'For the hundredth time, Christopher and I are just friends,' Kitty said in despair. 'Besides . . .'

'You're smitten with Charlie?' Susan offered.

Kitty gave Susan a knowing smile. 'I am rather, yes.'

Just as they turned the corner of the lane, the American airbase came into view, its sentry gates open as a bus full of girls entered, clearly having been recruited in from Ipswich by the social planners for the occasion. Kitty spotted Charlie pacing nervously. On seeing them he walked forward to meet them.

'Are we terribly late?' Kitty asked.

'Not at all. I'm terribly eager,' he replied. 'Hi, I'm Charlie,' he said, holding out his hand to shake Susan's.

'Susan,' Kitty's friend introduced herself and gripped his hand in return. 'I've heard *lovely* things.'

'Likewise.'

'I'll leave you two love birds to it,' Susan said. She kissed Kitty on the cheek. 'I'll find you in a bit. I spy my navigator.'

'Do you want a tour or do you want to dance first?' Charlie asked when Susan had moved off to hunt down her man.

'Ooo, I think a dance first, don't you? Before I run out of energy.'

The two entered the throng of couples dancing in the large grey metal aircraft hangar. Kitty was in awe of the sheer, vacuous size of it.

Hundreds of couples were dancing and a stage had been set up on one of the far sides. US and English flags were draped all around it, along with bunting. 'There's so much colour,' Kitty said. In a world of grey and khaki, blackout and the farmyard colours of her uniform, this hangar decoration was a feast for the eyes and the senses. The band was in full swing and Kitty took it all in, the trumpets and drums, saxophones and singers. The noise, the colour. She'd never seen anything like it. She spied Nancy, adding to the colour in a bright red dress that looked suspiciously crisp and new.

'You ready?' Charlie asked as one song finished and another started seamlessly.

'Oh I know this one,' Kitty cried excitedly as the band began to play 'Don't Sit Under the Apple Tree'. She looked at Charlie with wide, smiling excitement, her energy suddenly renewed.

Charlie held her hand, laughing with energetic excitement that mirrored hers. 'Then let's dance,' he shouted over the noise and pulled her into the throng. He spun her expertly, pushing her out and pulling her back in against him in time with the music and with all the other couples moving in similar style around them.

'I've never danced like this,' Kitty cried out happily, her dress flying up as she held on to Charlie's hands – although she didn't care about the dress. Neither did she care about her feet, already sore in shoes that didn't fit her swollen ankles now she spent all day working in gumboots; she was already so used to the familiar flat comfort. 'What's this music called?' she cried.

'Swing. Glenn Miller. They got him here for us tonight.'

And then the song ended and a slow number started. 'I'm not sure if I've heard this one,' she said, frowning as she tried to remember.

'"Moonlight Serenade",' Charlie said as the pace slowed and the volume diminished. He held her close as the music sung out around them. She fitted into his arms so neatly, resting her head against his chest, listening to the sound of his heart slow down, in line with the drum beat reverberating around them. A moment later, he rested his chin against her hair and everything felt exactly as it should. She felt so at ease with him. It was almost as if he'd always been here, always been in her life. She swallowed, understanding exactly how lost she was already. Or how found. She didn't know which. She just knew that she'd gone beyond liking him. *Damn this war,* she thought. *Damn it.* Because it presented too many opportunities for Charlie to be lost to her. Although if there hadn't been a war, she'd never have met him, never have started falling for him, never have allowed her heart to feel so irregular. She couldn't get a grasp on her conflicted emotions.

Kitty pulled back gently from Charlie's chest and looked up at him. Just seeing his face, made everything feel so perfect, so meant to be. It was like they were the only people in the room.

'Kitty,' he said her name softly.

She could only breathe in return, nodding helplessly because that's what she felt, helpless but in the best way possible. When she was with him she was lost, helplessly lost but happy and wanted. She didn't know what she was feeling. Everything. She felt everything.

'Kitty,' he said again into her ear, over the music.

'Yes,' she replied, too afraid of what might come next, what might not come next and everything after.

'I think I love you,' he said. He watched her, his eyes scanning hers, her eyes fixed on him in return. Her chest rose and fell as they both stopped dancing, just holding one another, watching one another.

'Really?' she breathed, the smile widening across her face, her heart racing firmly out of time with the slow, melodic band.

'Really,' he said seriously. 'I feel like I've known you forever. I don't know how it's happened in such a short space of time, Kitty, but I've fallen for you. I'm head over heels. I can't stop it and what's more,' he said, touching her cheek, 'what's more . . . I don't want to.'

Kitty breathed in, breathed out. 'Are you serious?' she asked softly. She had to know, had to know if she was being fooled.

'Yes,' he said as if she was mad. 'Yes, I'm serious.'

Kitty took her eyes off Charlie momentarily, as the band continued playing its slow song. Out of the corner of her eye, couples were kissing, Susan was holding her navigator tightly. There was something in the air tonight, something invisible but present, something bringing people together in a war that wanted so desperately to tear people apart.

'I know it's soon,' he continued. 'But I just feel it. I'm not in a hurry to postpone life simply because we're at war. I feel something and I just want to tell you. I just want to be near you when I'm on the ground. I want to be with you when I'm in the sky. I want to be near you, always.'

Kitty was silent, awestruck, in a way, watching this man pour out his heart to her.

'Charlie,' she whispered. 'Oh Charlie.'

'You gonna put a guy out of his misery and tell me if you feel the same?' he asked with a shy laugh. 'I mean, you don't have to,' he said quickly.

'Of *course* I love you,' she said in a burst. 'Of course I

do. You've . . .' She didn't know how to describe these overwhelming feelings rushing through her.

'I've . . .?' he prompted.

'You've taken my breath away. Ever since I first met you when you burst in through the pub door, shoving your way past me . . .'

He issued a low laugh.

'I've not been able to stop thinking about you,' she confessed. 'I dared not hope you felt the same way. I dared not imagine a future with . . . anyone because it's all so . . . big. The world out there at the moment is so big and you see it and you're part of it and I'm down here so far removed from it all and . . .' She stopped rambling but he didn't interrupt her, just waited for her, entranced by her words.

'But,' she continued, 'yes, I do love you and it scares me. It scares me so much because . . . what will happen if we pursue this. It's all so out of our control and it scares me, Charlie.'

'It scares me too,' he confessed, pulling her close against him while all around them couples swayed. 'You're right. I do see this war from up there.' He looked heavenwards. 'But you see it from down here too. And you know, my odds of survival, they aren't so great so we have to just take this for what it is. I love you, Kitty, and you love me and while I'm here, we have to hold each other tight and know that's what we've got for now. Is that enough for you? Ordinarily it shouldn't be enough, it wouldn't be enough. But for now, it's all we've got. Am I asking too much of you?'

She shook her head. 'You're not asking anything of me that I'm not already giving. My heart was yours. I don't know at what point you had it but it's yours and I love you. And we need to just take every day as it comes and hope for the best.'

Charlie agreed. 'We've got love, we've got this moment. And we've got each other. And then after that, it's out of our hands and it's not our fault.'

She nodded but some part of her already felt as if this was the end, not the beginning.

'I love you,' he said again, slower than the first time, and he held her close, whispered in her ear, 'I love you.'

'I love you too.'

The song came to an end and around them couples broke away or carried on. Some moved to the buffet to help themselves to food and drink.

'You hungry?' Charlie asked, whispering into her hair.

'Not a bit,' she said.

'Thirsty?' he asked.

She looked up at him adoringly. 'Not yet.'

'You maybe wanna go for a walk?'

She slid her hand into his. 'Yes please.'

On escaping the hangar through a side door, being mindful of the blackout, Kitty had never been so relieved to be hit with cool summer air.

'I didn't realise how hot I was getting,' Kitty said absently, looking up at the stars twinkling above them.

'You okay?' Charlie asked.

'Yes, just a little bit flustered. An impossibly handsome pilot has just declared his love for me and I'll confess, that kind of thing doesn't happen to a girl every day of the week.'

'It should,' Charlie said. 'In fact I can't believe I'm not beating men away from you as we speak.'

'That's my father's job,' Kitty teased.

'Maybe I should meet this father of yours,' Charlie said.

'That's exactly what he said, but let's walk before we run, shall we?' she said.

'Ha, okay.' He squeezed her hand as Kitty looked around the base in the summer twilight. For the few months the United States Army Air Force had been based on the outskirts of the village she'd never had occasion to set foot here.

'Would you like to take me on a tour? I've always wondered what went on behind these gates, where you sleep, where you eat, where you go for your briefings . . . I want to know everything. I want to picture you when I'm on the farm hoeing and mucking out the stables and catching rats, I want to know what you do . . .'

They walked slowly around, the summer sun setting, the evening slipping magically into night. The Americans were renowned for their raids in the glare of broad daylight so, in the stillness of the hot summer's evening, it was the echoing sound of fast music and not the roar of engines that provided the soundtrack to their meander as they held each other's hand.

They walked past the control tower, its squat pale green structure stretching only two stories high.

'I thought it would be bigger, taller,' she clarified.

'Doesn't need to be.' Charlie shrugged. 'You can both see *and* hear us returning from miles away, there's always so many of us.'

'I know. I count you all out and I count you back in. I always look for the artwork, the name.' A thought struck her. 'What is your artwork? What is the name of your aeroplane?'

He winked. 'I'll show you the old girl if you like?

'I *would* like,' Kitty enthused. 'Then I can really picture you.'

134

He gestured to a small brick building as they walked towards the living quarters. 'This is where I sleep.'

'I was told officers were billeted out of town in country estates.'

'They were. But there are quite a few of us now so some of us are here . . .' But she wasn't listening. She was imagining what it would be like to lie asleep with him, to fall into his arms, the sheets crumpled around them. The thought made her blush. Why had her mind gone there?

'And over there's the gymnasium and the racquet courts,' he said, and Kitty was grateful to him for forcing unladylike thoughts from her mind.

She glanced around, taking it all in in the last of the good light. Around the site, low-level corrugated metal huts had been dotted around haphazardly. Air raid shelters were dug deep into the ground with only a small brick path disappearing into the earth giving any hint as to what lay underneath. The enormous A-shaped runway stretched over a mile into the distance, and to the side of it rows and rows of giant, hulking grey bombers lined up on the tarmac in front of another large hangar that looked big enough to house at least two planes side by side.

Charlie put his arm around her waist as they approached the first row of planes. The sound of the music faded the further away they walked.

'This lady is ours.' He gestured to an aircraft with a picture of a half-naked redhead in lacy white underwear painted on the side. The words *Beauty Queen* were scrawled in bright red letters. Even in the twilight Kitty was perfectly able to see the image and she turned to Charlie with a knowing smile and one of her eyebrows raised.

'And who might *she* be?' Kitty laughed.

He laughed and held his hands up. 'An old girlfriend.' Kitty's eyebrow went even higher.

'Of our navigator. Nothing to do with me,' he added. 'There's only one girl for me.' He pulled Kitty towards him.

'There must have been girls before me,' she prompted, both wanting to know and not wanting to know.

'Sure, but no one serious.' The laughter had left his face and he was looking at her with a serious expression. 'I've never met a girl like you, Kitty. I've never been in love before. I don't know what I'm doing. I can't concentrate on anything.'

'Well you need to concentrate on staying alive when you're in this thing, please,' she said seriously, looking at his handsome features, his kind dark eyes, his laughter lines. If anything happened to him . . . God, it didn't bear thinking about.

CHAPTER 18

Summer, 2011

Kitty shifted in the doorway of the farmhouse kitchen and Amy jumped in surprise at finding her grandmother there. 'I'm so sorry,' Amy blurted as she looked down, shame-faced, at the diary she'd been reading. 'I shouldn't have looked. I'm so sorry,' she repeated.

Kitty looked from Amy to the diary. 'I only left the room for a moment, I shouldn't have left it out.' She scooped it up, cast Amy a disappointed expression and left the room.

'I . . .' Amy said to Kitty's retreating back, but she had no defence. She was mortified, her head rife with so many questions on the back of what she'd just read.

Amy made her grandmother a glass of water and went in search of her. She hadn't gone far, just to the sitting room. She looked tiny as she sat in one of the overstuffed cream sofas, the diary on her lap.

'Old ghosts.' Kitty tapped the diary with her fingertips, clearly holding no grudge against Amy's violation of privacy.

Amy nodded although she didn't really understand. She'd read fragments about farm work, a dance and how a man had captured her gran's heart all those years ago. Amy sat on the sofa across from her gran.

'I'm glad you found these. Really, I am,' Kitty admitted. 'I needed to have one last little look after all these years. Laying the ghosts to rest is something I should have done long ago. Sorting out the junk in the attic is a job for me really, now, while I'm still able. It's not something I want to leave your poor mother to do, or you girls for that matter, when I'm dead and in the ground.'

Amy had a thousand questions but she didn't feel able to voice a single one of them.

'How much did you read?' Kitty asked in a quiet voice.

Amy wished she'd not read those pages now. 'Nothing that made too much sense without context,' she said. 'A few pages. That's all.'

Kitty nodded and looked down at the closed diary thoughtfully.

It was Amy who spoke softly, breaking the silence. 'Gran?' she prompted.

Kitty looked up and into the eyes of her granddaughter. In those few seconds it seemed as if Kitty had forgotten Amy was there.

Amy put her hand in her pocket and lifted out the St Christopher. 'There's something else,' she said. 'I found this, I almost forgot about it.'

The pendant dangled from Amy's fingers and Kitty inhaled and then exhaled an, 'Oh.' Kitty had gone incredibly still. 'Oh,' she said again and then reached out slowly for it.

'My word,' she said to Amy. 'I thought I'd lost this. I thought it was gone.'

'I found it in the trunk with the diaries and albums.'

Kitty put her hand to her neck. 'I wonder . . . I wonder

if it fell from my neck when I was putting everything in the trunk. I'd thought it was in the field. I went looking and I cried for days when I thought it had gone. And it was in the trunk the entire time?'

'I guess so,' Amy said.

'Oh,' Kitty said again, looking at the tarnished pendant. 'Is it special? Did someone give it to you?'

'In a way,' Kitty said cryptically.

'Would you like me to clean it for you?'

'No thank you,' Kitty said. 'Now I have it again . . . I don't think I can let it out of my sight. I'll find the silver polish and I'll have a little go later.' Kitty went to put the pendant on the coffee table and then obviously thought better of it, choosing to clutch the pendant tightly in her hand instead.

'What happened, Gran?' Amy asked. 'What happened back then from your diary that still has the power to upset you now?'

Amy had never seen anyone smile so sadly. While the corners of Kitty's mouth lifted, her eyes stayed downcast.

'Oh, it was . . .' Kitty exhaled, opened her fist and looked softly at the pendant. 'It was a long time ago. These things, when you're young, they seem like the most important things in the world, things that no one else could possibly help with, could possibly understand, could possibly be going through themselves. But in the end . . .' She appeared to be choosing her words carefully and then closed her fist around the St Christopher. 'It all rights itself.'

Amy didn't know how to reply. Anything she said would be trite, uneducated when it came to these specifics. Although her gran was not being specific at all, now Amy thought about it. And what experience did Amy have in matters of the heart? It was Kitty who clearly bore all the experience here.

Kitty looked at Amy's confused face and it appeared as if she was steeling herself to speak, debating whether or not she should continue.

Amy prompted. 'Do you want to talk about it? About him? Was it remembering the man you wrote about in the pages that's made you sad?'

'Not sad so much. Just reliving it is . . . hard. I thought I might be alright reminding myself of what had been, but it was like going back in time – as if I was there, back at the dance in the airbase.' She smiled and then the smile fell. 'It was in the last year or so of the war that I met him,' Kitty said. 'We hadn't known each other very long but it was love. Everything happened so fast back then, in the midst of war when you didn't know if you were going to get bombed to death and be dead by the end of the day. Everything was heightened.'

Amy sat quietly, relaxed into the sofa, looked at her gran and waited for more. She could see her grandmother swallowing down some kind of fresh pain as she remembered the past. And then she brightened, lifted her shoulders, looked Amy in the eye. 'But all that was then. And this is now. And that young American chap of yours is very lovely. Perhaps that's what brought it all back. Perhaps this weekend is bringing it all back. I shouldn't have gone in the loft. The ghosts will lay themselves to rest without my input.'

Amy slumped, deflated. Her gran wasn't going to tell her then. Amy opened her mouth, started to prompt, but her gran gave her a look that said *and now we're going to talk about something else.*

'Time is knocking on and I've missed *The Archers*,' Kitty

said abruptly. 'Would you mind showing me once again how to catch up with it on that blasted i-thing your sister bought me? It asks me to log in every single time and I can never remember the password.'

Early the next morning Amy made herself a coffee to take down to the tearoom kitchen. She needed to steal a march on the cakes and scones or else there would be no way she'd get it all done in time, even with Caroline working flat out too. For the first time in a long while Amy couldn't find relief in baking, even though she had so much to do for the upcoming Heritage Day. Instead she couldn't get past the niggling feeling her gran was keeping her past secret. But why?

Ten o'clock in the morning always brought a rush of locals and this morning was no exception. As the bell above the door rang for about the tenth time in as many minutes, Amy paid no attention, up to her eyes as she was in another round of buttercream icing, so it was Caroline, working at the front of the shop, who greeted Jack first. She led him through to the kitchen with the words, 'It's your American.'

Amy replied without turning round, 'He's not *my* American. Also I need to talk to you about something important when you get a sec.'

'Caroline went about ten seconds ago but you can tell me if it'll help?' Jack teased.

Amy spun round, knocking the switch on the stand mixer up to its highest speed. A cloud of icing sugar flew up, filling the space between them. She fumbled to switch it off and waved her hand in front of her eyes, coughing on the powdery air. He looked at her with concern on his face until she finished.

'Well, that was graceful,' she said eventually, when her lungs had cleared.

Jack's expression turned from concern to humour. He was clearly trying hard not to laugh. 'It was certainly something,' he said, his eyes twinkling. 'You need a hand?' He gestured to her face.

'Thanks,' she said, but instead of Jack offering her a napkin, he wiped sugar from her cheeks with his bare hand.

His touch shocked her, sending a not-unpleasant shiver through her body. She wanted to back away, fix her icing-sugared face herself, but instead she was rooted to the spot as Jack's soft fingers brushed her skin. He glanced up to her eyes and Amy felt her breath slow, time stop. As if realising what he was doing, Jack took his hands away from her skin.

'What is this?' he asked after a few seconds.

Amy wasn't sure if he was referring to whatever was happening between them or to the cloud of white that had covered her and most of the work surface and floor. She chose the safest answer. 'Icing sugar.' Her voice sounded nothing like it normally did.

'Oh,' was all he said. They both stood, neither moving. Was he about to kiss her? Amy's breath quickened and then out of the corner of her eye she spotted Caroline in the doorway, a knowing smile on her face, holding two empty latte glasses.

Jack saved them, stepping away and saying, 'Amy, I brought something to show you. Caroline, maybe you can give me your honest opinion too if you have time?'

But Caroline attempted to make herself scarce. 'Bit busy but maybe later?' she asked, heading back into the tearoom.

Jack picked up the frames from the floor and blew icing sugar off them. 'I had these printed yesterday evening and

I just went to the framers. What do you think?' He laid four pictures of local Suffolk scenes on the centre island.

Places Amy recognised had been transformed with Jack's careful skills. A photo of the beach at Aldeburgh looked unending in black and white, its famous Maggi Hambling Scallop sculpture taking pride of place; the river running past Snape Maltings glistened in the sunshine; the house in the clouds at Thorpeness; and The Duck was in the largest frame, taking precedence on the quiet and ambling high street.

'These are *really* good, Jack,' she said in awe of his quiet skill.

'Thank you.' He gave an embarrassed grin. 'Would you still like to put them up on the walls? It's totally fine to say no.'

'Of course I'll put them up. They're beautiful. How much do you want to charge for each one?'

Jack named prices that Amy thought were more than fair and suggested a cut she should take for each she sold.

'And I still have that one of you in the wheat field that I want to print and frame for you as a gift. I just want to edit it a little first. It's beautiful,' he said as he moved towards the door. Amy blushed. 'The way the wheat's blowing, the light. The way you looked back at me just at that split second. Perfect.'

'Oh God,' Amy said, embarrassed. 'Thank you.'

He laughed at her awkward reaction. 'No problem.' He stood there, the corners of his mouth lifted into a smile. She didn't know what to say to keep the conversation going and so he said, 'I'll see you later?'

'Definitely,' she said louder than she'd intended. It had been so long since Amy had flirted confidently with anyone. She was making a complete mess of this.

'What is going on with you and the fit American?' Caroline said in wide-eyed amazement as she entered the kitchen after Jack had left. 'That man is into you,' Caroline continued. 'And you don't exactly look at him like he's a bag of sick.'

'Oh Caroline, that's gross.'

'He was wiping sugar off your face and his expression said he was about to kiss you. I'm so sorry about my timing by the way.'

'I don't think he was,' Amy said honestly. 'I don't think anything like that's happening. Although I do really like him. And anyway, he's not here for long so what's the point?'

'Because it's just a little bit of fun. Because it's a summer romance.'

Amy cringed. 'Aren't we a bit old for that kind of thing?'

'No,' Caroline dismissed her. 'He's only here for a few weeks, right?'

Amy sighed. 'Yes. And then he goes back to New York.'

'So just enjoy it for what it is. Flirt a little, kiss a little, see how much fun you have,' Caroline suggested. 'If you don't. I will.'

Amy narrowed her eyes.

'I'm joking.' Caroline held her hands up in defeat, laughing. 'I'm joking.'

CHAPTER 19

'Excuse me, how much is this?'

Amy looked up from arranging her sandwich-making supplies on one of her tearoom tables at the lady who'd asked the question. Amy wouldn't normally spill out from the kitchen into the tearoom but it was almost closing time and Caroline had taken over out the back with the final cake preparations for the Heritage Day. Eager to get buttering and filling the sandwiches, Amy looked up as the final customer pointed to the last-but-one photo of Jack's that remained on the walls, told her the price and then waited for the woman to snap up the picture, as had been the pattern of events ever since Jack had put his photos up a few days earlier. Jack's talent was proving very commercial for the both of them. She wondered if he'd want to continue the arrangement when he went back to the States?

Considering the sisters had been flat out baking and freezing for weeks, they were still both wide-eyed when they counted up how much of everything they had.

145

'We've got too much food, surely?' Caroline looked concerned.

'Always best to over-cater. Just in case,' Amy replied as she carried on icing, ready for the morning.

When the women arrived to set up, it was to find the Heritage Day organisers had pulled out all the stops and the old airfield was heaving with craft stalls, a dance marquee, beer tent, and vintage costumiers and makeup artists. Amy surprised herself by being excited at finding a retro hairdressers set up inside a small canvas tent, and she and Caroline had gone inside before the event opened to get victory rolls put in.

What with the yellow tea dress Amy had worn for the occasion and a slick of victory-red lipstick, even she had to acknowledge she didn't look half bad.

'We look like wartime film stars now,' Caroline enthused as they looked at each other appraisingly.

'You do. I'm not sure *I* do.' Amy rubbed at the bags under her eyes. She was sure they were noticeable. She'd still been up at two o'clock this morning, running through the stock for the day and putting finishing touches to the sandwiches.

As she parked the van back in a parking bay after having unloaded the last of the food into the tent, Amy had a chance to have a look around. The concrete bases of many of the old US Air Force buildings still remained, even if the shells of what used to be hangars, officers' mess and other outbuildings had long since crumbled. In the middle of it all was the control tower, intact, preserved and full of memorabilia donated for display today. She'd have to make a point to go inside and have a look if there was a quiet moment. It had been restored years ago, only open sporadically, and she wasn't sure why she'd never visited it before, especially when it was so close.

The great big A-shaped runway was still visible across the thin grass, although it had wide cracks running throughout and no plane would ever risk landing on it now. But there was no real way to get a feel for how it once had all been; the fear, the camaraderie, planes taking off and returning, or not returning as the case so sadly often had been. But so many people were in wartime garb that Amy almost felt a sense of something resembling history surrounding her. All of this her grandmother would have known, only with love followed by sadness from what Kitty's diary had said.

She stopped and scanned the horizon, jingling her van keys in her hand. For a few seconds she closed her eyes to try to imagine what it must have been like for Kitty back then, falling in love with someone so much that now thoughts of it caused such pain. But what happened? A rattling engine sounded as if it was on top of her and an old khaki open-top American military Jeep stopped beside her.

Inside were two men, one driving and a passenger. Both were in full Second World War American Air Force uniform. Amy did a double take as the manager of The Duck waved a greeting.

'David, you look great. Where did you get that uniform?'

'You can hire them for the day in one of the marquees,' he said, pushing his aviator sunglasses up the bridge of his nose. 'They're doing tours around the site in these Jeeps for charity. It's great fun. Where's your sister?'

Amy looked at him in surprise. 'My sister? In the tea tent sorting the napkins and tablecloths. Why?'

'Just thought I'd go and say hello before it all gets busy.' He gave her a sheepish grin. 'You want a lift?'

'Go on then,' Amy said and then realising she might be getting in the way of romance said, 'Actually, I think I've left something in the van. You go on without me.'

From her position on the other side of the wide expanse of tarmac, she could see David head inside the tea tent after the Jeep had dropped him outside. She smiled. David liked Caroline. They were both loud and over excitable. It was a match that might work.

On foot, she finally reached the marquee. Caroline was playing with her hair and David was leaning against the counter, looking forcibly nonchalant. Amy threw her sister a discreet thumbs-up and made herself scarce in the far corner, arranging extra chairs.

'God, I'm dreading this,' Caroline called over to her sister as David eventually left. 'This is the biggest thing we've ever catered.'

Amy stood up from pushing a coaster under a wobbly table leg. 'It's the *only* thing we've ever catered. We'll be fine. It's the same as the tearoom.' She scanned the large tent with well over fifty tables, each with four to six covers. She gulped. 'Only on a bigger scale. Is Mum still coming to lend a hand?'

Caroline nodded quickly, as the first customer headed inside, perusing the cakes.

'Don't worry.' Amy touched her sister's shoulder as she stood behind the counter. Outside she could hear more people arriving. 'Here we go.'

CHAPTER 20

The frenzy Caroline had predicted had come true as she took care of teas and coffees, Amy served food and their mother, Alison, cleared the crockery from tables and began washing up. The organisers had sorted a sink and huge hot water urn for teas and coffees for them. There was no way they could have coped with the turnover of dirty plates and saucers without.

The women didn't get a chance to chat until the lunch rush finished. 'It'll be afternoon teas next, Caroline. Brace yourself.' Amy smiled, high on life and the elation of a job well done. The afternoon tea menu was printed in old-fashioned swirly writing and was suitably 'wartime' in tone, minus the rationing. Customers were happy. *She* was happy and loving every second of it, although her sister looked as if she'd had enough.

'Why don't you nip off and take a break?' Amy suggested. 'Mum and I can hold the fort and then she can go when you get back. See if David's still looking dashing in that outfit.'

Caroline smiled but couldn't hold eye contact. 'I might just do that actually.'

Amy handed her mum a piece of cake and ushered her over to a chair to rest her feet. For the next few minutes Amy fiddled with the hot water urn to check it was still doing what it should, poured teas for customers and delivered them to their tables. With a slight lull in trade, she approached her mum. 'Where's Gran? Is she coming?'

'Not today, no,' Alison replied.

'Not today? It's only on today. She's going to miss it all. Is she okay?'

'I popped in this morning to check. She said she just didn't fancy it. She seemed perfectly well.'

'What? But . . .' Amy didn't know what to think. Why was Kitty purposefully missing out on something as fun as this? The diaries. Had reading them struck so much sadness into her that she couldn't face any sort of reminder of that time?

Alison popped the piece of lemon drizzle cake in her mouth, waiting for her daughter to finish her sentence, but Amy didn't know what to say.

Amy's mother had been a complete rock today, running around for her children. Amy owed her a hug later and a huge bunch of flowers. Amy looked at her mum. For all the fussing she normally did, she was a fabulous mother; encouraging both girls to do whatever it was that made them happy. Kitty had always been the same too. Amy's thoughts turned back to Kitty. Her grandmother had been fiercely in love with another man before marrying someone else. But that didn't feel like the entire story. Amy wondered if Alison had the slightest inkling about Kitty's life before her daughter's arrival and if she should drop a hint to test the water? She thought how strange it was that her gran, who had always been very 'what you see is what you get', had experienced a whole other life and love all those years ago.

But through it all, Amy tried to shake off the feeling there was something she was missing.

The afternoon teas were going well but at this time of day, the beer tent was also in full swing. Amy and her mum only had twenty or so covers to attend to when Caroline burst into the tea tent with David in steady pursuit. They were both red in the face and giggling like children.

'The dance tent is boiling.' Caroline fanned herself with a tea menu. 'We've been throwing shapes to some wartime tunes. Those pensioners really know how to party.'

Another figure appeared at the tent opening and Amy glanced over David's shoulder to see Jack. He strode over with a huge smile on his face. He was in jeans and a T-shirt and Amy was a little disappointed he'd not dressed up. She could imagine him in a pilot outfit quite happily.

'I knew I'd find you here,' he said to Amy and then waved his hand to greet them all.

Amy returned his smile. 'Were you looking for me?'

'I was looking for coffee but you'll do,' he teased. 'I actually wondered if you were due a break any time soon? And if you wanted to walk around with me? Have you seen much of it yet?'

Amy shuffled. 'Not really but I'm not really supposed to, I can't leave Mum.'

Alison jumped to attention. 'Of course you should go. We're not rushed off our feet like we were this morning. And Caroline's back now. Aren't you darling?'

Caroline took the hint instantly and started putting her

151

apron back on. 'Yes, go, go. See if you can convince Jack to get his hair Brylcreemed in the dress up tent.'

David pointed to his own coiffed hair with a grimace. 'It's really greasy. I wouldn't.'

'Yeah I might skip that.' Jack smiled and then turned to Amy. 'Ready whenever you are.'

'Where do you want to go first?' Jack asked as they wandered through the middle of proceedings. 'The dance tent?'

'I might need a bit of Dutch courage before I foxtrot or whatever it is they're doing in there. Beer tent?'

'Warm beer or something else?' Jack said with a knowing smile.

'Suffolk cider if they've still got any left. If not, warm beer will be fine.'

Jack pointed to a patch of grass where the old runway ended in a crumble of concrete and asked if she wanted to wait for him while he queued. Other people were scattered around the grass picnicking so Amy lay back on an empty patch of land and blinked up at the clouds as they passed overhead. She was in danger of going to sleep in the sunshine as Jack returned, casting a long shadow over her.

'Sorry that took so long. It's insane in there.' He produced two plastic pint glasses and then sat slowly next to her, being careful not to spill their drinks. 'Cheers,' he volunteered his glass and Amy put hers against his gently and then smiled. His normally dark brown eyes looked light brown today as the sun shone into them.

'Thanks.' She dragged her eyes away from his and sipped her cider. 'Delicious.'

They sat in comfortable silence for a few moments watching two children run past towards the tea tent with

152

their parents in hot pursuit. All around them people chatted and grazed on picnics. Jack put his drink down on the grass and lay back on his elbows, his gaze up at the blue sky and passing white clouds.

'You're so lucky,' he said.

She glanced down at him from her cross-legged position. 'Do you think so?'

'Sure.' He nodded. 'England is wonderful and Suffolk is beautiful. It's a picture postcard. Actually I found a picture postcard of the village my grandpa sent home to his mom during the war. It hasn't changed at all since then. Not one bit from what I can tell. Maybe some yellow parking lines but it's like time has stood still. It's completely magical.'

Amy didn't need telling. 'But New York's wonderful too,' she offered.

He rolled his eyes. 'Please. It has its good points. Museums, pizza joints that stay open all night. And if I want a bottle of vodka at 4 a.m. a takeout service can bring one to me in minutes. But this space, this greenery and this freedom to breathe, I hate that we don't have that; outside of the park I mean. And I don't get much chance to wander aimlessly round Central Park. There's always a reason not to. Work or . . .'

'Or?' Amy questioned.

'Or more work actually.' Jack grimaced.

'You sound like you don't want to go home.'

He sat up and took a swig of his drink. 'I don't. Not really,' he said quietly.

'It's holiday syndrome.' Amy shrugged. 'You'll get home and you'll soon snap back into it all again. It's what always happens on holiday. But life carries on.'

'Well, I'll have the chance to test your theory. I have to go home tomorrow.'

'Tomorrow?' Amy's heart plummeted. 'I thought you were here for a few weeks yet?'

'My grandpa's flown in with his buddy from the war especially for today and so they and my dad are staying on for a few weeks as planned.' He nodded. 'But I got asked to work on an assignment for an old client. Their in-house photographer is sick and the money was far too good to turn down, so . . . needs must.'

'Oh.' Amy plucked a piece of grass from the ground. Jack was going home. She knew he was going eventually, she just hadn't thought it would be so imminent. She decided not to think about any possible romance with Jack. There was no point. Instead, she'd enjoy today and then get on with her life.

After they drained their glasses, Jack stood, collected their empties and held them stacked in one hand. 'Do you want to dance?' He offered her his other hand.

'I'd love to but I can't promise I'm not going to step on you.' Amy took Jack's hand and allowed herself to be pulled up from the grass. He held her hand as they walked, smiling down at her when she glanced up at him.

'We'll tread on each other's toes together,' he said conspiratorially. She looked down at his warm, strong hand in hers. It felt wonderful, a feeling she'd not felt in such a long time – that closeness to someone. And now he was leaving.

Inside, the band was playing tunes by Glenn Miller and the floor was full to bursting with families dancing with their small children, or elderly couples reliving their youth. Around the edge a few bored teenagers were sat on chairs, playing with their phones. Jack pulled Amy onto the edge of the dance floor and put his hands around her waist. 'Let's do this.' He grinned and led Amy as the band played the quick beat of 'A String of Pearls'. Jack's strong hands were around her waist as they moved in time to the music. She told herself to stop enjoying the feel of him holding her quite so much. It was going nowhere.

At the end of the song, Amy congratulated them both for having only trodden on each other once. She was getting warm but was having far too much fun to stop now. She couldn't remember the last time she'd danced to anything, let alone tunes as lovely as this.

The band announced their last number for the afternoon and the melodic sound of 'Moonlight Serenade' began. The beat was so much slower than that of the previous tune that Amy found herself being pulled closer to Jack as they slowly danced. At first he looked into her eyes with a smile, and after a momentary awkwardness at being so close to him, Amy started to get over it and simply enjoyed the dance. After a few seconds his hands moved and one held the small of her back, while he positioned the other one between her shoulder blades. Amy enjoyed the embrace and moved closer to Jack so that her face was almost on his warm chest. The gap closed and he rested his head gently on hers as they swayed.

She was being swept along with the music and closed her eyes as they danced. It felt as if they were in a bubble, just the two of them. The music, or maybe it was the alcohol on a near-empty stomach, was having a strange effect. The scent of his aftershave together with the feel of his hands was intoxicating. She lifted her head from his chest and snuck a glance at him but he was already looking down at her. His gaze moved from her eyes to her mouth, and he angled his head ever so slightly. She waited for his lips to connect with hers but suddenly he stood up straight and raised his hand to wave a greeting to someone. Amy glanced back to see Jack's father and two elderly men waving as they were preparing to leave the dance tent.

Amy felt about eighteen years old again and as if she and Jack had just been caught doing something they shouldn't.

'I think they saw us.' Jack laughed.

The number ended all too soon and as the final bars played they reluctantly pulled away from each other.

CHAPTER 21

Amy smoothed her yellow tea dress down to avoid looking at Jack. Something was happening between them that really shouldn't be, given that he was going home so soon. They joined in the applause that the band had earned and while Amy watched the musicians as they put down their instruments for a break, she could feel Jack's gaze fixed firmly on her.

She was too embarrassed to catch his eye again and they spoke at the same time.

'I owe you—' Amy started.

'Do you want to—' Jack laughed. 'No, no, you go first.'

They left the dance tent and Amy was grateful for the fresh air. She'd only been dancing for a few minutes but felt flushed. Perhaps it was the cider, or the close proximity of dancing with Jack. Either way she was warm.

'I owe you money,' Amy said as they walked slowly. 'Quite a bit of money actually.'

Jack looked taken aback. 'How do you figure that?'

'All your pictures have sold. All but one.'

'No way.' He stopped and gave her a doubtful look.

'I told you they'd be a hit. And they were. Can you do more?'

'I can do more.' He shrugged and then looked at his watch. 'Today?'

'No, not today,' she said, laughing. 'I've been thinking, if you send me the files, I can get them printed and framed and put them up, if you trust me with the files, of course. It's going to be too much for you to try to sort.'

'Why is it going to be too much for me to sort?'

Amy looked at him with laughter in her eyes. 'You want to organise it all from New York?'

'I don't mind.' He smiled. 'It's my job after all.'

'You're going home tomorrow. If you still want your gorgeous photographs displayed in my sleepy Suffolk village tearoom then you're going to have to meet me halfway here. I can't be forever hassling you if I'm running out?' Amy gave him a sly smile.

'You can hassle me. I wouldn't mind.' He'd stopped and his head was tilted on one side, his smile playful.

Flirting with Jack was harmless and only for today as he was flying home tomorrow. And what was the harm in a little casual flirting?

'Okay.' She held up her hands in defeat. 'If you have time to sort it all out from the other side of the Atlantic then be my guest . . .'

He held his hand out to shake hers. Amy clasped his hand.

'Pleasure doing business with you,' she replied.

Jack laughed. 'You're so English.' But he didn't let go of her hand and as his smile slowly faded, the intensity of his gaze deepened. 'I've really enjoyed spending time with you,' he said, their hands still clasped. He looked down at their entwined fingers, his thumb rubbed gently on hers.

Amy's breath caught. 'Me too.'

'So,' he said in a low voice. 'Now we're kind of in business together, I suppose I should take you out and schmooze you a little. Get you on side so you don't go rogue and find another photographer to pit me against.'

She laughed. 'You never know what might happen in the future.'

A pause and then: 'Have dinner with me?' The way he said it, looking directly into her eyes, made heat rise in her face. Did he have any idea how seductive he was, even when he wasn't trying? Amy's heart did something mad in her chest.

'We've only got tonight,' he reminded her.

And that was the phrase she didn't want to hear, the phrase that meant she knew they were both wasting their time, the phrase that grounded her, bringing her back to reality. What was she doing? She couldn't – shouldn't – invest any more of her heart into something like this with Jack, no matter how much she wanted to. She was going to get hurt. She was going to spend a few blissful hours in his company tonight at dinner, she was going to like him, *really* like him. And then he would be gone, to his home on the other side of the world. She would get hurt. She was already in danger of getting hurt. This was all so utterly, unbelievably pointless.

'Jack . . . I don't think it's a good idea. You're going home tomorrow. Your home is on a different continent. And however lovely dinner would be with you, and I know it would be lovely . . .'

'I think I know what you're going to say,' he replied. 'And

159

I'm feeling the same thing. I know it's kinda mad to ask a girl on a date when I can't do anything about it afterwards. I just thought it might be nice to get to know you. But then . . .' He shrugged.

'What if we really like each other?' Amy voiced, ever so softly.

'And there's nothing we can do. I know. I know,' Jack conceded.

'We should just leave it as it is,' she said. 'It's for the best.'

He sighed. 'Yeah I know. I guess we'll talk anyways about photographs . . . and . . . um . . .' He looked lost, dejected, as if this wasn't the way the conversation was supposed to go at all.

Amy nodded. 'We will.'

'Okay,' he said. Neither of them knew quite what to do. 'I guess I'm gonna . . . I guess I'm gonna go, just have a look around a bit more or . . . something . . .'

Amy nodded again. This was it. He was going. And as he gave her a small wave, turning and leaving the tent, her feeling of elation at how well the day had gone, had been replaced now with complete misery.

CHAPTER 22

When Amy returned to the tent without Jack, Caroline knew something was up. 'That was a bit quick. Are you okay?' she asked.

'I should be. But I just feel awful. Where's Mum?'

'Gone to the van quickly to get more napkins. What's wrong?' Caroline stopped what she was doing and Amy gave her sister the edited highlights.

'And you just let him go?' Caroline questioned disbelievingly.

Amy gave her sister a pleading look. 'What else was I going to do?'

'*Not* let him go,' Caroline said simply and then followed it up with, 'That man really likes you. Or rather I thought he did. What did he say that made you end things so sharply?'

Amy took a deep breath. Then in a quiet voice, 'He asked me out for dinner.'

Caroline frowned, uncomprehending. 'And you replied by . . . sending him on his way?'

Amy nodded.

'Did you not think . . . maybe I'll go to dinner, maybe it'll be nice. Maybe it'll be an evening of flirty fun and then maybe Jack and I will text a bit, call a bit and if it's too good to leave there, see where it goes?'

'I don't think either of us wants that complication in our lives,' Amy said.

'Getting on a plane isn't that complicated,' Caroline countered.

'Emotionally it is,' Amy replied quietly. 'And I don't think I want that level of emotional complication, or to lead myself somewhere with Jack that might just hurt me, even if it is only dinner and a goodbye. I've got so much going on in my head and with the business, we're only just getting off the ground—'

'So what?' Caroline interjected. 'I think you're just making excuses.'

'Excuses for what?' Amy asked sharply.

'You tell me,' Caroline challenged. 'Nice men don't grow on trees. Trust me. I've been looking.'

'It's complicated. He lives so far away. Why would we even bother?'

'*He* seems to be bothering. It's you that's holding back and what's a bit of logistics if you really like someone?'

'*And* aren't we jumping the gun a bit?' said Amy. 'We don't even know if that kind of flying-back-and-forth thing is on the cards. I don't know if he feels like that at all.'

Caroline nodded sagely and followed it up with, 'Well that's okay then because you're not going to find out now. Problem solved.'

'Yes,' Amy said doubtfully. 'Problem solved.'

'And this way,' Caroline chimed in again, 'you'll be able to look back in years to come, on your deathbed, and think

. . . I'm so pleased I never had time for romance because I had so much more time to work instead.'

'Hmm, yes *exactly*,' Amy said brightly and then worked out what her sister had just said. She could feel her features crumpling into a frown.

The women were silent, and neither of them moved. It was as if Caroline was waiting. Amy was waiting. But for what?

It dawned on Amy that she *might* have made a mistake. 'Right,' she said. 'What should I do then?'

'What do you think you should do?'

'I should probably go after him, shouldn't I? But what do I say? I'm going to look crazy.'

'Say whatever comes into your head . . . whatever you really want to say,' Caroline offered. 'But I think if you stand here any longer, you've definitely blown it.'

'You're right,' Amy said. She paused at the tent entrance. 'Thank you.'

'Just go!' Caroline said with a grin.

What would she say to him? She had no idea. Amy ran it through in her head as she worked her way through the crowds, but no explanation sounded remotely normal.

She couldn't find Jack anywhere as she politely moved through groups of tourists. Where had all these people come from? It was as if every tent had emptied of humans. They were all making their way somewhere. A disjointed voice sounded over the tannoy, making Amy jump. She shielded her eyes from the sun and listened to the voice inform the crowd that the memorial unveiling would be in five minutes, over by the control tower.

Amy was swept along. The last thing she wanted to do was watch a plaque unveiling so she went towards the beer

163

tent, wondering if Jack felt the same. But he wasn't there so she followed the crowds, keeping her eyes peeled for any sign of him. A semi-circle of people had naturally gathered around one side of the control tower as the speech started. One of the control tower walls had been newly decorated with ornate white plasterwork of wartime bomber planes in formation. A red curtain hung draped over the middle section, hiding what Amy assumed was the plaque. She slotted herself into the front of the crowd as it slowly formed. The sun beat down on her head as the man at the front spoke and she scanned around for Jack.

'We owe tremendous thanks to the men and women . . .' the voice continued. Amy had missed the start of the speech and tried to pick up what was being said. Glancing around the crowd on the opposite side, her heart lifted as she finally caught sight of Jack with his father and one of the elderly men she'd spotted in the dance tent who Amy took to be Jack's grandfather. As she caught Jack's eye she smiled uncertainly, but he looked embarrassed, glancing away quickly. The very last thing she'd wanted to do was offend Jack but she feared that was exactly what she'd done. Her momentary elation was over and she looked down, despondently. Would he welcome her backtracking now, or should she just leave it? She didn't know what was for the best.

'The men who flew gave their all for freedom, with the odds stacked heavily against their survival. Only around twenty-four percent were expected to survive unscathed . . .'

Twenty four percent? God, that was a frighteningly low figure. 'And so, to honour the men of the 487th Bomb Group, who sacrificed their lives so the ideals of democracy might live, we are proud to unveil this memorial.' The speech ended and as the red curtain was pulled back. The plaque commemorating the valiant efforts, successes and tragic losses of the USAAF in Suffolk received the round of applause that the men's heroic efforts was due. As the crowd dispersed, people moved forward to take a closer look and read the text while others left in favour of the beer tent and entertainment. Jack's family moved forward and waited patiently to view the memorial but Jack was nowhere to be seen.

CHAPTER 23

Why *had* she stalled earlier? On reflection, she'd not been as happy in the past few years as she'd been in that last hour sitting on the grass and then dancing with him. It was this realisation in particular that shocked her the most, making her reassess what she'd been doing all these years. But Jack was leaving. Why was she doing this to herself. There was no clear-cut answer and that's what she had to tell herself, as well as telling him. And time wasn't on her side.

Amy wandered over to the memorial and looked at the words. The twenty-four percent survival rate played in her mind. She smiled at a few of the elderly American men and women who were chatting to each other nearby, reminiscing with their old friends and making new ones. Where was her grandmother? Why wasn't she here, experiencing this and enjoying the day?

By the time the memorial event had finished and they'd loaded up the van and driven the short distance back to the tearoom, the women were tired and their feet ached. Caroline shut the boot of the van after they'd dropped a tired Alison home and unloaded everything. 'Glass of wine in The Duck?' she suggested.

Amy looked down the road towards the twinkling lights of The Duck. Dusk was settling and the bar was inviting. Amy nodded. Even if Jack wasn't interested after her rebuttal, Amy did need to pay him for the photos she'd sold. And it would be nice to say goodbye properly. 'Just the one though. Then I need to get some sleep.'

The bar wasn't as busy as Amy thought it might be. As she glanced around, her breath caught in her throat as she saw Jack sitting alone on a barstool, reading a book. The effect he had on her told Amy everything she needed to know about how she felt. She was in trouble. Or rather, her heart was.

Caroline ordered their drinks further down the bar and left Amy to it.

'Hi.' Amy fidgeted next to him.

He turned, tilted his head to one side to look at her and closed his book. 'Hi,' he said questioningly.

Her mouth went dry just thinking about what she'd say. Instead of speaking, she fumbled with the roll of money and held it out to him.

He took it. 'Oh,' he said. 'Thanks.'

'I wanted to see you before you went,' she said. 'I wanted to apologise. I—' Amy was cut off as David presented Jack with his mineral water and then made an exit.

'Do you mind if I have a sip, I'm gasping.' Amy looked at the glass and Jack handed it to her and then watched her with amusement. She sipped then returned the glass to the polished wooden bar. She'd completely lost her train of thought.

'What was I saying?'

'You were apologising,' Jack said gently, pushing a barstool out for her.

'That's right.' Amy climbed onto the stool and then didn't know how to carry on, what to say.

'I think you need this more than I do.' He pushed the glass of water in her direction and signalled David for another one for himself. Amy drank a few mouthfuls until her tongue no longer felt like sandpaper.

David approached with bar menus and Jack's replacement water. 'Are you eating tonight?'

Jack nodded, reaching for the menu. 'Thanks. I could eat. Amy?' Amy looked at Jack. Was this what he wanted? Was this what *she* wanted, to spend time getting to know someone she already knew she liked only for it to end in less than twenty-four hours' time? What in God's name was she doing?

'I'd love to,' she said, and after a quick glance they ordered. 'I'm really sorry,' she continued after David had taken their order. 'About earlier.'

'Why are you sorry?' Jack asked.

'You surprised me. Or I surprised myself,' Amy clarified. 'I've not been out to dinner or been . . .' She grappled for the right word. 'Interested in getting to know someone the way I am with you in . . . years. I've been too focused on work and that's kind of crazy. And you're so lovely and I'm really intense at the minute. And you're leaving, which doesn't help,' Amy babbled on, reaching for the wine they'd ordered and pouring them both a healthy measure. 'And you asked me to dinner and I said no and I realise that was just so rude. And then we just left it there and I don't think I explained myself very well.'

168

Jack was smiling. 'You explained yourself very well. You were only saying what we're both thinking.'

'I just can't see how this will go,' Amy confessed, putting her fears out there and hoping, praying Jack didn't make fun.

He didn't. He sipped his wine and said, 'Neither can I. For now, right now I mean, it's just dinner. It's just two people who found themselves really enjoying each other's company, just having dinner. Two people who really should know better because they live nowhere near each other, just having dinner,' he added with a low chuckle.

They did both like each other. He'd voiced it out loud. And it made her feel better and worse in equal quantities.

'Also,' he continued. 'It's kinda funny how you turned down my dinner invitation and now you're having dinner with me while apologising for turning me down.'

Amy laughed, looked at him. 'So I am.' He was funny, kind, handsome. And he lived nowhere near her.

They sat close to each other, dining at the bar and by the time they'd reached their main courses the atmosphere had finally cleared. Amy's tension had melted away. She was focusing on enjoying it for what it was in this moment. Jack leaned in towards her whenever she spoke and there was the strangest moment when, after two glasses of wine each, a rogue strand of hair had worked its way into her eyes and Jack had instinctively leaned forward and moved it for her. His touch had jolted her – unexpected, desired. It was something she'd not felt in so long. It did things to her it really shouldn't have done. She tried to concentrate on the conversation rather than the fact she'd just been knocked sideways by an electric jolt. The lights were dim, table lamps providing a yellow glow, flickering candles adding to the atmosphere.

Amy realised Jack was looking intently at her, waiting for a reply to a question she'd obviously missed.

He laughed, repeated himself. 'I asked how you ended up working with your sister?'

'Oh, it was an easy decision to ask her to get involved. I couldn't possibly do it on my own. When the two sisters who ran it before decided to retire, it seemed only natural that Caroline should come and help. She was in a bit of a rut work wise, doing admin for a car sales showroom. They moved her to the back office. She's got a good head for figures but she missed that daily interaction with customers. I asked her if she wanted to help me and she said yes. She was excited to join the tearoom. She really mucks in. At some point she'll realise she's made for better things than running around in a tearoom, then I'm alone.'

They glanced over at Caroline laughing raucously at something David had just said.

'She's a real people person,' Amy said, proud to call Caroline her sister.

'I see that,' Jack agreed with a smile. 'So two young sisters take over from two elderly sisters. History has a funny way of coming full circle and scooping everyone up with it.'

'I never looked at it that way,' Amy mused.

'And so what are you planning on doing with the tearoom in the long-term?'

Amy sipped her wine. 'I feel like I'm on a job interview,' she teased.

'Hey, you grilled me on where my career is going so it's only fair I get to find out about you in return.'

'Alright,' she agreed. 'I suppose,' she started, 'that I found

170

today really energising, exhilarating. Despite the fact it was hard work and busy, it was fun, good fun. Although tiring. I'd maybe like to do a bit more catering,' she said thoughtfully. 'I supply this place and I offer celebration and wedding cakes.' She glanced around the misshapen plaster and oak-beamed walls of the hotel's small bar. 'It's been a good taster for something . . . *more*. I now know we can do events. I don't think I'd want to do more than one or two a month and maybe not on that scale. But maybe if I rented a bigger commercial kitchen somewhere nearby it would be . . . easier. Hire in staff for specific occasions. Who knows? I need to think about it a bit more.'

'It sounds like you've thought about it enough to know it could work. Today was great. You'd be great.'

He looked admiringly at her and Amy flushed, mumbled, 'Thanks,' and took another sip of wine to hide her embarrassment.

'So what are you going to do when you go back to New York?' Amy asked.

'What do you mean?'

'Well, you said you've had enough of photographing stunningly attractive models.' She said it with a glint in her eye. 'But you've cut your holiday short to do just that, haven't you?'

'Not quite,' he replied. 'I've cut my holiday short, yes, which I'm annoyed that I've done now. I don't know why I did it. I just can't say no, which is a fault I need to work on if I'm ever going to have a life. But I'm not going home to take photos of girls. It's a project my ex-girlfriend needed help on.'

For a split-second, Amy stiffened. 'Oh,' she said in surprise.

It was as if he'd read the expression in her eyes. 'It's not like that,' he explained quickly. 'She works for a real estate

171

company. Some celebrity is selling their apartment and she needs a photographer she can trust to take pictures of the place – you know, not to steal things or go poking their nose into their mail or their trash. They pay really well. Too good to turn down. And every single cent helps if I'm to sell up and move out of the city.'

Amy's head shot up. 'You're going to leave New York?'

'That's the plan. I'm not sure when. Or where I'll go, come to think of it. Somewhere quieter. Somewhere upstate. New York City is for twenty-somethings hungry for . . . well, hungry for anything and everything. I'm in my thirties. I'm not hungry for whatever it is the city has anymore.' He picked up his drink and Amy watched the beads of condensation on the side of the cold wine glass run down to meet his fingers as he held it. When he put it down, she put her hand out, instinctively touching his hand. He wrapped his fingers round hers in return and looked at her. He sighed, looked heavenwards.

Amy's heart thumped.

When he next spoke it was softer, quieter. 'I'm sorry I'm leaving tomorrow.'

Amy looked up and into his handsome face. 'Me too.'

Jack offered to walk her back to her flat. Hand in hand, they walked in silence past the rows of lopsided, timber-framed buildings, enjoying the sound of a solitary owl in the trees in the distance. Amy could get used to the feeling of Jack's skin touching hers as their fingers connected.

When they arrived at the front door to her flat above the tearoom they stood awkwardly. Or rather she stood awkwardly while Jack exuded his all-American confidence. She wondered if she should invite him in for coffee, but then where would that lead? He was leaving. She was never going to see him again as it was and a one-night stand wasn't really her style, even if it was with someone as lovely and as handsome as Jack.

She was pulled from her thoughts as Jack spoke. 'I don't fly until the evening. I'd like to spend the day with you tomorrow. If you're free?'

Amy smiled. 'I'd love to but . . .'

'But?'

'I have to work,' she said desperately.

His hand was still holding hers and he rubbed the back of it with his thumb. It sent tingles through her body. 'I understand. I'm delaying the inevitable. I just don't want to say goodbye,' he admitted.

'Neither do I.' The tingles were suddenly replaced with raw unhappiness and there was a bittersweet silence between them. This was it. He was leaving. 'Maybe I could ask my mum if she'd cover for me,' Amy declared desperately. Oh God, her mother would kill her. After having roped Alison in at the Heritage Day, Amy severely doubted her mother would be happy to be on her feet two days in a row, but she could only ask.

He smiled, a warm, infectious smile.

'If I can get my mum to cover, what would you like to do tomorrow?' she asked.

'My grandpa wants to visit a cemetery in Cambridge.'

'Oh,' she said in surprise. 'That's . . . niche. And you want me to come with you? To a cemetery? That's a strange place to take a girl on your last day in England.'

Jack laughed. 'I realise that now I say it out loud. But it's a special cemetery. It's an official war graves site. It's where all US personnel from the Second World War are buried.

Those that were stationed here and died here, I mean. My grandpa wants to pay his respects to friends he lost.'

'In which case, I'd be honoured to join you, thank you. I hope Mum can cover for me,' Amy finished doubtfully.

'I hope she can too.' Jack touched Amy's cheek with his thumb and butterflies flew in her stomach. He leaned in slowly and it was as if time stood still. There was nothing – no passing car – to break the magic of the expectation of Jack's kiss. She closed her eyes and waited for his lips to softly touch hers. When he kissed her, it was as if everything else in the world fell away and there was only her and Jack standing together, connected now in such a magical way.

Desire rushed through her and she put her arms around his waist as he kissed her harder and deeper. And then when they eventually moved apart, he issued a low chuckle. 'I've been desperate to do that since that first night you threw beer all over me.'

She smiled. 'Really?'

'Really,' he replied, dipping his head and kissing her again. 'I should go,' he said reluctantly.

Amy nodded, still holding onto his waist. 'Yes,' she said softly. 'You should.'

Jack waited until she was safely inside before he turned to walk down the street towards the hotel.

From a few paces away, he turned. 'Good night, Amy.'

'Good night,' she replied from the doorway. She closed the door and leaned against it. Her heart was racing and she laughed with happiness.

CHAPTER 24

Alison arrived at the tearoom promptly at 8 a.m. 'Thanks for covering, Mum.'

Alison saluted. 'I'm happy to help. We made quite a team yesterday.'

Amy put her hand on Alison's arm. 'Mum, you're a lifesaver. Where would Caroline and I be without you?'

'Oh be quiet.' Alison waved her hand to brush the compliment away as the two women began opening up the tearoom.

'No I mean it. You really have been our rock. You've been our everything. We don't deserve you. Well, I don't anyway.'

'You do, darling. With your gran, we are four fierce women,' her mum issued the rallying cry, followed by, 'You know I did always worry that growing up with only a female presence in your worlds might possibly damage you in some way. Not having your father around when it was far and away the norm . . . But you've both turned out to be wonderful human beings – different characters and personalities, but fine and successful young human beings.'

Amy smiled. 'Thanks, Mum.' She paused to watch Alison as she moved around the tearoom. What would she do without her mum, her sister, her gran? She knew she was lucky. 'Caroline will be here soon.' Amy looked at her watch.

Alison was already tying an apron round her waist. Having stepped in before on the odd occasion, she looked at home behind the counter and turned to flick on the coffee machine. 'I can manage until then. Off you go. Have fun.'

Amy had sent a quick text message to Jack telling him she'd be joining him and his family. He'd replied almost instantly to say how happy he was that she could make it, which made Amy soar. But before they were due to meet, there was something she needed to do.

The farmhouse was eerily quiet. Although Kitty lived alone there was usually the quiet rumble of human existence – the kettle boiling or the soothing tones of Classic FM playing from the pretty blue digital Roberts radio she and Caroline had clubbed together to buy Kitty last Christmas. But not today. Kitty's breakfast things were still on the table, which was most unlike her neat and orderly grandmother. Amy moved further into the house and found her grandmother in the pale blue sitting room, staring out of the window. She coughed at the threshold to the room and Kitty spun round. She was clutching something to her chest. Amy recognised the same wartime diary Kitty had been reading last time.

She felt as if she'd intruded, although it was common practice to enter the house without warning through the kitchen. Today, this moment felt different. Kitty's eyes stared at Amy as if, for a second or two, she couldn't quite fathom who her granddaughter was.

'Are you alright, Gran?'

'Yes, dear.' Kitty indicated the diary. 'I was just . . .' She glanced around the room as if searching its walls for the right words.

Amy's heart went out to her. 'Another trip down memory lane?'

'Something like that.'

Amy sat on the settee but didn't flump into it the way she normally did. She sat tentatively at the edge of it, her knees together, her feet crossed at the ankles. 'Why didn't you come along to the Heritage Day yesterday?' Amy asked gently.

Kitty looked at her blankly.

'To the memorial unveiling,' Amy said. 'You were missed.'

'I told you I wouldn't be there,' Kitty reminded her. 'I haven't been back to that airfield since Char . . .'

'Since Charlie . . .?' Amy guessed, when her grandmother looked as if she was offering no end to the start of her story.

'Well perhaps only once after that. The day it was sold. I went to take one final look the day your grandfather parcelled up and sold all the land. And I just . . . couldn't face going back there yesterday. It wouldn't look the same, wouldn't feel the same. I didn't want to see it.'

The tick of the oversized carriage clock on the mantle was the only noise for a few seconds. Amy's mind whirred. Whoever this Charlie was, he had meant so much to her gran – enough that Kitty had felt unable to revisit the airfield all these years later. It had been so long, and Kitty had loved her grandfather Christopher so wholeheartedly. But there was obviously something poignant about Charlie that Kitty couldn't shake off, even now, all these years later. Amy wondered if maybe she could try to trace him or at least find out what had happened to him. Perhaps war records would shed some light, although Amy didn't know how on earth to begin that sort of investigation.

'What happened, Gran?'

'It wasn't meant to be,' Kitty said simply, looking at the floor. It was clear it was taking every ounce of energy she had to relive what looked like a painful memory. Amy sat even closer to the edge of the settee, waiting . . . just waiting.

Kitty raised her gaze from the floor and looked sadly at Amy.

'Gran, what happened to him?'

CHAPTER 25

1944

A fitful night's sleep meant Kitty slept through the shrill ring of her alarm clock, its bells ringing loud and clear inside her head before she realised it wasn't a dream and reached out to halt the horrible sound. As she blinked into the daylight there were a hazy few seconds where she hadn't fully registered the events of last night and she smiled as she remembered Charlie's kiss, his declaration of love.

She was blissfully happy and she grinned from ear to ear. Even the odious task she'd been dreading doing today on the farm seemed almost pleasant. Nothing could dampen her spirits.

While two new Land Girls had arrived to help with the harvest, Nancy had just completed her rat-catching training with poison bait and was tasked with keeping rats from Christopher's farm – so they wouldn't eat all the crops – as well as some of the neighbouring ones. She was considered a skilled worker now and had been enjoying discussing every part of her training with Kitty and Christopher over the last few days, teaching Kitty all she'd learned. The two girls were going to tackle the vile job together in order to protect the animals and crops and this now meant Christopher didn't need to hire in a rat catcher and pay out extra, precious money to them in such straitened times.

As Kitty walked to the farm, she wondered if anyone could possibly tell how in love she was. Would anyone see the happiness in her eyes? Charlie was going to meet her father soon, that's how invested they both were in this relationship. Because it had grown into a relationship. They were in love. She laughed with joy just thinking about it.

Rat catching was among the most revolting work Kitty had to do as a Land Girl but it wasn't the most gruelling, and learning from Nancy was enjoyable, in its own way. The laying of the sugared bait in order to catch the rodents struck Kitty as particularly cruel and in no way appealed to her sense of fair play – a tease to the hungry rats who would taste something so wonderful, that held such promise, and then find it had all been a disastrous trick.

Kitty's back ached from helping lay the bait and clearing away the dead rats. She'd been surprised how many there were. Christopher's mother had come to inspect a handful of dead rats near the stables, a handkerchief held against her nose the entire time.

'Don't worry. They don't have plague no more these days,' Nancy declared.

Christopher's eyebrows shot up as they watched the Land Girl shrug and continue clearing up dead rats around a startled Mrs Frampton. Kitty tried not to laugh as she cleaned. Christopher glanced at her and stifled a smile.

'Kill that rat. It's doing Hitler's work,' Mrs Frampton said in her cut-glass tones from behind her handkerchief.

Kitty looked around for a rogue rat. God, not another one. She thought they'd got them all. 'Where?'

'I think they've all gone now, Mother.' Christopher hid a smile.

'They bloody better have. We've been at it for hours,' Nancy confirmed.

'I'm quoting the poster,' Mrs Frampton muttered quietly and then turned and left the three of them to it. It was the first time in weeks Kitty had seen the woman in the flesh.

Christopher hauled the sack of dead rats away but gave Kitty a look that confirmed he found his mother as hilarious as the two Land Girls did.

The girls settled in for lunch in the sunshine. Nancy had just started seeing a radio operator and usually wolfed her sandwiches down and then lay in the field, sleeves rolled up, shirt buttons daringly undone down to her bosom, catching a few rays of sun behind the tractor while waiting for him to pop over and say hello. But today she was reading a magazine about her favourite Hollywood film stars. If Kitty ever had any energy to read she preferred *Weekly Illustrated*. But instead they chatted and shared their food. Nancy ate hers and the majority of Kitty's.

'Go on,' Kitty said. 'I'm not hungry.'

'You'll waste away, you will,' Nancy said between mouthfuls of Kitty's fish paste sandwiches.

Kitty laughed. 'I doubt it.'

'You ain't scrawny. I'll give you that. But you don't eat much. I'm the same. Can't look at a bowl of raw spuds without bursting out of my dress.' She looked down at her overalls. 'Not that I wear a dress much these days. Did last night, for that dance at the airbase. You looked pretty by the way.'

181

'So did you. Where did you find enough coupons for that flame-red dress? It looked new.'

'It was. I've got my ways,' Nancy said cryptically and then confessed. 'Black market. Dad sent it to me. No idea where he got it from. Back of a lorry probably.'

'That's a strange place to sell clothing from.'

Nancy looked at her as if she wasn't sure if Kitty was joking or not. 'You being funny?'

'I don't think so,' Kitty said uncertainly.

'It's nicked, probably,' Nancy explained.

'Oh. Right.'

'You're quite innocent you, ain't you?'

'Maybe,' Kitty said testily.

'You enjoy last night? Get a tour?'

'I did, yes. Saw Charlie's plane. What about you?'

'I didn't look at the planes. You been inside them bunk huts where they sleep?'

Kitty didn't think anyone had been allowed in there. She shook her head and Nancy gave her a wink. 'I have.'

'Really? Why?'

Nancy roared with laughter, the victory rolls in her hair shaking with movement. 'Why d'ya think?'

It took Kitty a few seconds to understand Nancy's meaning. 'Oh,' she said simply. 'That's . . .' But Kitty didn't know what it was.

'So innocent,' Nancy said, lying back and soaking up the last of the summer sun. Kitty, cross-legged, stared across the field to the oak tree where she'd picnicked with Charlie. She missed him already and she'd only seen him last night. Was it like this for everyone? The madness, the intensity with which two people could fall in love? Every second more special than the last? Every moment not spent together complete, undeniable torture?

'Aren't you worried about . . .' Kitty bit her lip, wishing she hadn't just spoken.

'About?' But when Kitty didn't answer Nancy propped herself up on her elbows and gave her an enquiring look.

Eventually Kitty said, 'About having a baby? It's such a risk before marriage.'

'Oh.' Nancy lay back down on the ground. 'No.'

'No? Why ever not? Are the two of you marrying then?'

''Course not. And my man wears something. A French letter, he calls it. Silly name really. Sounds far more romantic than it really is. Bit of a mood-killer actually, but sadly necessary. I don't want a bloody baby. And he don't want me to have one neither.'

Kitty was startled. Did everyone know about, what was it Nancy had just called them, French letters? Kitty had no idea what they really were, just that they would stop a baby somehow. There was a lot she needed to learn.

Nancy's eyes were still closed but she picked a bit of grass and played with it absentmindedly. 'If I were to have a baby and no husband,' she waved the bit of grass around to emphasise her point, 'my life wouldn't be worth living. My dad may like a bit of dodgy dealing but he don't want me to get knocked up. About some things he's a traditionalist.'

Kitty looked down at Nancy thoughtfully.

'My family would never forgive me,' Nancy continued. 'My friends would think I'd lost my marbles. Mrs bloody Frampton would fire me on the spot. The WLA would kick me out, so no more Land Army for me. No job. I'd be stuffed. Royally stuffed. Nowhere to live. No way to earn any money.' Nancy whistled. 'I ain't the cleverest girl I know, but I sure as hell ain't getting a baby put inside me for a few minutes of fun. I ain't that silly.'

'What would you do if . . .'

Nancy opened one eye. 'I wish you'd finish your questions.'

'What would you do if you did get pregnant?'

Nancy shuddered. 'Doesn't bear thinking about.'

'Yes, but if you did?'

The Land Girl sat up, looked at her watch and started buttoning up her shirt. She sighed. 'I suppose . . .' she started. 'I supposed I'd see if my man would marry me. Although . . . I mean, I fancy him quite a bit but I don't want to be shackled to someone like him. Bit flaky. Not forever, no ta. Not just because of a baby.'

'So then what?'

'I'd have to find one of them God-awful backstreet abortionists. Perish the thought but that might be the only thing to do.'

Kitty's mouth dropped open. 'What are they?'

'Bloody hell.' Nancy chuckled. 'I didn't know it was going to be a lesson in biology today. Well, the clue is in the name. They're sometimes midwives who know what they're doing.' Nancy shuddered again. 'And sometimes they're not.'

'And what do they do in order to get rid of the baby?' Kitty enquired, risking sounding even more innocent than ever.

Somehow she knew she wasn't going to like the answer.

'I don't know. Thank God. Never had to find out. But a friend of a friend went to get rid of her baby. She went through with it but she was weak as anything afterwards and ended up with some kind of poisoning illness. I often wondered if they gave you something to drink or if they just used knitting needles, like what I've always been told did the trick.'

'Knitting needles?' Kitty was horrified. She could imagine full well what they were for. 'How awful,' she exclaimed.

'Oh listen, Kitty, love. Don't worry about me. I won't be getting a baby in me for a very long time yet. Not until I get a honking great wedding ring on my finger.'

Kitty couldn't help but agree.

CHAPTER 26

The next morning she and Nancy were in the field again, repairing the combine harvester as the Land Girls prepared to start work on the biggest task yet, only one of the mechanisms kept locking up every time they tried to start it.

The Americans were making their way back home from another early morning raid somewhere over Europe.

'Back already?' Kitty questioned. 'They've not been gone long.'

'France, I reckon,' Nancy guessed as the din of the aircraft sounded in the distance, the roar of engines growing louder as they neared. The metal shined off the planes in the late morning light as they made their way back to the base, wheels down as they passed overhead. Kitty and Nancy usually counted them out in the morning, waving enthusiastically to wish them luck. She liked to think they were waving back, but in reality they were probably staring at the skies with dread, wondering if they'd make it back alive – at what point in the journey they'd encounter flak or be fired at by enemy anti-aircraft gunners.

Kitty watched the planes as they flew in, one after the other, spaced well apart, as she and Nancy stared up, their task forgotten. Kitty stood with her hands on her hips, easing the ache in her back that had started forming.

'We'll give it one more go and if we can't fix it we'll have to see if one of the other girls has got a magic touch or give up and fetch Christopher,' Nancy said. 'Do you know where he is?'

'Finishing milking the cows, I think,' Kitty said absently. 'It's still so early.'

Nancy sighed. 'One of us will have to run a pale of milk up to the farmhouse so the dragon can have her morning cuppa soon. It's got to be your turn,' Nancy announced.

'Sorry?'

'You're miles away this morning. You up there, in the skies, with him?'

But Kitty wasn't listening. Her gaze was trained on the last of the planes as it flew back in. Something was wrong.

Nancy followed her gaze. 'That one's wheels ain't down.'

Kitty looked as the plane flew over their heads, firing red emergency flares as it passed. They were so used to the deafening noise that she'd barely paid attention but now her eyes were fixed on it. She couldn't make out the markings to identify which aircraft it was as it came past. Her eyes were locked on the smooth undercarriage. The wheels hadn't come down.

Kitty stiffened as they watched the plane fly over the line of trees that divided the field from the beginning of the airfield. The plane dipped out of sight. She prayed it wasn't Charlie. Ten men were inside that plane. Were they full of fear of the danger ahead as they approached the runway?

There was a dreadful shriek of metal scraping on tarmac,

unlike anything Kitty had ever heard before. Nancy grabbed Kitty's arm in shock and the two women stood, mouths open, unable to see through the line of trees. The ghastly noise went on and on. Kitty dropped the wrench in shock as the scraping noise continued.

'Oh my God,' Nancy cried as the sound of tearing metal continued from the other side of the trees.

A flicker of fear went through Kitty. The men inside. What was happening to them? Why were the trees in the way of their view? Why couldn't she see what was happening? Kitty started running towards the noise.

'Where you going?' Nancy called.

'We can help, can't we?'

'Don't be daft.' The sound of ripping metal, a sound Kitty would never forget, finally ended. 'They'll have plenty of help and there's very little we can do. The speed that thing was going . . . they'll be the other end of the runway by now.'

Kitty put her hand to her heart, her chest rising and falling at such a rate. She'd never heard or seen a plane crash before.

'I can't believe that just happened.' Kitty's breathing came quick and fast. 'What do we do now?'

Nancy picked up the wrench. 'We fix this sodding combine harvester.'

Charlie was late the next day. She was used to him coming and going from the village without notice or warning. Sometimes he'd be gone for a few days but he'd told her to expect that now that they were pushing their way further into Europe. She'd deduced he'd been dropping bombs over oil refineries as she kept reading about such successful Allied raids in the newspapers. She often wondered which raids Charlie had been involved with and which he hadn't.

But today she'd been expecting him. Kitty had borrowed Nancy's bicycle so she could dash home for her lunch and get back to the farm all within the hour. And now she was running out of time. Kitty tapped her fingers against the edge of the wooden pub door. The paint was flaking off but there was no paint to be had this side of the war. She wasn't helping the door's survival and she picked a fleck of paint out from underneath her nails, continuing to tap her fingers hard against the door. Charlie knew what time the pub closed for lunch and it would be useful to get her father in a good mood when he wasn't working. Once they'd met, once they'd got this out the way, it would be a weight off Kitty's mind and would be easier for Kitty to step out with him. She didn't like all this sneaking about. She was proud of Charlie, proud for her dad to meet him.

Susan approached, waving happily to her. 'I'm on my way to post some letters. Want to come for the walk?'

Kitty looked past Susan briefly. 'Um . . .'

'Waiting for someone?'

'No,' Kitty teased. 'Not at all . . . just getting a breath of fresh air.'

'Oh, right.' Susan laughed. 'He's very nice. But then I think you probably already know that.'

'I do,' Kitty said, blushing. 'I do.'

'Will you say that to him when he asks? *I do*?' It was Susan's turn to tease.

Kitty blushed even harder. 'You mean to marriage? That's a bit adventurous, Susan. He's not even asked and we've not known each other very long. Besides . . . if we marry

189

then . . .' Kitty didn't know what came next if that eventuality occurred.

'There goes your plan to forge a path in the Women's Land Army.' Susan winked. 'Off to America you go . . . lucky thing.'

'I suppose so, yes.' Kitty said, thinking. She wasn't disappointed, just stunned. None of this had occurred to her. She dared not dream. Charlie was the kindest, most handsome man she'd ever met. There was no way she was going to mourn the loss of being a Land Girl for a new life with him, if that's what was going to happen. But America? She was getting ahead of herself.

'When do *you* leave?' Kitty changed the subject.

'Two days!' Susan trilled. 'I'm so excited.'

'What kind of work will you be doing?' Kitty had no idea what girls did in the other services. She'd never really taken the time to investigate. It had always been Land Army for her.

'Oh all sorts I'd imagine, although I'm not *really* sure. I assume it might be terribly hush hush for no reason at all and I'll be doing something awfully boring. But anything's better than being utterly useless.'

'Hear hear,' Kitty chimed in.

'How's Christopher treating you?' Susan asked.

'Well. He's kind. Always has been. Bit lonely perhaps? Spends all his days outside working like a dog and then all his evenings at home with his mother. Perhaps he's just tired. Like me really. Farm work's harder than I thought it would be even with more Land Girls helping with the harvest. Fun, useful, but tiring.'

'Christopher always was a dreamboat,' Susan mused. 'Never once looked at me though. Always seemed to be mooning about after you.'

190

'Don't be silly. Of course he wasn't. Besides, he was always far too grand for the likes of us.'

'Ah I'm not sure if it was he who was grand or if it was his batty old mother pretending they were. My mum always said Mrs Frampton suffered from illusions of grandeur.'

Kitty thought about Mrs Frampton and the way she did have a tendency to look down at her and the other Land Girls, despite the fact they were the ones keeping her farm going – alongside Christopher, of course. 'Yes, you might be right,' Kitty agreed.

'Listen,' Susan asked. 'You will write to me, won't you? I'm not sure what I'll do without you to keep me laughing. I know you'll be busy with the pub and the farm and Charlie but I really will miss you. I've never been away from home before and I'm not really sure what to expect.' Her voice wobbled.

Kitty smiled and held her friend's hands warmly. 'Of course I will. If you promise to do the same. I'll miss you too, you know.'

Susan smiled tenderly and waved as she continued on towards the post office and Kitty mused on how it really was *all change*. And then Charlie approached on Kitty's bicycle, slower than he normally rode. His posture looked . . . wrong.

She called his name and he looked up; the skin around his eyes was bruised and his face was cut in several places and there was a large gash on his cheek. He attempted a smile but it clearly hurt and he let his jaw go slack again as he approached her.

Kitty ran towards him. 'What's happened? You're hurt. It was you wasn't it? You were in that crash.' She held his face in her hands and then he slowly, ever so slowly

191

dismounted from the bike. He looked at her, his eyes almost glassy.

He nodded, slowly. 'I think I need to sit down.' He looked around for the bench and Kitty led him over to the one a little way down the road.

Charlie winced as he sat down and all worry about introducing him to her father dissipated. There were bigger things to worry about.

'Ah, that's better.' He tried to smile.

'What happened up there?' Kitty looked at his hands. They looked as tanned and as perfect as they always did; a stark contrast to the bruised mess that was his face.

'Damned wheels didn't come down.' He looked at her.

'How? How did that happen?'

'Mechanism for the landing gear got stuck.' He shrugged. It sounded so matter-of-fact but it had almost killed him.

'Are you alright?' She knew it was a stupid question. He looked anything but alright.

'Now, yes. Yesterday, no.'

She grabbed his hand. She had almost lost him. She could barely think straight. 'Why are you here? Why aren't you resting?'

'I've *been* resting. I wanted to see you,' he said. 'Do you want know the strangest thing about it?'

Kitty nodded her head and waited as she stroked his hand.

'You're supposed to see your whole life flash before your eyes when you're about to die. But I didn't see anything other than you.'

'In the field below you? When you flew over?'

'No.' He shook his head. 'Is that where you were? I just saw you, in my head, I guess. When I knew we were gonna hit the ground, when I knew anything I did at the controls wouldn't help us one bit, I just thought of you.'

Kitty swallowed. 'Charlie, I could have lost you. You could have been killed.'

He smiled weakly. 'Ah I'm still here. It'll take more than that kind of . . . uncontrolled landing to finish me off.'

'What about the rest of the crew?'

'Fine. All fine. We're all bruised and shaken. The ball turret gunner climbed up before his compartment underneath smashed to pieces. God, the noise. Metal on runway. I'll never forget *that* sound.' Charlie shuddered.

'Me neither.' She leaned into him as they sat on the bench, not caring if anyone saw her. This was love. She wouldn't lose Charlie. She just wouldn't. Kitty could feel his warmth through his uniform. He put his arm around her. The effort forced a pained noise from him. 'Charlie, shouldn't you be in hospital?'

'Doc's given me the once over. I can walk. And just about ride that bicycle. Nothing's broken. I smashed my face into the controls though. That's why I look even more handsome today than usual.' His laugh turned into a cough. He put his mouth against the top of her head, nestling in against her victory rolls. 'I love you,' he whispered.

She dared to squeeze him a little more. 'I know you do. Charlie, I love you so much. Please be careful. Please stop nearly getting killed.'

He laughed into her hair. 'If that was my brush with death, then I'll take it.' He sat up and took his St Christopher pendant out from underneath his shirt collar. It dangled at the end of its long silver chain. 'Maybe this guy has been looking out for me after all.'

Kitty sat up and looked at it. 'It's lovely.'

'My mother gave it to me before I left for England. It feels like a lifetime ago. I feel like I've been here forever.'

Kitty nestled further into his chest. How was he still alive?

'I want to be with you,' he continued. 'I'm so serious about you. I can't keep away. I love you so much.

She said it back and they held each other, Kitty mindful of his injuries.

'Do you still want to introduce me to your father? He might not be so hard on me seeing his daughter at odd hours of the day because today . . . today I'm all beat up. He might take pity on me. What do you think?'

Kitty looked at him thoughtfully. 'I think it's sneaky,' she said with a smile while inside her stomach somersaulted. 'And while I hate to admit it, that's not actually a bad idea.'

'Really?'

'I'm dreading it obviously,' Kitty said. 'And I apologise in advance if he gives you the grilling of your life about your intentions.'

'Intentions?'

'Don't fathers always ask about intentions? That's what Janie says. But I'll only keep dreading it if we put it off and this way we get it over and done with.'

'My thoughts exactly,' he said, smiling and hurting his face in the process. 'Ow,' he said under his breath. She kissed his cheek, ever so gently, and then his mouth.

'Careful,' he said, glancing around.

Kitty gave him a devil-may-care look. 'It doesn't matter who sees us now, does it?' she said, standing up. She inhaled slowly, then exhaled. 'We're about to enter the lion's den.'

'And so, Mr Williams,' Charlie said to Kitty's amused father, who'd said nothing the entire speech, 'to finish, I have nothing but the best intentions towards Kitty and in short . . . sir, I'm in love with your daughter.'

Kitty couldn't have been happier hearing these words spoken aloud to her father. It warmed her every time Charlie confessed his love and this occasion was no exception.

Silence reverberated through the kitchen above the pub. Kitty shifted on her feet, unsure of her father's reaction.

'Are you now?' Kitty's father replied. 'You're in love with my daughter,' he repeated.

'I am, sir,' Charlie replied, standing his ground and then he physically wobbled and Kitty's father relented.

'Sit down, son. You're making me nervous.' Her father's eyes flicked towards Kitty.

'Thank you, sir.' Charlie pulled out a dining chair and sat while Kitty turned, assuming it was now safe to take her eyes from the situation and start making tea.

'And this has been going on since . . .?'

'Only a matter of weeks,' Charlie said honestly, glancing at Kitty for any sign he should stop talking.

Kitty nodded. It was alright. It was all going to be alright.

'And you have the best intentions?' Mr Williams asked.

'Certainly, sir.'

'And what might they be?'

'Pardon? I'm not sure I follow,' Charlie said.

'What are your intentions towards my daughter?' Mr Williams said slowly, as if Charlie was an idiot. Kitty stopped making tea and turned back towards the scene in the kitchen. It was not safe to make tea. It was not safe at all.

'Oh, I see,' Charlie replied. 'Well,' he threw Kitty a smile, 'I love her and . . .'

'And . . .? Kitty's father prompted. 'Do you intend to marry her?'

'Dad!' Kitty cried.

Charlie inhaled and glanced at Kitty. 'We've not . . . really . . . spoken about it yet.'

'Why?' Mr Williams asked.

'Dad!' Kitty chastised again.

Charlie paused, as if weighing up the right words. 'In truth sir, how do I put this . . .' he said. 'Take a look at me. I'm an honourable man. But I'm a bruised one, who's lucky to be alive. I don't want to offer Kitty something that might not ever happen. I don't want to propose to her and then—'

'And then die?' her father cut in.

'Dad!' Kitty cried in exasperation.

Charlie nodded. 'Exactly. I could stand here and tell you I'm going to marry your daughter . . . if she'd have me . . . of course.'

Kitty could barely breathe.

Charlie resumed. 'But it might not happen. To me, that's not the best of intentions, to promise to marry her and know full well keeping that promise is out of my control. But if I finish my tour and she wants to be my wife . . .' Her heart soared as he flicked his gaze to Kitty, leaving his sentence unfinished but the meaning was clear.

The silence in the room that descended was electric. Her father turned to her. 'I take it this is news to you?' he asked.

Kitty looked at Charlie. He smiled slowly.

'We haven't spoken about marriage or . . . anything,' Kitty said, thinking on her feet. 'But I understand,' she said truthfully. 'I do. I understand your concerns.'

'I want to be with you,' Charlie said. 'And I want your father to know how serious I am about you. But I can't propose to you *yet*. I can't offer to marry you. If there wasn't a war on, I would.'

It was her father who spoke next. 'If there wasn't a war on you wouldn't be here.'

Charlie laughed suddenly. 'That much is true. And I wouldn't have met Kitty and I wouldn't have fallen in love. But it is love, and for now that's all I'm able to offer her. I hope that's enough.'

'Kitty?' her father asked. '*Is* it enough?' How her father had ended up mediating this strange situation was beyond her.

Kitty nodded. Of course it was enough. Of course it was. 'Yes,' she said, her heart still so full. 'Yes, it is.'

'Then it's good enough for me,' Mr Williams said. He looked from Kitty to Charlie. 'But you know, son, promise of marriage or no promise of marriage . . . I can see it in her eyes . . . Kitty's heart will still break the same if something happens to you, regardless as to whether there's a ring on her finger or not.'

'That was unexpected,' Charlie confessed when he and Kitty were alone together outside the pub. 'If I ever get captured by the enemy I think I'll be just dandy. Nothing will ever be as bad as that interrogation. At one point I wanted to answer your father with just my name, rank and serial number.'

Kitty laughed, hiding her eyes behind her hands. 'Oh God, I know. I'm so sorry. I had no idea it was going to be *quite* like that! Although you started talking about intentions . . . not him.'

Charlie pulled her hands away from her eyes and held them in his. 'I know. What was I thinking? But it's fine. The worst is over. I didn't imagine on meeting him that I'd have to justify *not* asking for your hand in marriage. I think I'd have been less nervous, on reflection, if I'd been actually asking his permission to marry you.'

Kitty gave Charlie a warm smile.

'I know we haven't talked about it,' he said uncertainly. 'But you do understand, don't you? You understand I can't possibly ask you to marry me while my life isn't my own to live?'

'Don't say that,' she said quickly.

'You know what I mean,' he said. 'I'm sorry that's how you found out but . . . I can't marry you when . . . I don't even know if I'm going to be alive this time next week. Yesterday's crash really brought that home to me.'

She let out a deep breath. 'I know. I do understand. I've not asked anything of you,' she said, 'and you've not asked anything of me. but you've got my heart and I've got yours, and for now I know that's all that can be.'

'It's what makes sense for us, right now,' he confirmed. 'But the minute this goddamn war is over . . .'

'Don't,' she said. 'Don't jinx it. Just let it be what it is and if it becomes something else, if we're allowed anything else, then that's a gift.'

'Okay,' Charlie said. He kissed her hands. 'Anything else is a gift. Is it jinxing it if I tell you that I've only got five left? I daren't say it aloud. I wish I hadn't now.'

'Five?' she asked. 'Five what?'

'Missions,' he said quietly. Then he pulled out his St Christopher. 'If this guy keeps his end of the bargain,' he teased.

She touched it, closing her eyes. *Please keep him safe,* she thought, not quite believing a pendant could do such a thing. But willing to hope, just in case.

Kitty rested her hand on his uniform but let the tips of her fingers touch the bare skin above his collar.

'We can have a little bit of time together now, if you'd like? I can't fly for a week, maybe two depending on what the doc says about my recovery.'

Kitty brightened. He'd be safe for a while longer at least. And then a thought struck her. 'Can you hurry up and get better and then you can get these five missions completed.'

'I know,' he sighed. 'The sooner I get up in the skies the sooner we get to be together, properly.' They were silent, holding each other in the street outside the pub.

CHAPTER 27

The next evening Charlie was waiting for Kitty under the oak tree where he'd said he'd be. The sun was lowering in the sky and he took his jacket off, painfully, for them to sit on. They sat under the shade of the tree canopy, looking out towards the field.

His eyes looked less sunken than yesterday. His cheeks held more colour and the bruises had dissipated. Kitty reached over and stroked his face. 'You look so much better.'

'I *feel* a lot better. I'm also on some wonderful meds. Doc prescribed me something to keep the pain at bay.' He gave a sideways smile. 'My face hit the controls pretty hard.'

'I could see that.' Kitty smiled then looked out towards the tree line.

She shuddered as she remembered watching the plane slide out of view, heading straight for the ground. And all the while it was he who'd been inside. God, the terror he must have been feeling, in addition to the pain.

They talked for a while, of Charlie's mother and the latest letter he'd had from her. How his mother said she felt better but how Charlie knew, deep down, that she was lying to him – trying to make him feel less guilty about having signed up for a second tour, although there were only five missions left. Just five.

'Have you told her about me?' Kitty enquired shyly.

'Not yet. But I will.' He took her hand and kissed it. 'In my next letter I gotta tell her I've fallen in love. It will cheer her up and I just know she'll love you, just the way I do.'

Kitty laughed. 'Perhaps not quite the way you do,' she volunteered.

Charlie smiled. 'I can't get enough of you, Kitty. The way you laugh. The way you smile. The way you say my name. Say it now.'

She did.

'Say it again.'

'Charlie.' She said it quietly.

He lay back on the ground and sighed. 'Life is almost perfect.'

If it wasn't for the fact his mother was ill, if it wasn't for the fact there was a war on. She looked over and saw that Charlie had scooped up a handful of daisies from the ground. He was using his fingers to cut small holes in the stalks and had started threading the flowers together to make a chain.

A companionable silence fell happily over them, Kitty propped on her elbows, Charlie working quietly away beside her. With a great effort of will he sat up and placed the daisy chain on her head like a crown. He looked at her with a smile as she gave him a curious expression.

'Would you like children?' he asked. 'I'm not jinxing us,' he said quickly. 'I'm just asking an innocent question.'

Kitty mused on it. 'Yes, I think I would.' She shifted on his jacket. 'Do you?'

'Yes.' His reply was instant. 'They'll be beautiful. Just like their mother.'

'You're jinxing it,' she said in a sing-song voice.

'I'm not. I'm being hypothetical.'

'Hmmm,' she replied. 'Hypothetically, where would we and our beautiful children live?' she dared.

'On my family's farm . . . if you want? You think you could do that? You think you could leave England?'

'Hypothetically, you mean?' she teased.

He laughed. 'Exactly.'

She looked at him meaningfully. 'Yes,' she said, her voice turning serious. 'Yes. I could. I would. I love you.'

'I love you,' he replied. 'Someone like you, and someone like me . . . could be together forever,' he said.

'Hypothetically?'

'I can feel it,' he said. 'A hypothetical version of us . . . will be old and grey, playing bridge with our friends, sitting in our garden together, watching the sun set. The war will seem like a distant memory. We'll be in a farmhouse, just like that one . . .' He pointed to Christopher's house.

'The hypothetical versions of you and me . . .?' she teased.

'Exactly,' he said with a smile, looking up at her from his position on the ground. 'I want to be with you forever,' he said.

'Charlie, I don't want to curse whatever this is with expectations for the future,' she insisted. 'Instead, we need to *not* plan for the future. And in order to stop your planning I've decided I'm simply going to have to kiss you.'

He laughed. 'I'll take that exchange.'

She turned into him, kissing him lightly on the mouth, careful not to hurt his bruised face. She rose to her knees so she could kiss him easily. He pulled her onto his lap and ran his hands through her hair, stroking the nape of her neck. His touch was so tender, so maddeningly gentle as he stroked her skin lightly. She wanted more from him, more than this, just more.

She risked touching him where his shirt collar met his neck, running her hand along and up towards his jaw and against the grain of his light stubble brought about by the end of the day.

Their kiss deepened and she moved her hands onto his chest, enjoying the feel of his hard torso through his shirt. Her heart raced, thudded, the sound of it reverberating through her ears but she couldn't stop herself. She loved him, wanted him. She pulled back from the kiss, just briefly. They were in sight of the farmhouse, should anyone be looking. But the sun was setting and within moments the sky would be dark, the area by the tree already in darkened shade from its canopy. No one could see.

He touched her hair, his hand brushing gently down her face, her neck and then he paused, watching her. She nodded, a silent response to a silent question. He moved tenderly, delicately, as he brought her back down towards him again, kissing her.

She undid his top button and then looked up, gauging his reaction. He watched her intently, his chest rising and falling. Slowly she undid the next button and ran her fingertips delicately across the top of his chest.

He looked directly at her. 'Are you . . . What do you . . .?' He couldn't seem to find the words and neither could she.

She nodded again, her gaze on his.

The corners of his mouths lifted. 'Are you sure? Do you think anyone can see us from here?'

'Possibly?' she replied and then reached down for his hand, helping him to his feet. Charlie stood, obviously aware of his pained body, and gave her a curious expression. Kitty bent and took his jacket from the floor. She walked with him to the other side of the oak tree, where the canopy met the edge of the wood, out of sight of the farmhouse, and laid his jacket down on the shaded grass.

She stood awkwardly, all trace of confidence suddenly gone with the act of laying his jacket on the ground. He reached forward and took her hand, pulling her down with him slowly.

As she started undoing the remainder of his shirt buttons, he reciprocated, unclipping her regulation dungarees, unbuttoning her blouse, Kitty helping him with the fiddly little buttons. He peeled her clothes from her, taking in her body, her underwear. She helped him out of his shirt, his arms almost bound by pain. As she stripped him, she ran her hands down his hard chest as she reached for his trousers. If anyone did stumble upon them she'd have no idea, she could hear only her own heart. She left her hands resting against Charlie's stomach, his belt half undone in her hands. He murmured her name and when she didn't move he opened his eyes.

'You okay? You want to stop?'

Kitty shook her head. 'No.'

Charlie removed his trousers and underwear, peeling Kitty's from her until they were both naked. She looked at his firm body and her own ached almost uncontrollably for him. She wanted nothing more than to be swept up with him, to be made love to.

He was slow at first, kissing her neck, her mouth, her breasts until she wrapped her legs around him, guiding him towards her. She cried out and he paused.

'Am I hurting you?' he asked.

'No,' she whispered and his rhythm deepened. She looked past the silky strands of his dark hair and up through the canopy of leaves to the clouds beyond.

He resumed, moving rhythmically, faster, clutching her hand within his, their fingers entwined until her body felt something immeasurable, far beyond her comprehension or control. And afterwards, they lay together, Charlie's hand still in hers, his lips soft against her neck, planting gentle kisses against her hot skin, tickling her until she had no choice but to laugh. He lifted his head to look at her, his expression was that of concern.

'I'm going to marry you,' he said.

'Don't, you've jinxed it,' she said meaningfully.

'I should have . . .'

'Should have what?'

'I didn't use anything,' he said, his expression of concern deepening. 'I didn't use anything. I can't believe . . . I was too caught up. It was the last thing on my mind.'

'Mine too,' she said, but strangely she wasn't as concerned as she probably should be, even after the startling conversation she'd had with Nancy. This was Charlie. This wasn't someone who'd get her pregnant then leave her. He wanted to marry her. 'I think I was too worried about it being my first time, about doing the wrong thing,' Kitty said. 'A French letter . . . that's what Nancy called them.'

'We get given them, Air Force issue,' Charlie said absently. 'And you didn't do anything wrong. It was all on me. I was so swept up with you. I just didn't . . . I didn't think about it.'

'You get given them?' Kitty asked. 'I didn't know that.'

'Will you marry me?' he asked.

205

'Charlie, you can't just ask me like this while we're naked in a field.'

He laughed. 'I can. I just did.'

'No,' Kitty said. 'The answer is no. This isn't how you want to propose to me. You want to wait until you're no longer in danger and I understand that.'

'But if you're—'

'Why don't we wait and see if *I'm* anything and then let's go from there.'

He paused and looked at her, the level of concern the same as before. 'Are you sure?' he asked.

'Yes. If I'm pregnant and I'm going to have to do some reading as to how one knows . . . then I'll be begging you to marry me, don't you worry. But knowing you want to marry me . . . that's good enough for me.'

He looked uncertain. 'I don't know. It takes so long to get permission to marry from the powers that be. They actively discourage it. I'm going to put an application in anyway,' he said, frowning with thought. 'I'm going to get the ball rolling.'

'An application? You've just unromanticised marriage.'

He laughed. 'I know.'

'And you've jinxed it.'

'I know that too.'

'I'm still saying no,' Kitty joked. 'That way I've unjinxed it.'

He rolled her back into the grass and kissed her. 'You're a hard woman, Kitty Williams. But I am so in love with you.'

'I know,' she said, kissing him back. 'I know.'

When they'd dressed, Charlie made sure Kitty's hair was neat and they moved round to the front of the oak tree and gathered the ginger beer bottles. They drank the remainder of their warm drinks and Charlie pointed at the tree trunk where carvings of lovers' initials had been etched into the bark.

'We're not the first to fall in love round here.' He smiled as he drank. He turned towards Kitty and then turned back to the trunk. 'Hold on,' he said as he produced his penknife from a pocket. He walked towards the tree and stood for a few minutes, his small flick-knife working into the wood. 'There.'

'Are you vandalising?' Kitty smiled. She looked at his handiwork. Nestled among the other lovers' initials was theirs. *C&K 1944*. Charlie had etched a heart around it. Part of her never wanted to leave this spot, never wanted to part from him. She didn't want to wish time away but she wanted these next few weeks to speed past so his five missions would be over and all would be well.

He drained his bottle and smiled down at her. 'Until the end of my life, I will never stop loving you, Kitty.'

CHAPTER 28

Despite what she and Charlie had discussed, in the back of her mind Kitty couldn't help but wonder what would happen to her – to them – after the war, after Charlie's five missions finished or whichever came first. It felt as if the war would go on forever but Charlie had said he wouldn't continue, wouldn't sign up for another tour. And so, all things being well . . . he might remain in Suffolk for a time, while she remained a Land Girl? She might become his wife, in a matter of months and then she might go back to the United States with him so he could be with his mother, although they dared not speak about any kind of future. And if she was pregnant then it simply didn't matter. They were going to be together. In some form or another it would all be alright.

Over the next few weeks, Kitty was grateful she could be productive and useful for the war effort while Charlie had been back at the controls and she hadn't seen him since he'd re-joined his crew. They'd had two precious weeks together with him in total safety, but at the back of her mind she'd wanted him flying so he could finish and be done. Then they could start their life together. He'd flown yesterday and she knew he was due out again today. Two missions out of five. The bruising had lessened around his eyes, his cuts and grazes healed to fine lines, his body no longer in any pain. He now had only three missions left before he completed his tour. Charlie hadn't wanted to make anything of it, firmly choosing not to count down, telling her he regretted having told her how many he had left. It felt like bad luck. But Kitty *was* counting down. Three left. Just three. Who knew when the next ones were? It could be days until he flew again.

'Hello, love,' her father said when Kitty walked through the door one evening. 'Have you had too long a day to help your old father out tonight?' He looked hopefully at her.

Kitty was dead tired after helping Christopher rebuild a collapsed dry stone wall but said, 'Of course I'll help. Just give me a few minutes to get out of these dungarees. I'm dropping dried mud everywhere.'

By the time Kitty had changed into one of her regular day dresses and freshened up, she half expected Charlie to be in the bar, drinking with his crew, his friends, making eyes at her from across the room. She wondered where he'd been today that had kept him away from the pub this evening. Another successful mission, she hoped, so he would be closer to the end of his tour of duty. Whichever city or town it was that was going to be obliterated she simply didn't want to know. And Charlie never wanted to talk about it. If it had been awful, it drove him to drink and she could hardly blame him.

Kitty pulled a pint for an airman in front of her. She

made idle chit chat about the day, the weather, points of interest in the village and when the man didn't move on, enjoyed listening to talk about his hometown and his family. He missed his home, that much she could tell. What would it cost her to sit and listen, to talk to a man who was ready to give life and limb to help the war effort – a man who didn't have to be here, who had volunteered to fight Hitler when he could be tucked up at home in sunnier climes, thousands of miles away, living life in the land of the free. That's what she and Charlie might be doing soon.

A flicker of panic rose as she remembered she wasn't supposed to be jinxing it, not just yet. And then there was her father. At least he was too old to go to war, to fight. He'd be safe behind the bar of The Duck, pulling pints for other men willing to put themselves in harm's way day after day, night after night. Janie, too, would be gone. Wouldn't it be funny if they ended up living near each other? Where was Bobby from? Kitty had forgotten. She must make a point to ask.

'Speak of the devil,' Kitty said as Janie's head appeared at the door and she looked around the bar.

'Good timing,' Janie declared. 'I've made a bit of tea for you. Bacon and fried potatoes.'

'Thank you, but I've got to help here,' Kitty replied with a look that said *I'm so tired.*

'You've been in the field all day. Eat first, help after. I'll eat mine and come and help as well.' Kitty followed her sister upstairs, taking the stairs two at a time to speed things along. She perched at the table while Janie served up their basic supper.

'Dad forgot to eat lunch again today. I found the fish paste sandwich I'd made him curling at the sides about an hour ago,' Janie said and then quickly started eating her food.

'Oh, Dad,' Kitty said exasperatedly to her father, who down in the pub couldn't hear them. 'Of course he forgot to eat. He can't take care of himself. What on earth will he do when you go to America?'

'Or when you go for that matter,' Janie stated, putting a plate over their father's tea to keep it warm. He clearly wasn't coming up to eat. Kitty would eat hers quickly and then go down to help.

'I can't think like that,' Kitty said. 'Or rather, I shouldn't think like that.'

'You've got to take your happiness where you can find it,' Janie said. 'You always think the worst. It can't be easy being you when you always find a way to worry about something.'

'That's because there's usually reason to worry. We're in the middle of a war in case you hadn't spotted that.'

'I did spot that, actually,' Janie said, giving her sister a look. 'I watched a factory burn to the ground yesterday afternoon in Ipswich as it happens. Reported as soon as I could and did what I could to save people but waiting for the firemen to arrive was . . . harrowing. The screaming . . .' Janie trailed off.

'Ipswich has really been through it these past few years,' Kitty said sadly. 'I don't like you there, you know.'

'I know. But it's something useful, isn't it? And it's outside, bit like you but not quite as arduous. If I'd been in a factory job yesterday afternoon I might have been killed. At least this way I'm looking up at sky and . . . sometimes at Hitler's lot coming for us.'

'Janie,' Kitty said, silencing her sister. 'God it doesn't bear thinking about.'

'You're my younger sister,' Janie said. 'I should be worrying about you.'

'You don't need to worry about me.'

'Maybe not today,' Janie said. 'But what about later on . . . what about when we aren't living together anymore? What will I do without you?'

'You'll have Bobby.'

'I know, but he's not you, is he? I'll be in South Carolina. Bobby says it's really far away from Iowa where your Charlie's from. We'll never see each other. America's a huge place – and it's even further from Dad. And I do worry about you. I'd do almost anything to protect you, you know that don't you?'

'What's brought this on?' Kitty asked as she finished her bacon and potatoes.

'Oh it's everything, isn't it. It's the war, it's the raids, it's you working now properly and growing up and it's me leaving and it's Dad not eating and . . . oh I don't know. I'm just aware since Mum died that you've been the strong one and perhaps I should have been looking after you better.'

'You're my sister, not my parent.'

'Be that as it may, I've decided to look after you a bit better. If you need me, for anything . . . you do know you can turn to me, don't you?'

Kitty hugged her sister. 'I know.'

Janie held Kitty at arm's length and looked at her, smiling before Kitty left the kitchen to resume her duties behind the bar. 'Don't get taken advantage of will you, by Charlie. He seems nice – from the one or two times I've met him down in the pub. But Kitty . . . don't let him . . .'

'Let him . . .?' Kitty prompted.

'Have his way with you.'

212

Kitty blushed. It was a bit late for that sort of talk. 'He's not like that.'

'Darling,' Janie said knowingly as she put their plates in the sink and they started downstairs to help their father. 'They're all like that.'

In the bar, a short while later, a man coughed in front of her and Kitty looked up at him. It was a few seconds too late but she plastered her usual smile onto her face, always aware that she was not only a girl pulling pints but that she represented something friendly to these foreign fighting boys while war raged around them. She was dog tired and trying not to look it so Charlie didn't think he was walking out with a dishevelled farm girl, which he was actually doing now Kitty thought about it.

'What will it be?' Her hand was already on a beer glass, expecting the usual order.

The man cleared his throat again and glanced around. Kitty looked around too, wondering what or who he was looking for. She raised an eyebrow and her false smile turned into a real one.

Behind him a few crewmen trickled in through the door, their faces morose. 'May I have a word?' he asked. 'I've been asked to give you something. It's outside. That okay?'

'Er . . .' Kitty said doubtfully.

'Captain Young asked me to give you something.'

'Oh Charlie, of course, that's fine. Hold on a sec.'

She wiped her hands on a tea towel and told her father she just needed a moment's air. He looked concerned but one of the crewmen who'd just stepped through the door was attempting to engage him in conversation, asking if they could play the old upright piano and his attention was drawn away from her. The piano was rarely used but when it was it was often rude ditties and so her father had put a stop to that, worrying about Kitty and Janie's innocence. If only her father knew. She left him to negotiate with the crewman.

Kitty and the airman stepped into the cool night's air. She hadn't realised how much she needed to breathe fresh air instead of the beer and cigarette-addled smog inside the pub.

The crewman was twisting his cap in his hands. 'We met a few weeks back. At the dance. At the hangar.'

'Yes,' Kitty said. 'You're one of Charlie's friends? One of the crew? I remember you now. I'm sure Charlie introduced us.' The man nodded.

'That's right. I'm the navigator. Jimmy. James. I mean, whatever you prefer to call me.'

Kitty extended her hand to shake and then remembered something. 'It's one of your sweethearts the plane is named after.'

'Yeah,' he said as if he wasn't listening to her. The man looked around awkwardly and Kitty's gaze followed his. To her left was a bicycle and she glanced at it before looking back at Jimmy expectantly. 'Is this my pushbike?'

When the man didn't speak, Kitty took it upon herself to coax him along gently. 'Is this what you need to give me?'

'I was told,' he started. 'No, I was *asked* that if anything should ever happen, I should come find you here. And I should tell you myself. As soon as I could. And I should bring you this.' He gestured at the bicycle.

Kitty looked at it in the fading summer light. She felt faint as she realised the significance of his words.

Kitty's heart thudded quicker and quicker in her chest. 'Why have you brought it? What do you mean *if anything*

214

should ever happen?' She didn't want to know. At the corner of her mind, something awful wormed its way in.

Jimmy twisted his cap in his hands tighter and tighter.

The voice that came out of her mouth didn't sound like hers. Her breathing quickened. Her voice sounded panicked. 'What's happened?'

Jimmy shook his head. 'I am so, so sorry,' he said.

Tears pricked her eyes. 'Why are you sorry? Don't be sorry. Just tell me what's happened to him?'

'He said you were gonna be married, after the war. He said he was gonna write you a letter, something you could have if . . . but I looked through his things as they'll just pack his stuff up and send it all back to his mom. And I don't think he did the letter yet.'

Her voice shook. 'Why are his things being sent home to his mum? What's happened to him?' she begged. Oh God, no. 'Please, please just tell me.'

'I'm so sorry,' Jimmy repeated. His next words were a whisper, barely audible on the night breeze. He said the two words Kitty had been dreading, the two words she'd been repeating in her head for the last few seconds. 'Charlie's dead.'

Kitty slumped against the wall and the navigator dashed forward to grab her. She could feel herself weakening, her breathing coming quick and fast. She couldn't speak, couldn't think, couldn't move. She slid down the wall of the pub as her legs gave way.

Jimmy looked around and took Kitty by the arm, levering her away from the wall of the pub and across the road towards the memorial and its accompanying bench. 'Come with me,' he said gently. 'You should sit down.'

He sat alongside her but she hardly felt his presence. She

couldn't think straight, couldn't see through her tears, which fell free and fast. He handed her his handkerchief. She could feel her body almost convulsing as tears fell. It wasn't grief. Not yet, more disbelief, fear, upset. A movement across the square made her blink tears from her eyes and she tried to focus, as hope rose inside her that Charlie would walk along any moment now. That they would walk into the pub together and everything would be alright. There might still be a chance.

'What happened?' Her eyes were red and already sore.

Jimmy looked at the ground between his feet. 'We were hit. It was bad. Never stood a chance. Thick cloud everywhere. Guns firing.' Jimmy shook his head, disbelief written all over his face. 'By the time we realised the damage that'd been done it was too late. We were in a bad way. Chunks of the plane missing, one of our engines caught light. She was trying to go into a dive but they were holding her tight up front. Charlie told us to bale out, said he'd stay at the controls until we were all out. He'd keep it level, try to keep it up so we had time to attach our 'chutes to our harnesses. It wanted to go down so bad. It was limping. We jumped and Charlie didn't. The plane descended pretty fast and he never left the plane, never pulled his 'chute. I think he got hit while still at the controls. The plane went down. He was still inside.'

A cold, sick feeling crept over her. He'd died. How could he have died and she hadn't known; she hadn't felt it. She thought if anything should ever happen to him that she'd feel it. She would just know. It was a stupid thing to think. She hadn't felt Charlie crash all those weeks ago and she'd actually watched it happen. And now it had happened again. And she'd not known, not felt it. She'd been on the farm and in the pub, deliriously happy, hugging herself with glee that she was in love and loved in return.

How wrong she'd been. The man she loved had died. 'When?' she asked softly.

'A week and a half maybe? We got picked up on the ground by the Brits and worked our way back here. But Charlie . . . he . . .' The man trailed off, his sad expression never lifting.

She had no words of comfort for his fellow crewmember, his friend, his brother in arms. Her throat felt tight, constricted. She couldn't speak.

Jimmy, awkward and obviously still stunned by the loss of his friend, moved over to the bicycle. 'Like I said,' Jimmy muttered, 'Charlie asked me to bring this to you if . . .' He trailed off. 'Where should I put it?' Jimmy wiped his eyes with his sleeve.

Kitty stared at the bicycle. This wasn't happening. It couldn't be. 'I'll . . . take it,' Kitty forced a whisper.

Jimmy let her take the bicycle from him. 'I'm so sorry,' he said again. He shuffled nervously in front of her as if he didn't know how to say goodbye and leave her to her grief.

'It's fine, you can go,' she said and he looked grateful. He raised his hand in a goodbye and muttered a parting that Kitty didn't catch. She was glad he was gone, she wanted him gone. She needed to be alone. She eventually gathered enough momentum to walk away from the bench and round to the back sheds and parked the bike, hiding herself on the grubby floor among the pub detritus and old beer barrels awaiting collection from the brewery. The pot boy emerged, left the back door open and shoved some rubbish in among the metal bins, clanging the lids as he did so. He didn't spot her. She stared straight ahead, unblinking, unfeeling. She felt numb, dead. Silent tears descended her face but she couldn't feel them, couldn't feel the action of crying.

As the pot boy closed the pub door behind him she couldn't help it. Great wracking sobs finally escaped from her and for the next few hours, no one knew she was there.

CHAPTER 29

Kitty felt hollow, her body shaking with shock. She didn't know how long she'd been slumped on the cold, hard ground inside the shed. She cried until she thought she had no tears left. Her eyes were sore, her chest ached with the pain of her broken heart. It might have been only an hour or it might have been four but eventually she picked herself up from the floor and wiped her face. Slowly, she put one foot in front of the other and focused on getting to her room where she could hide forever, shut herself away. The back door was still unlocked and as Kitty walked in, she was confronted with a scared-looking Janie.

'Where have you *been*? We heard about Charlie. I looked outside for you where that airman said he'd left you. He asked me to check on you hours ago and I couldn't find you. Where have you *been*?' she pleaded again.

Kitty shook her head, attempting to struggle past her and towards the stairs.

'Talk to me,' Janie cried. 'Please.'

Kitty could only shake her head. 'What time is it?' she said with a dry mouth.

'Midnight,' Janie said. 'Dad's been frantic. He went out looking for you.'

'I'm sorry,' Kitty said automatically. 'I was in the sheds.'

Janie pulled Kitty towards her. 'Oh, Kitty. I'm so sorry.'

'They sang songs for him,' Janie said glumly into Kitty's hair as the two girls held each other.

'Is that all Charlie will get in the way of a goodbye from his crew?' Kitty said unhappily. 'So used are they to saying farewell to dead friends.'

Tomorrow it would be different, unless another crewman died. The dead man was toasted one day and reduced to a memory the next. Crewmember replaced crewmember. Pilot replaced pilot. Letters to loved ones would be written from commanding officers. And then they were consigned to a figure, a statistic as the war raged on and more men died.

She was supposed to be telling her father she was marrying. He'd only had three missions left. Charlie was supposed to be here but instead he was somewhere in Europe in his coffin of a plane. Visions of Charlie sat at the controls, saving his friends, swam in her head. Visions of their life together disappeared out of view.

She had no idea how she picked herself up and carried on. For weeks after she felt dead inside. She'd seen girls in the village mourning the loss of their bomber boy sweethearts one day and then merrily accepting a drink from another man in uniform weeks later. She would not be one of those girls. Charlie had been different. Charlie had been special. So wise and knowing. So kind, so loving and so ready to be loved. He'd had a good soul. He'd had his whole life ahead of him and they were supposed to have been spending it together.

'Why him?' she cried into Janie's arms as her sister embraced her in the flat above the pub.

After her mother had died, Kitty had been told by anyone who cared to offer an opinion that it would all get easier in time. The grief would disappear slowly, day by day, bit by bit until all that was left was a fond and loving memory of the times spent together. 'Life goes on,' plenty of village women had said to her father as well, while openly having their eye on him. But it hadn't for her father, who had never remarried, who had loved her mother so fiercely that he'd never looked at another woman the same way.

Kitty would be the same. She just knew she would. She would never love another man the way she had loved Charlie Young. He would occupy her heart until the day she died.

CHAPTER 30

Autumn, 1944

The brave face she plastered on over the following month as summer edged its way into autumn was only in response to the strange and worried looks she received from her father in the pub and from Nancy and Christopher on the farm. Kitty made sure to throw herself into the daily routine, completing the tasks well enough so that no complaints were issued and then leaving the farm each evening after a polite goodbye.

She was empty. Even all these weeks later she was simply hollow. And no matter how many days passed, the hollowness increased like a dark well she couldn't escape. It invaded every waking moment. Out of the corner of her eye Kitty often thought she saw Charlie. She'd long got past seeing him in the pub when she knew he wasn't there. It had happened every day at first until she knew her mind had been playing tricks on her. But it was in the field, in the barn, mucking out or during some other inane task when her mind was finally occupied, just for a moment, that she felt him near her and thought she might have caught sight of him – just a glimpse. But then when she'd looked up he had never been there. Her mind was playing tricks on her. She wanted to be comforted. If he was there, if he was truly there, looking out for her, it should have made her happy. Instead it only served to reinforce the fact he was dead. Or that she was going mad. She hoped beyond hope it was madness. Pure and utter madness. Then soon she would be able to drift inside her own mind and forget the real world existed, forget about the fleeting moment of happiness she'd had with Charlie – such a brief moment out of her entire life but it had meant so much. And because it hurt so much she wanted the madness to come and take her away and in doing so, replace the pain.

Her fake smile fell away in the pub one night when she was clearing glasses. An overwhelming feeling of tiredness came and her vision blurred. She didn't know what she wanted to do first, throw up or fall asleep. Was this a migraine? She'd never had them before but Janie did and this was similar, no? The moment passed within seconds but as bedtime drew near she steadied herself against the bannisters, pausing for breath. But her fingers missed, she stumbled, her vision blurred into blackness and she fell to the floor.

When Kitty awoke it was to find she was tucked up in bed, Janie and the village doctor both hovering over her, Kitty's wrist in his hand as he timed her pulse. Her vision was blurred still and she blinked. He smiled as she opened her eyes, waited until he'd finished counting her pulse and then he gently placed her arm back on the bed.

'Nice of you to join us, young lady.' Dr Gilchrist had been Kitty's doctor for only two years, replacing the elderly

223

doctor that Kitty had known since childhood. She tended not to bother with doctors too much these days. They were expensive and she never got sick. She worried about the cost of him being here now, unnecessarily.

Janie gave her a smile. 'I've been so worried about you,' she said.

Kitty smiled wanly.

'Hot, sweet tea all round,' Janie said and left the doctor to his work.

He asked her questions about her general health, looked in her eyes and wanted to know so many details about how Kitty conducted her day that her head hurt afresh.

'And you've not been feeling like this for long?' He narrowed his eyes.

'No. Just today. It's been tiring, working on the farm. I've never fainted before.' It was the grief, the grief was killing her. She looked towards the window next to her bed, willing the doctor to leave. She knew why she'd fainted. But she didn't want to speak. Didn't want to tell him that grief had begun its destruction of her. How had her father gone through this when her mother died. How did anyone go through this without it killing them in turn? She wanted to be alone with thoughts of Charlie, no matter how painful it was. She never wanted to move again. Never wanted to see another soul.

'I worry about the farm work *and* working alongside your father in the pub. He mentioned to me he was getting some proper help. I'll shimmy him along on that front because I think you've been overdoing it somewhat, wouldn't you agree?' The doctor smiled kindly.

'All the young men are away fighting other than the pot boy who's too young to serve,' Kitty said tonelessly. 'It's just me and Janie and we've both got war work now. And we refuse to leave Dad to it on his own and . . . oh God . . . I think I'm going to be sick.' She leaped from the bed.

'Steady,' the doctor said as she ran to the bathroom, throwing up into the toilet. There wasn't much to show for her efforts as she'd hardly been eating anything. She instinctively reached for her toothbrush to clean her teeth. The doctor looked at her from the threshold of the door.

'You might have a nasty virus, or a bug. Let's get you settled back in bed and I'll take your temperature now you're awake.'

'It's not a virus,' Kitty said pragmatically, making her way back to bed. It was all dawning on her finally. It was the sudden nausea that had done it. She put her hand on her stomach.

'You have a pain? May I feel?'

Kitty couldn't speak. The lump in her throat where she was swallowing down tears wouldn't allow her.

'May I feel?' he repeated, more kindly than the first time. Kitty nodded and pulled the bedcovers down.

Dr Gilchrist gently felt her abdomen. 'Perhaps we should think about appendicitis?' he said with a hint of concern as he felt. As he pushed down he looked up at her for her reaction. A questioning look was in his eye.

'I'm pregnant, aren't I?'

'Is that what you think? Do you . . . do you *know* you are?' he asked as he felt, looking at her all the while.

'Yes,' she said. She'd been hoping for it, and dreading it.

The doctor breathed in, his hands leaving her stomach. 'When your sister telephoned me she said you had someone and that he'd died,' he said.

She nodded. 'Last month.'

'I see,' he said softly.

Her eyes met his and she held his gaze, willing him to tell her she was wrong, willing him to tell her she was right. Charlie was gone but if he'd left her with his baby, she needed to know either way, needed to plan, needed to keep it, needed it to be safe. It was the last part of him and she had it, she had it safe within her.

'I think it's been six weeks or maybe a little bit more since . . .' she said, tailing off.

'I see,' he said with a rueful expression, which said everything. She was pregnant. She couldn't remember the exact date they'd made love, nor when the doctor asked her, could she remember the date she'd last bled. She didn't need to know any of that. Not now. She only needed to know if there was a baby inside her and how she would keep it safe.

CHAPTER 31

Days later, dawn broke over the village and Kitty stood by the window, watching the sun rise over the medieval rooftops. She felt numb, destroyed, and try as she might no plan had come to the surface that enabled her to stay here. She'd discussed everything with the doctor that she couldn't with Janie or with her father. Once the idea of carrying Charlie's baby had cemented itself and she'd recovered her wherewithal in order to work out what she should do. it had finally occurred to her that she was, in fact, totally and utterly in trouble. She was lost, completely lost. She couldn't bring shame to her father by having a baby while being unmarried. It didn't matter to anyone that Charlie had planned to marry her. The entire village would know her situation and none of them would drink in her father's pub anymore. She would be the cause of his downfall. Her shame would be his. But she wasn't ashamed of her baby. She wasn't. She loved it, so fiercely. So fiercely. It was hers, it was Charlie's, it was theirs. But it was going to be a problem if she stayed here. And she couldn't. She couldn't do that to her father. Her baby couldn't cause her family distress. She hadn't told them about the baby and nor would she. She closed her eyes as the sun's early morning rays glared into them but no tears came. She had cried enough over the last couple of months and now she had no more tears left to shed. Now her sole focus was on being practical.

She was leaving, sneaking out like a coward but it was for the best. It was all for the best. Nancy's words from their conversation rang in her head. She would not find a seedy backstreet to rid herself of the child. She would not punish the baby. But neither would anything be normal ever again if she stayed here like this.

As the sunlight streamed into her room, Kitty gathered clothes in a carpet bag, her ration book and gasmask. If she waited for the bus, which was often late, she risked people seeing her. Perhaps she could bicycle her way to the train station instead, find a little flat in Ipswich or London where she could share with a few other girls. But how would she pay for her share of the rent? She might be able to work for a few months and save. But how much would she be able to save before any prospective employer discovered she was pregnant, and then dismissed her? She was ruined, but she could not let the baby's life go the way of those other few village girls who had found themselves in similar situations. The baby would be called names, made an outcast in the village, ostracized forevermore. She could not be responsible for that. She had to leave, had to set up somewhere new and pretend she was widowed. Kitty steeled herself with a strength she didn't feel, and left the pub, creeping past the stair that creaked, through the back door, closing it quietly behind her and retrieving her bicycle from the sheds. With shaking hands, she tied her belongings on to the saddle pack on the back fender of her bicycle, climbed on and cycled away from the village.

CHAPTER 32

From the wide lane in front of the Frampton farm, Kitty could see the oak tree in the distance, bathed in full light. She stopped and put her foot down to still the bicycle. The oak tree and the edge of the field were the scenes of almost all of her happiness, where she'd picnicked with Charlie, worked happily alongside Nancy and the other Land Girls then stood and listened as Charlie's plane had crashed, the near miss he'd thought was the sign his luck stood firm. Kitty issued a hollow, angry cry. He'd been wrong, so wrong. She glanced towards the farm as she propped her bicycle up against the farmhouse wall. The other Land Girls were not yet up from their hostel digs and even Christopher didn't start the day quite this early.

Kitty moved through the field, drawn to the tree. She felt as if she was being pulled towards it. One last look was all she wanted before she left forever. One last look at the place she'd been so happy with Charlie. She reached up to touch the engraving he'd made with his penknife, after they'd made love and drank ginger beer together. *C&K 1944*. It was so fresh, alongside the other engravings – remnants of couples in love in a time of war. It was all that was left of him. She touched her stomach. Not quite all that was left. She ran her fingertips over the letters and then rested them over the C he had carved. She had to leave it behind but she would picture this always.

She stood in the place where they'd made love. The sunlight was starting to dapple through the spreading branches and green leaves. Out of the corner of her eye the sunlight danced over something small shining on the ground.

Kitty bent, stooping to pick it up. Charlie's St Christopher pendant shone in the morning sun. Confusion flooded her mind, the significance of it being here almost evaded her. At first, she was startled, and then a smile crept over her face as she realised she would have something to remember him by after all. And then she remembered St Christopher was the patron saint of travellers, and the significance it held for a bomber pilot like Charlie. He'd worn his pendant around his neck for luck when he flew. Only the last time he flew he wasn't wearing it. He'd discarded it, knowingly or by accident, when they had stripped each other under the shade of the tree.

Kitty fell to her knees and cried. She had done this. She had been responsible for his death. It was her fault he hadn't been wearing his pendant, her fault his plane had crashed into the sea. Kitty wanted nothing more than to die. She wound Charlie's St Christopher around her fingers, half believing that if she clutched it hard enough it might bring him back. Her body shook with tears and she could take it no more. She wanted to be dead. She wanted nothing more than to be dead. She fell down to the ground, letting dizziness and grief take her to a place of blackness, a place far far away where none of this had happened and where she hadn't caused the man she'd loved to die.

Kitty blinked, slowly coming to. Her mouth was dry, her head hurt and she was vaguely aware she was in a bed so much softer than her own. Above her the ornate, Regency-style plasterwork ceiling only added to the confusion.

'Hello,' Christopher said softly.

Kitty stared at him blankly.

'Are you feeling a bit better now?'

Why was Christopher here? Where was she? She didn't know what to say. She simply nodded, although it wasn't true. She felt awful.

'Would you like a sip of water?' he asked, lifting a glass to her lips when she agreed.

'Thank you.'

'Quite alright,' he replied kindly after she'd sipped. He sat back down on the edge of the bed. For a few moments, neither of them spoke.

'I would like to fetch the doctor,' he announced quietly.

'No,' Kitty said suddenly. 'No thank you, I mean.' She remembered her manners.

'That's what you said when I picked you up off the ground, and I didn't do it then because you asked me not to.'

'Did I?' She didn't remember any of that. Why was she here? Why was she at the Frampton farm? She retched, narrowly avoiding vomiting over what looked to be an expensive eiderdown. Christopher was prepared and held a bowl for her but she didn't need it in the end.

'I'm so sorry.'

'Don't be,' he replied.

'Is this your bedroom?'

'Yes,' Christopher said. 'The sheets are clean,' he said with a smile. 'Since the war we've not had the staff so the guest rooms have been mothballed. I'm not sure what Mother would say if she knew you were here.'

'She doesn't know I'm here?' Kitty asked.

'Not yet. I sort of . . . smuggled you in and then she went out a few moments ago to Ipswich for some shopping.'

'You smuggled me in?' Kitty laughed and then stopped as the terror of everything fell over her. She was pregnant. Charlie was dead.

'Why am I here?' she asked.

'I was rather hoping you could tell me that,' Christopher replied. 'I saw you walk through the field. I watched you for a moment, wondering why on earth you were here so early and why you weren't wearing your usual WLA clothes and why you were by the tree. It was all so odd. I'm glad I watched you because I saw you collapse.'

'I collapsed?'

'Yes. I came to fetch you. I ran at quite a lick, I'll have you know.' He aimed for lightness and through her anguish, Kitty tried to smile. 'And I carried you back here. When I got to you, you had this in your hand.' He held out the St Christopher to her.

She looked at it and then lifted her hand from the bed, taking it from him. 'Thank you,' she said, clutching it to her heart.

'You don't have to tell me what's bothering you, but I wonder if it might help in some way, if you wanted to get something off your chest, I'm a very good listener.'

'I can't,' she said, starting to cry. 'I'm in so much trouble. I'm so . . . ashamed.'

'Come on,' Christopher said gently. 'It can't be all that bad?'

'It is. Oh Christopher, it is. It's the worst.' She looked him in the eye. 'The moment I tell you, you'll throw me out, you'll fire me from the farm, you'll write a letter to the Land Army telling them what I've done and I'll never work in agriculture again. I can't tell you. You . . . you'll never talk to me again. My father will never talk to me again. My life is over,' she said, sobbing.

'No,' he said vehemently. 'Of course it's not over. And I can't speak for your father but I shall do none of those things, Kitty. You must know me by now. We've known each other years, off and on. I'm not the kind of man who'll do any of those things. Have you . . . have you stolen something . . . from me . . . from here, from the farm, I mean?'

'No,' she said loudly. 'No, of course not. I would never steal.'

'Then, Kitty, what on earth do you think would possess me to throw you out, put you out of employment? You have to tell me now. You just have to.'

It took some time but as Kitty looked into the eyes of her old childhood friend, she eventually told Christopher everything. She didn't have the energy to hide anymore. It was too late for lies, too futile. She needed help, suggestions.

She confessed her fears, that she'd be outcast in this small village. That so would her baby. That the baby would be called names if they stayed. Everyone here knew she was unmarried. She told him her worry that her father's business would suffer if regulars chose to drink their ale in another of the village's pubs as a result of her tarnished reputation. That she couldn't do that to her family. But if she lived elsewhere she had no idea what she'd do for money, how she'd earn any. How she'd never be considered employable while pregnant, even in this time of war when women were stepping into the roles vacated by men. And then when she had the baby . . . what then? Where would she live, *how* would she live?

Christopher listened. He made no judgement and at the end of her story said, 'Why don't you stay here for a while, with me?'

Kitty shook her head. 'I can't. Thank you but I can't.'

'Why not?'

Kitty laughed, although not unkindly. 'As much as I would love to bury myself away in the rambling old farmhouse with my childhood friend, I can't. I'll pass the shame on to you. I can't. And it would only be a temporary solution to my problem.'

But his words, his gestures were kind and she reached out to touch his hand.

'And I'm *not* your problem,' she said between tears.

'You're not my problem, no. You're my friend.'

'And what's the point of me staying here even for a short while? It's delaying the inevitable and it wouldn't be a permanent fix,' she admitted.

Christopher reached out across the eiderdown and held her hand. He looked into her eyes, his own deep with meaning. 'It could be permanent,' he said softly. 'If you wanted it to be?'

CHAPTER 33

1945

Kitty had never felt pain like it. The screams coming from her mouth didn't sound like her own, didn't feel like her own. Her eyes were full of tears and the sting of salt as sweat beaded down her forehead and blurred her vision.

'Mother's gone for the doctor,' Christopher said, rubbing her back.

It would have been more appropriate for Mrs Frampton to have stayed with her and for Christopher to have fetched the doctor but Kitty, in pain and almost delirious, had grabbed Christopher's hand and refused to let him leave. Instead Mrs Frampton, put out and muttering how inappropriate it was for the father to 'bear witness to all that,' had gone to fetch Dr Gilchrist.

'I'm not sure what he can do though,' Christopher had said. 'Surely we need a midwife.'

Kitty shot him a look between screams. The quickening in her lower abdomen had intensified and she knew the baby was coming imminently. Mrs Frampton had left it too late, or the baby was coming far too quickly. Christopher continued rubbing her back. 'I love you, Kitty,' he said. 'My beautiful, brave wife. It will all be alright. I promise.'

'Help me,' she called weakly. She started pushing. She had no choice. She didn't want to push but she needed to.

Christopher's mouth fell open. 'No, not now. It's too fast. You have to slow down. You have to wait for . . .'

Kitty pushed. It was as if her whole body was being ripped in half. Christopher, wide-eyed and unbelieving, swore loudly, rolled up his shirt sleeves and climbed onto the far end of the bed. She'd never heard a cry so tiny, so helpless and then loud, exaggerated wailings emanated from her baby's mouth as clever, loving Christopher delivered Kitty's baby.

After Dr Gilchrist had been and gone, examining both mother and baby and deeming them in fine health, Kitty nursed the baby and looked down, marvelling at how such a small thing had managed to grow so silently inside her all this time and how it had entered the world in such a loud way. Kitty wondered how each of them had survived the ordeal and how women the world over went through this without complaint. She looked at Christopher who, in turn, was looking at the baby suckling Kitty's breast. He was smiling and Kitty tried to catch his eye.

'The wonder of it all,' Christopher said quietly when their gaze connected.

'How did you know what to do? How did you know how to help me give birth?' Kitty asked as she watched the baby pause its suckling. As quick as it had fed, it fell asleep.

'I've delivered a few lambs in my time,' Christopher said. He sat next to her at the top of bed and kissed her hair. 'And I didn't have much of a chance to think about it. There she was. You did it, Kitty. You did all the work. And look at her, such a beauty, so perfect.'

Kitty looked at her baby. 'She is beautiful, isn't she?'

'Of course she is,' he whispered. 'She looks like her mother.'

'We're so lucky. I'm so lucky,' Kitty whispered back. She turned her face to look at the man who had come to her rescue.

'I'm the lucky one,' he said. He looked adoringly from Kitty to the baby. 'Shall I take her for a while? Let you sleep?'

Kitty yawned and nodded. 'If you'd like to . . . Yes please.'

'Come on, baby girl,' he whispered as he gently lifted the baby into his arms. 'Come and have a walk around the house with Daddy.' He cast a shy glance at Kitty, who smiled reassuringly.

'We'll try out some names on you and see if any sound right,' he suggested. 'Then we'll see what your mummy thinks when she's had her nap. Let's start with the "A's" and see how we go.'

Kitty watched as Christopher held her daughter to his chest and moved towards the door. As he closed the door quietly behind him, she listened to his tread in the hallway and his quiet, calm chatter to the sleeping baby. She had to make it work with Christopher. For the baby's sake, for her own sake and for his, because he was a good man who had already become a wonderful father.

CHAPTER 34

Summer, 2011

The sitting room was still. No air flowed through the open windows and Amy was beginning to feel engulfed but she didn't know by what. She'd been holding her breath. Slowly, she exhaled. 'Oh, Gran,' she breathed. 'Oh, Gran.'

'But that's not all of it,' Kitty said.

Amy got up from the settee and moved next to her grandmother. She wrapped her arms around her, holding her while Kitty shook gently, crying, small silent sobs. 'What do you mean, that's not all of it?' Amy stroked her grandmother's silver hair, entwined in a silky knot, attempting to soothe her. It was something she'd never had to do with her gran and it felt such an alien gesture. And then she tried to work out what had happened. The man Kitty had been in love with, the man Kitty was engaged to, Charlie, hadn't left her. But he hadn't known Kitty had been pregnant when he'd died, which was probably for the best. The worst had happened. He'd been shot down. He'd died. Christopher, who had secretly, quietly loved Kitty all those years had stepped in and married Kitty.

'I think I'm telling you the story badly,' Kitty said, sobs subsiding. 'There's more.'

'More?'

'About Charlie.'

Amy's phone buzzed and Kitty wiped her eyes. 'Sorry, hang on, I'll just get rid of them,' Amy said. But the damage was done and Kitty wiped her eyes determinedly and stood up.

'It's only a text, not a call so—' Amy started.

'Don't you have a date?' Kitty asked.

'Yes, but he can wait.' Amy waited for her gran to tell her whatever else it was that was still bothering her. What else could there possibly be?

'I'll be fine, my darling. Don't keep him waiting. Good men like that don't stay around forever, take it from me,' her grandmother said. 'Please go and enjoy your date. We can talk more later.'

'Okay, Gran,' Amy said reluctantly. 'Shall I pop back after? I hate to leave you like this.'

'Pop back after, darling. I'll be in a better frame of mind and I don't want you to miss your date because of me. He seems a lovely chap.'

'He is, Gran, but he's leaving to go back to the US so . . . it's just for today really.'

'Sometimes today is all we have. Now go, enjoy yourself.'

As Amy drove back towards the village, hoping Jack would still be waiting she realised she had so many questions, about Christopher, about Charlie and about her own mother. Was Alison not Christopher's daughter then? Oh God, was that what the rest of the conversation was going to be about? Of course it was. Kitty had been pregnant with Charlie's baby. Alison was born in 1945. It all made sense. Charlie's baby. Alison wasn't Christopher's baby. Did Alison know this? Did she already know – had she already been told, years ago? Did that then mean that Christopher wasn't Amy's grandfather? Oh no, no that couldn't be the case. It just couldn't. Questions fell on top of questions until Amy's mind was a blur of quick thoughts she couldn't keep on top of. She knew that she couldn't even speak to her mother about this until she'd been back after her day out with Jack in order to establish the remaining facts. They weren't important, Kitty had insinuated. But this seemed like the most important thing in the world right now, or at least it was to Amy. Amy's grandfather might not actually be her grandfather. The thought sobered her and she parked her car with half a mind to start the engine up and go back to her gran's and ask.

She was a few minutes late but Jack was waiting by his hire car, wearing a smile with a level of happiness she didn't mirror. She forced her face into a smile. With his white shirt sleeves rolled up and his blue chino shorts giving Amy a glimpse of his tanned limbs, he looked every inch an all-American male. She waved half-heartedly as she walked towards him and they exchanged a kiss on the cheek.

'Are you okay?'

She nodded, fibbing. 'I've just been to see my gran.'

'Everything alright?'

'Yes. No. Sort of. I think my family history is a little more complicated than I would ever have imagined.'

'How so?' Jack asked.

'I think my grandad's not my grandad,' she said simply. 'I think it's someone else, someone who died in the war.'

'Oh wow,' Jack said. 'Really?'

'Yes, really. I think . . . I don't know what to think actually.'

'I'm . . . sorry?' he said. 'Is sorry the right word? Feels like a strange word.'

'I don't know what the right word is. It's confusing. I'm confused.'

'You still wanna come today?' he said in such an earnest tone that Amy momentarily cast aside her thoughts and nodded in response. He was doing things to her heart she knew would get her in a world of trouble. *You can't fall for this man. He's leaving. A summer romance that lasts only a few hours isn't worth it.* But as she looked at him, she knew it might be worth it. A few hours with Jack would be worth any pain caused by him leaving. She just had to enjoy the time she had with him and then he would leave and that would be that. It was just for today. She needed to think about her family drama later on, back when she went to see Kitty, which she'd promised she would do. It would all keep for an afternoon, no matter how much Amy wanted to know, right now, exactly what had gone on all those years ago.

'I couldn't stop thinking about you last night,' he confessed.

'Really?' Amy replied. She had to look away out of embarrassment.

'I want to kiss you again,' he said.

'Stop,' she chastised playfully. 'We're in the middle of the street. Anyone could see.'

'I don't care if they do.'

'Well I do,' she said, laughing.

'You didn't care when I kissed you last night on your doorstep.'

'That's true,' she replied. 'Perhaps we should ration kisses, especially given that your family are on their way over to us.'

Jack waved at his father and grandfather as they walked closer to them. 'Rationing kisses?' he whispered to her. 'That's kind of on-brand for a day doing wartime things.'

Amy laughed. It felt so natural being with Jack. Everything just felt so easy.

'It's lovely that you're joining us,' Jack's grandfather said. 'It's a real pleasure to meet you.' He held his hand out for Amy and she shook it gently, noticing how his eyes crinkled in the same way Jack's did when he smiled.

'And you,' Amy said warmly. 'Thank you for letting me tag along. I never knew there was an American War Cemetery in England. I've heard of the Commonwealth War Graves in France and Belgium. I've always wanted to go and see them, pay my respects. But I didn't know there was an American War Cemetery in the next county.'

'I suppose it's not really a tourist attraction,' Jack's grandfather said kindly. 'So, are you ready to stare death in the face and climb into a car with Jack behind the wheel?' he said jovially.

Amy burst out laughing. 'Oh you've experienced Jack drive, have you?'

'Hey, I'm not that bad,' Jack chipped in.

As his grandfather climbed into the front passenger side he said, 'Jack, maybe you can sit in the back with your . . . friend. And your father could drive this time?'

Emmett agreed quickly. 'That sounds like a good idea.'

'For all of Jack's many good qualities,' his grandfather said, 'driving is not one of them. The cemetery is supposed to be a day out, not our final destination.'

Amy laughed so hard and Jack did his best not to laugh

and to try to look put out but he failed. He climbed in alongside Amy in the back. 'Thanks, Grandpa, what's happening? You're all ganging up on me. I'm not *that* bad,' he grumbled.

An hour later they arrived at the Cambridge American Cemetery and Memorial. Amy blinked into the sunshine as she walked through the archway and into the cemetery. What she saw made her stare in awe. She hadn't been sure what to expect but it wasn't this. Rows upon rows of neatly laid out white gravestones, cross-shaped, stretched into the distance. It was almost a semi-circle spanning out in front of her. A flagpole to the far left flew the Stars and Stripes and a long oblong pond glinted in the sun as it led down to the visitor centre. They weren't the only people there, but like those that were also visiting, they fell into a hushed silence. The only sound was Amy's sunglasses case snapping shut as she pulled out her shades, attempting to shield her eyes from the glare of the sun's rays on the white stones in front of her.

'For a cemetery this is kinda pretty,' Jack muttered as they scanned their surroundings.

His grandfather shuffled next to him and adjusted his walking stick.

Amy looked over at him. This day was all for him, really. She was just tagging along and she wondered now if she should really be there, invading his privacy as he looked for his friends, long since fallen and buried here.

Jack looked down at Amy and mouthed, 'You okay?'

'Yes,' she said warmly. 'I'm going to leave you guys to it, I think. Take all the time you need. I'll just have a little wander around and look at some of the names on the stones.'

Jack smiled and nodded as Amy gave a little wave and wandered on to the path that would lead her around the cemetery. A part of her wondered if she might be able to find Charlie Young buried here, the man who may or may not be her biological grandfather. The thought stilled her again. Although Christopher had died when she'd been small, it was throwing her just thinking he wasn't her real grandfather. She needed to know but she wasn't going to find the answer here – that much she knew. But she could find Charlie at least by finding his grave – if he was buried here – and then she'd tell Kitty, and if laying ghosts to rest really was her grandmother's plan this week, this was one way to do that, surely?

Charlie Young was American and had been posted here before perishing in the war so the American Cemetery would be the most suitable place for him to have been laid to rest, wouldn't it? It was a bit of a long shot, but if she found his grave what would she do? Would she photograph it for her grandmother? As Kitty had said, old wounds had already been opened – but would this just make things so much worse?

It was an odd feeling, knowing that if she did find his grave here or his memorial, she would be paying her respects to someone her grandmother had been completely and totally in love with so long ago. Her grandmother had had a life that had been rich, full and as she'd said in her own diary . . . frightening.

Amy focused her energies on scanning the names on the graves as she walked. They were laid in rows and it was impossible to read each of the gravestones without actually stepping off the path and moving between them.

Finding him here felt unlikely now she took in the size

of the site and the sheer number of headstones. Two thousand, maybe even three? She couldn't tell. This would take hours. The well-kept grounds and the immaculate headstones were a beautiful testament to the dead but it felt awful knowing underneath this patch of ground lay American men who'd volunteered to help defend the world from evil. They'd paid the ultimate price and had given their lives.

Amy walked over to a plaque commemorating the crew of a distressed bomber. They had stayed with their plane until the last possible moment, keeping it in the air long enough to save a nearby village from death and destruction. The ten men inside the plane had sacrificed themselves to save others. It all felt a bit too close to home. Amy tried to swallow down the lump in her throat as she realised it was the exact same thing that Charlie had done, stayed at the controls and kept the plane in the air so the rest of his crew could parachute to safety from a safe height. For Charlie it had been too late, and he might be here somewhere, in among the graves that were purposefully laid out like a baseball field on land donated by the nearby Cambridge University.

A gardener was tending a grave nearby and Amy moved over to take a look, at the name of the grave. It was of a woman named Emily, who had been part of the American Red Cross.

'Oh,' she uttered and the gardener glanced round and smiled. 'I wasn't expecting to see any women buried here,' she explained. 'Although I'm not sure why I wasn't expecting it. I thought it would just be men.'

The gardener stood up. He looked as if he was choosing his words carefully. 'We've a few women buried here,' he explained. 'It's also a non-denominational cemetery so we've got different religions, Catholics, Jewish buried side by side.'

'Have you?' Amy asked as the gardener stooped to pick up his kneepad and trug.

He nodded. 'And,' he continued, getting into his stride, 'we've the names of a few famous people here too.'

'Really?' Amy wondered. 'Such as?'

'We've Joseph Kennedy, brother to President JFK?'

Amy's eyes widened in surprise.

'His plane exploded,' the gardener continued in a matter-of-fact way.

Amy's mouth dropped open and she shivered, even though it was far from cold.

'And we've got Glenn Miller, the big band leader.'

Amy recalled dancing to one of his tunes with Jack at the memorial unveiling. 'Glenn Miller's buried here too?'

The gardener shook his head. 'No, neither of them are buried here. Their names are over there . . .' He pointed to a long white stone wall that ran along the edge of the cemetery. 'On the Wall of the Missing.'

Amy looked over at it. Interspersed at various sections were huge stone statues of men, standing sentinel dressed in uniforms to represent the various roles the Americans took up in the war at sea, air and on land.

Now she was confused and her face must have been showing it because the gardener clarified. 'Glenn Miller's plane was lost at sea so his body wasn't recovered.'

Amy could see where this was going.

'The same with Joseph Kennedy,' he continued. 'His body was also never recovered and so their names are on that wall.' He pointed again. 'Along with over five thousand other men and women whose bodies were never found. They're remembered over there.'

'Five *thousand*?' Amy's heart sank again. If Charlie's plane

247

crashed, then of course his body wouldn't have been found. Why hadn't that occurred to her before? His name might be over there, in among thousands of other names.

The gardener smiled. '*Over* five thousand, I'm afraid.'

This just got worse and worse. Amy braced herself. 'Right, so I need to look over there then I think.'

'Are you looking for anyone in particular?'

'I am, yes.'

'In which case let me help you a little bit further. The names aren't in alphabetical order I'm afraid.'

'You're joking. Why on earth not?'

The gardener chuckled lightly.

'So you need to look in the correct section, land, air, sea and then you'll need to scan down. They're in the right order once you get to the right area of the wall. You'll see what I mean when you get over there.'

Amy thanked him for his help and started to walk towards the Wall of the Missing. On the way over she spied a large pillared white building that reminded her of something from Ancient Rome. She followed the path round to peer inside and see what it was and if it was open.

She spotted Jack, who was just leaving the building, and walking towards her.

'Hey.' He put his hand up to wave. 'It seems . . . wrong, I guess, to ask if you're having a nice time at a cemetery.'

Amy laughed. 'I am. Thanks. Are you?'

Jack sighed. 'It's fascinating. It's kind of unbelievable really. So many dead. So many *here*.' He gestured towards the white headstones. 'I need to make more time for my grandfather,' Jack mused. 'He could have ended up buried here at any moment during the war. Instead he's back all this time later mourning so many friends he lost so long ago. He's sitting inside the chapel.' Jack gestured to the white building. 'He's been in there for ages so I'm leaving them to it for a while.' Then he gave her a devastating smile that did things to Amy's insides, and held her gaze. 'Thought I'd come find you.'

'I'm glad you did.' They stood in silence, looking at each other for a few seconds as if each of them were waiting for the other to do something. Eventually they spoke at the same time.

'Have you seen the Wall of the Missing?' Amy asked.

At the same time Jack stepped forward, looked into her eyes and said, 'I'm not ready to go home yet.'

'I'm not ready for you to go home yet either,' she confessed, stepping closer to him.

Jack held his smile as they walked towards the Wall of the Missing and then laughed slightly, almost as if to himself. 'This is the strangest date I've ever been on by the way,'

Amy laughed back. 'Me too. But I'm pleased I'm here with you before you leave. I'm pleased you asked me.'

'I'm pleased you said yes,' he replied, reaching down and holding her hand.

Amy looked at their hands entwined and then up at him. His dark hair had fallen over his eyes and he pushed it back and looked up towards the sunshine. Amy looked away. This was doing her no good and yet she couldn't stop wanting it.

They approached the Wall of the Missing where there were four huge white stone statues dressed in wartime attire. Each face was serene and Amy looked at the items that they held and wore such as a gun or a lifejacket or flight mask that represented the area of combat in which they'd served.

'They look like they're guarding the names of the missing,' Jack said, sentimentally. Amy looked past them towards the wall. Above, a plane flew over, low and slow, but Amy ignored it as she started scanning the smooth white wall in order to find the air section and begin the hunt for Charlie's name.

Jack's gaze was fixed firmly to the skies. 'Would you look at that,' he marvelled.

Amy followed Jack's gaze. In the blue skies above them the recognisable engine noise sounded. 'Is that a Spitfire?' she asked.

Around them the few people also looking at the names on the wall looked up, shielding their eyes against the sun. Excited murmurs rang throughout them.

'My war plane knowledge is not good but, yes, I think that is a Spitfire.' Jack laughed as if he also couldn't believe they were watching a fighter plane from the Second World War while they were standing in the middle of a Second World War cemetery. 'It's like going back in time. What do you think it's doing here?'

'Duxford airdrome isn't too far from here.' Amy watched the Spitfire circle overhead. 'I went there once on a school trip. You can pay to be flown around in a Spitfire from there.' She looked at Jack. 'Maybe that's what someone's doing.'

He looked back down at her. 'I really like you,' he admitted out of nowhere.

'I really like you too, Jack,' she said honestly. She wasn't used to this, this level of openness in men, this level of openness in herself. Amy didn't dare suggest that he fly back in a few months, or that she attempt to visit him. It was just one *very* short-lived holiday romance.

'So, what are we looking at here?' He squeezed her hand and Amy squeezed his back.

'I'm going to scan for a name,' Amy said. A warm feeling flowed through her as his thumb started circling her hand as he held it. She could barely concentrate. 'You're in charge of finding Glenn Miller and Joseph Kennedy. You get points if you find them.'

'Glenn Miller and Joseph Kennedy are among the missing on this wall?' Jack's eyebrows shot up as Amy nodded. 'This place is just full of surprises.'

CHAPTER 35

No matter how hard Amy looked, Charlie's name wasn't there. As she reached the last name in the United States Army Air Force section for the third and final time, Jack approached her.

'That took me forever but I found him.'

Amy brightened. 'You found him?'

'Glenn Miller.'

'Oh right.' Amy had forgotten about that.

'I found Joseph Kennedy straight off the bat but Glenn Miller was a tough one. It didn't help that Glenn wasn't really his first name. It was Alton. Who knew? Anyway, he's over here.'

'Oh. Well done.'

Jack gave her a concerned look. 'You okay?'

She screwed up her nose. 'Yes. I was just looking for someone I thought might be here. But he's not and it's not really *that* important.' Although it was important. She wanted to at least have a place-marker, somewhere she could tell her grandmother where Charlie was remembered. It could have been somewhere Kitty could have visited, laid flowers for the man she'd loved and lost.

Jack looked up towards his family and gave them a wave as they walked over. Amy cast a quick final glance at the wall as they walked past and towards the visitor centre. Jack told his family they'd found some famous names but that Amy had been on the lookout for a particular one. Amy fell into step with Jack's grandfather as he walked slowly.

'Really?' Jack's grandfather asked Amy. 'Who?'

'Someone who died in the war. Someone my gran knew. But he's not here. Or if he is, I can't find him. I've conceded defeat.'

'They might be able to help in the visitor centre?' he suggested. 'They can tell you which number grave to look for or whereabouts on the wall to look. They told me earlier where I could find my tail gunner so I could pay my respects.'

'Thanks.' Amy didn't feel too convinced. 'I'll try.'

It was bright and airy inside the visitor centre. The modern building housed a collection of colour boards and photos. Stories on the walls showed the sacrifice the few had made for so many while based in England.

The woman at the front desk was busy giving someone directions to a grave and so Amy wandered off to have a look at the artifacts. There were videos showing the various key players from the American side and what it had been like for the Yanks, as they'd affectionately been known, living in England. Packets of Lucky Strike cigarettes, chewing gum and nylon tights were on display from the time. It was what Amy thought of when she considered the Americans and the provisions they'd been famous for doling out. And here they were, in a glass case, as prime examples of how the Americans had made friends in England. Clichés were clichés for a reason, Amy thought.

She looked at a series of documents that the Americans had been required to carry, including passes into the nearest town, and wondered what life would be like if even her *time* was rationed, as well as food. Next to her, Jack took hold of her hand and looked into the glass case. As she looked up at him, he continued looking directly ahead but squeezed her hand.

'Hey, come look at this,' he said and gently pulled Amy towards something large and metal on the floor. There was no indication as to what it was so Jack crouched down and looked at it closely. He looked through a binocular shape on top and then muttered, 'Wow.' He stood up.

'What is it?' Amy asked.

'Take a look.'

Amy bent down and looked through the fixed huge metal binoculars as Jack had done. She was looking through a bombsight, watching a navigational video play aerial footage from a bomber aircraft during the war. It was black and white, grainy and claustrophobic. Through the viewfinder, while the ground below looked vast and wide, the bombardier's vision was limited to a thin line straight down. The field of vision was far too narrow, far too constrained. She grasped for the edges of the bombsight as dizziness and claustrophobia encased her. She looked away and stood up.

'Is that what they had to look through in order to line up the bomb target?'

Jack nodded. 'I guess so.'

'That's awful. I couldn't see a thing. And there was so much cloud.' Amy shuddered. 'God, I can't imagine being up there in a bomber. What a terrible job.'

'Did you see the shots being fired up at them from the ground on that video?' He gestured to the bombsight.

Amy shook her head. 'No?'

'Well you'd have been dead pretty fast then,' he teased. Amy bent down and looked again. There was so much going on. It must have been terrifying and the field of vision so limited. Jack looked around the room and Amy stood up, followed his gaze over to his grandfather. 'To think they volunteered for all of that. What a hell of a way to die.' He took his hand from hers and put his arm around her instead. She felt warm from his touch, wanted.

They read a few more of the boards, taking in information about military campaigns Amy knew nothing about. She told herself that next week she'd go to the library to order a book about the Battle of the Atlantic. It was important, according to the boards, and she was ashamed she'd never even heard of it.

The lady at the front desk became free and so Amy and Jack wandered over. 'How can I help?'

'Hi.' Amy smiled brightly. Just behind her, near the exit, Jack's father and grandfather gathered, making themselves ready to leave. They waited patiently.

'I have a bit of a strange question,' Amy started.

The woman smiled. 'Go on.'

'Is every serving American who died while based in Britain buried here?'

The woman said, 'No. We had a lot repatriated to the United States after the war.'

Amy stood straighter. 'Repatriated? Why?'

'The American government offered the families the opportunity to have the bodies of their loved ones back, at the government's expense of course, so they could be buried in the States. A lot, a few thousand actually, chose to take up the offer, to have their loved ones in a grave they could visit easily near their homes. But over three thousand chose to leave their loved ones here, not to disturb them any further and let them be at peace here.'

Amy thought for a moment. 'Right,' she said. So it was possible that Charlie's body, if recovered, had been flown home as one of the many thousands of bodies that had been repatriated. Or he was out there in the cemetery somewhere, or his name was on the wall but she just couldn't see it.

The woman waited for further questions.

'I'm looking for someone,' Amy explained. 'Although I think his body wouldn't have been recovered and so his name would be on the wall rather than on a headstone here. Only, I can't find it on the wall.'

'Tell me his name and I'll look him up. If he's not here, and buried in another of our cemeteries back in the States or in Europe, I'll be able to find out. And if his body wasn't recovered and he's listed as missing, I should be able to tell you that too.' The woman's fingers hovered over her keyboard.

'Okay.' Amy rested her hands on the desk. 'He was shot down and went down with his plane, I think. And he was a pilot so I guess he'd have been a captain?'

The receptionist smiled. 'It's alright. I just need a full name preferably.'

'Charlie Young,' Amy said.

Behind her there was confusion as Jack's grandfather spoke loudly. 'Charlie Young?' he asked quickly and Amy spun round.

'Yes. Why?' she asked, her eyes moving between the three men who were staring at her in equal amounts of bafflement.

Jack's grandfather spoke. 'That's my name.'

256

CHAPTER 36

Amy looked at Jack's grandfather. 'What?' she asked. But no one spoke. All eyes were on him. 'Your name is Charlie Young?' she asked. 'But . . .' She pulled herself together. 'There must be more than one Charlie Young,' she suggested. 'I don't think you're the one I'm looking for. The one I'm looking for is . . . dead,' she finished bluntly.

'Is your last name Young?' she asked Jack quickly. He nodded, confusion still written on his face. It had never occurred to her to find out Jack's family name. She didn't think she'd even told Jack hers.

'How did the Charlie you're looking for die?' Jack's grandfather asked, a frown on his face.

'He got shot down. He was a bomber pilot and . . . he got shot down,' Amy finished helplessly.

'Okay . . .'

'And you're very much alive,' she pointed out with words that sounded silly even to her own ears.

'I was a bomber pilot and I got shot down,' he said.

Emmett and Jack's eyes swivelled back to Amy. 'But I'm obviously . . .' Jack's grandfather started.

'Alive,' Amy finished for him. It was time to be proactive. All her information came out in a rush. 'My grandmother was in love with someone called Charlie Young. They were together in the war, but only for a short while, and then he got shot down. And she was told he had died. And so, I was curious to see if he was buried here or if his name was on the wall.'

Jack found his senses. 'Shall we go outside and discuss this? We're attracting so much attention.' The visitor centre had quietened while everyone around them listened intently.

It was Jack's grandfather who spoke first when they were outside again in the bright sunshine. Jack looked between Amy and his grandfather. Everyone was expressing different levels of confusion.

'What was your grandmother's name?' Jack's grandfather asked quietly.

'Kitty Williams,' she ventured.

He closed his eyes. 'I think I need to sit down.'

They led him to the closest bench. He wasn't speaking and Amy didn't know what to think. She didn't like this. This wasn't supposed to be happening. How could this Charlie be her grandmother's Charlie? How? It didn't make sense. And if it was him, why wasn't he dead as Kitty had thought?

She tried to maintain a note of calm in her voice. 'The Charlie Young my grandmother wrote about in her diary,' Amy started, 'was in love with her, apparently. But he got shot down over Europe.' She spoke slowly, working it all out as she talked. 'He kept the plane up for as long as possible, so my grandmother was told, allowing his crew to escape. They baled out. He saved them. And then his crew reported that no further parachute came from the pilot. That Charlie's plane went down with him still inside. That he'd died. One of his crew came to find my gran when they returned back to the base. They came to the pub where she worked and told her all of this. There was no doubt whatsoever in the crew's mind that Charlie had died. They all watched it happen.'

On the bench in front of her, Charlie nodded. 'That all sounds about right,' he said. His voice had changed. He sounded far away. 'I did crash. But I didn't die.' He gave a rueful smile. 'The plane was bust up pretty bad and it just fell like a stone.' He spoke slowly. 'There was nothing I could do to keep it up in the end. We were on a raid into still-Occupied Europe, and by the time we knew we weren't going to make it there alive we were just over parts of France that were Liberated after the D-Day invasion. I needed the crew to jump. I baled out so late that even though my 'chute had time to open, I hit the ground *that* hard I thought I'd broken every bone in my body. It wasn't as bad as it could've been, I guess, considering the plane was still carrying all its bombs. I heard, years later, my crew were picked up by the Allied forces on the ground whereas I jumped straight into the hands of the Nazis.'

Amy stared down at Charlie. 'But . . .?' Amy didn't know what to ask, didn't know how to take this in.

'I was captured almost immediately,' he sighed, as if all these years later the painful memory was still as fresh as the day it had happened. 'I was transferred around POW prison camp hospitals until the war ended. I was in real bad shape when I crashed and I didn't know which way was up, who I was, where I was. My dog tag had my name on it, but if I hadn't have had that on, I couldn't have told you my name, where I was from, where'd I'd been stationed, nothing.

'Memories . . . they're sometimes all you have in a place like that. I had none. I had nothing to cling to. Absolutely nothing for such a long time.'

Emmett sat on the bench next to his father, comforting him. Jack was still, as he and Amy stood in stunned silence.

It was Emmett who spoke next. 'I knew you'd lost your memory. But I never knew about a girl called Kitty.'

Charlie gave Emmett a pained look. 'How could I ever have told you that before your mother there was someone else I loved so much it hurt to leave her? And I did, I did love your mother, I want you to know that.'

'But before that there was Kitty,' Emmett said simply.

'Yes,' Charlie continued. 'There was Kitty.' He looked at Amy, continuing his story. 'I guessed that my mother had died while I'd been inside the prison camps. I worked out that much for myself when my faculties returned to me and I returned home to find out it was true. It had been so long. She'd been so unwell. It wasn't supposed to be like that. Nothing ended the way it was supposed to,' Charlie continued. 'Only I didn't want to admit it, that me being on a second tour, being taken prisoner, was the cause of me losing everything. I found and lost Kitty. I lost my mother without having had a chance to comfort her in her final days, without having had the chance to see her again. But as for Kitty, when memories of her came back to me . . . I didn't know what to think. It all felt so hopeless. It had been so long. Would she still want me? I just hoped that whatever had happened to her and wherever she'd gone in those final months of the war that she was safe – that she was well, that she was happy.'

Amy slumped onto the bench next to Charlie – Kitty's Charlie, who had survived. It could all have been so different. She realised she was going to have to tell her grandmother that Charlie was actually alive, that he was now here. Part of her wondered if she should. And then of course there was everything that had been playing on her mind all day, ever since she'd seen Kitty that morning.

'Charlie?' Amy asked. 'I think you're my grandfather.'

Charlie narrowed his eyes and Jack looked totally lost.

'What?' Jack said loudly. 'What?'

Charlie smiled gently. 'What makes you think that?'

'My mum . . . Kitty was pregnant with my mum.'

Charlie's mouth dropped open.

Jack was in panic mode. 'You and I would be cousins,' he said. 'Wouldn't we . . . Amy?' He swore.

Amy looked at him in a mix of horror and confusion as this fact dawned on her too.

It was Charlie who took the lead. 'When was your mother born?'

'December 1945.'

He paused. 'Then I'm not her father.'

'What?' Amy asked. 'But Kitty was pregnant when you left.'

'Was she?' Charlie asked. 'Really?'

'Yes, it's why she married my grandfather. He stepped in when she was pregnant with your baby. It's why they married,' Amy said.

'But I was shot down in the September of '44. If your mother was born in December '45 . . .?'

'You were shot down in *September*?' Amy's maths wasn't great but even she could see that a pregnancy wouldn't last that long. 'But . . .' she said. 'I don't understand. What had happened to the baby that Kitty had been pregnant with, Charlie's baby?

Jack and his father looked lost. No one spoke, each of them processing what Charlie's revelation meant to them.

'How do you know she was pregnant with my baby?' Charlie asked slowly.

Amy blinked. Was she misunderstanding what she'd been told earlier that day? No, no she wasn't. 'Because my gran told me.'

Charlie nodded. And then, 'When? When did she tell you this?'

'Today, this morning.'

'Oh my God, she's alive,' Charlie said, but it was almost a whisper.

'Yes,' Amy said.

'I assumed . . . the way you were talking about her that she'd passed away.'

'No . . . she's alive.'

'Oh, wow,' Charlie said, sounding exactly like Jack for a moment. He was silent, thoughtful. The spitfire flew overhead, making its return journey back to Duxford. No one looked up this time.

'Dad?' Emmett said when the engine noise overhead had dissipated.

'Is she still . . . is she still married?' Charlie asked.

'She's widowed. My grandfather died when I was only four years old.'

Charlie nodded. 'So she's been alone this whole time?' he said disbelievingly.

'Yes.'

He smiled wanly. 'So have I. I wish I'd known. Although

. . . I don't know what good it would have done, to either of us.'

Amy didn't have the answer to that.

Jack looked at Emmett. Both men were wearing the same puzzled expression. No one had the answer to any of this.

'If she meant so much to you,' Amy asked softly, 'why didn't you go to her? After the war when you remembered her, I mean. Why didn't you try to find my grandmother?'

Charlie raised his head, looked at Amy sadly. 'I did.'

'I . . .'Amy said, confused. 'What? No. She thought you'd died. She told me you'd died. But . . . you went to find her?'

'Yes. It was the very first thing I did the moment I could.'

'But if you went to see her . . .?' Amy started. 'Why does she still think you're dead?'

CHAPTER 37

Summer, 1946

Just over a year ago when the war had ended, Charlie had stood at the gates of the prison camp where he'd spent the remaining few months of the war and had watched with tears in his eyes as the US Army arrived to liberate them. By the end of May 1945, all American POWs imprisoned in Europe's Stalags had been freed, but a year later Charlie had no idea if he was the only POW mad enough to be returning to Europe after having been demobbed in the States. But he had someone to go back for.

He'd joined the other 100,000 American service personnel who'd spent their war as a POW and had been placed on a ship home to America to await demobilisation. Although after all this time he wasn't sure what felt like home anymore. He didn't really have a home. He couldn't remember anywhere other than Iowa but when he got there it wasn't the same.

Charlie had guessed his mother had died and whatever help she'd had in his absence, had left too. Maybe those boys had joined the fight in Europe after all because the farm was in ruins and had clearly been like this for some time.

He'd stood, assessing everything around him, the dust in the remote farmhouse, the barns – still standing, just – the crop decaying into the ground, corn husks rotting around him. For a fraction of a second it felt so familiar, but it wasn't a memory of here. It was a field in a different place, a different country. The name of the plane he'd flown suddenly came to him. *Beauty Queen.* But he couldn't remember why it had been called that. He waited for more to come but it hadn't. Try as he might, no more memories came.

And soon after, he'd made a start. His livelihood depended on it. He owed it to his mother's memory to make this farm work, come what may. Every ounce of energy he had went into rejuvenating the corn fields, creating new life from the decaying field. He lived and breathed the farm, hiring in workers who'd returned from the war in need of employment, a young woman to help with bookkeeping so he could be out doing manual work.

When the farm was in less of a hellish state, he'd walked through the fields and stood still, assessing everything he owned, everything he'd done. He'd worked so hard to put this all right but there was still a long way to go. But despite the help, he still felt so alone. It just felt wrong to be alone. He knew at one point in his life he hadn't felt like this but he couldn't have said when that was. There were memories there – memories of feelings he'd once known, a person he couldn't remember. But slowly, so slowly it was painful, he remembered a drinking competition. Writing his name on the wall of . . . where . . . the officers' mess? Or somewhere else? A pub? A bar? Somewhere. He shook his head, hoping to shake a memory into his mind. Somewhere. Somewhere in England. Where though? It didn't matter. It wasn't important.

A German doctor in one of the camps had once told him sometimes losing your memory was a way to protect yourself, a way to save your own sanity and to compartmentalise when you'd been through trauma – in addition to it just being something that happened when you banged your head real hard in a crash. Although Charlie wasn't too sure what he was protecting himself from by losing any recollection of being a pilot in England. Maybe what the doctor told him had been lost in translation. But as he stood in the field one evening – the sun lowering in the wide open sky – drinking an ice cold beer, a wind passed through the farm, making a door inside the farmhouse slam and sending the oak trees in the distance into a flutter, their boughs bending and leaves rustling forcefully. He narrowed his eyes, looking at the trees as they moved in the breeze. It all felt so familiar, as if he'd been standing in a similar field, looking at a similar oak tree somewhere else.

There was something there, in the back of his mind, the back of his memory. He could see it, he just couldn't reach it. It was a memory of home, of feeling as if he was home and it wasn't here. As much as he'd thought it was – home wasn't here. He looked up at the leaves on the row of oak trees and it all felt so incredibly familiar. He remembered the planes he'd flown but try as he might he couldn't remember the faces of the guys he'd flown with, nor their names. He remembered the sun shining down on him during a summer in a country far away, but not exactly where. And after a while, long after he'd finished his beer and he was still in the same spot he'd been stood for hours, he vaguely remembered country lanes and riding a bicycle with a girl on the handlebars.

And then, the girl's face came into his mind. And ever so slowly, and ever so desperately, he began remembering.

Now it was Kitty that felt like home. He had to go to her. They had to be together. It was written in their stars. The woman he loved, the woman he was going to marry was in a tiny village in a corner of England. His heart pulled him towards Europe, towards Kitty. He just had to go back to her. And so that's what he did.

After the rickety old bus deposited him in the village he glanced around at the shop windows in Market Place. They didn't look any better stocked than they had done when he'd last been here and he was surprised to find that with the war long since over, rationing still held strong.

No one paid any attention to the man in civilian clothing who moved quickly through the square. He carried his suitcase towards The Duck. The pub looked exactly the same as it had done when he'd last been here. He wasn't sure what he'd been expecting but the moment he saw the pub his heart soared and he picked up pace, almost running through the door. He wasn't sure how he was going to begin with Kitty, what he was going to say. Hopefully she'd run into his arms and it would be as if he'd never left. They wouldn't need to say anything. They had been in love. He knew this for sure.

At this time of day and with the Americans long since gone from the village, the pub was almost empty – so different to when he'd last been here. It was all so different now. He stood at the door and looked towards the bar. No one was serving. He'd not expected that.

From the store room at the back came the sound of clattering glasses. Charlie's heart raced. He hadn't bothered looking at his reflection in the shop windows on the way past. He had no idea what he looked like. Hell, probably. He was a shadow of his former self. He knew that. Before capture he'd looked after himself in the airbase gym. But any sign of the muscles he'd acquired had all gone as he and his fellow inmates wasted away slowly on small prison rations. He'd tried to eat well when he arrived home so he would be strong enough to work on the farm, but found his heart wasn't in food anymore. It was just fuel. He looked different. He knew he did. He smoothed down his hair and waited. He hoped Kitty still recognised him. He hoped she still loved him.

A young woman rounded the corner and stopped as she caught sight of him. 'What will you be having?' the girl asked.

'A beer, please,' he said, wondering how to phrase the question he wanted to ask. He took a stool by the bar and waited, glancing around hoping for Kitty.

The woman placed the beer on the counter, told him the price and held her hand out while Charlie counted the change. He'd never quite got the hang of English money. She offered to help and he thanked her.

'Are you Kitty's sister?' he asked.

The woman looked at him. 'Yes.'

Charlie smiled. 'I thought I recognised you. Janie, right?'

'Yes,' Janie said again, puzzled. 'Who are you?'

'Charlie,' he said, waiting for some hint of recognition. She stared at him. 'You're not dead.'

'No.' He laughed. 'Not yet at any rate.'

'Why are you here?' she asked sharply.

'I came for Kitty,' he said.

She continued to stare. 'Why?'

268

'Because I love her,' he said simply.

'No,' Janie replied to his surprise. 'No, you can't just come back here after all this time and expect to pick up where you left off. That's not how life works.'

He stared back, stunned. 'Nothing about these past couple of years has been how life works. But it's not been my fault. Is she here? Is she okay?'

'She's fine,' Janie replied. 'She's more than fine. She's happy, settled, married. You can't just walk in here and disrupt that. I won't let you.'

His eyes rounded and he stuttered out the words, 'She's married?' Of all the outcomes he played through in his mind, all the eventualities . . . he hadn't envisaged this. 'She's married?' he asked again. 'No, she can't be.'

'I'm sorry,' Janie said softly, 'but it's true. She thought you were dead. She was devastated. She collapsed in grief the moment she was told. I couldn't find her for hours. She was a mess. But that was two years ago. Two years. Where in God's name have you been for two whole years?'

'I've been in a POW camp,' he said forlornly.

'And you didn't write to her? Not once.'

'I couldn't. I didn't know which way was up, I was badly hurt in the crash and my mind . . . I wasn't myself. But I'm here. I'm here now.'

'And it's too late,' Janie said sharply and then she adopted a softer tone. 'Regardless, it would have been too late if you'd come back even a couple of months after you disappeared. She was already married.'

'She married so soon after I crashed? I don't believe you.'

'It's true,' Janie said kindly. 'I'm sorry to tell you that but it's true.'

'Why?'

But Janie wouldn't say. 'I would say you'd have to ask Kitty that but I can't let you anywhere near her. You have to promise me you won't disrupt her life, their life? They're happy, content, a family. You storming in now won't do any good. It will do quite the opposite. You'll reverse everything Kitty has worked so hard for. You understand that, don't you?'

Charlie stared at the bar.

'Even you being here, like this. Word will spread there's an American. Someone will place you. Word will get back to Kitty and I can't have you upending everything. I swore to her I'd protect her. I swore I'd be a better sister and I swore I wouldn't let anyone hurt her. I need you to go. *She* needs you to go.'

'She's *married*,' he repeated. Tears formed in his eyes and he wiped them with his sleeve. 'I can't . . . Did she even love me?'

'Yes, she did. She did but she's married and she's happy,' Janie said desperately. 'So I need you to go. I'm sorry but this is the way it has to be. You see that, don't you?' she said quickly, anxiously.

Charlie nodded. 'I guess. I . . . don't know.'

'You do know,' Janie said. 'You do know that you can't go anywhere near her. You can't be here. You have to let her live her life. Please,' she said urgently. 'Please.'

He nodded, slowly. 'Who did she marry? Just tell me that, and I'll go.'

Janie stalled. 'You'll go home? If I tell you . . . you'll go home? Back to America?'

'Yes. Just put me out of my misery. Just tell me . . . and I'll go.'

Janie paused and then, 'Christopher Frampton.'

He inhaled, exhaled, tears fell from his eyes again. 'Oh.'

'He's a good man,' Janie said. 'If that helps at all.' Although the expression on her face showed she knew it wasn't going to help in the slightest. 'We couldn't have hoped for a better husband for her. He adores her. And . . . they have a child.'

'Oh God,' Charlie cried. 'They have a child?'

'Yes. So . . . you really can't go and upset things now. You see that, don't you? You can't go and destroy a family, because that's what you'd be doing. She loved you. She loved you so much that if you go there now, I know what's going to happen. I know she's going to go with you.'

Charlie looked at her. 'Really?'

'Yes. She'll go with you,' Janie said. 'Because she won't be able to help herself. She's still so young, impressionable. She was in love with you, and while I'm sure love has grown between them, it's not like it was with you. I can see that. I'm not blind. But she's happy, looked after and she's a mother. They're a family. Do you want to be responsible for ruining that, for destroying them, for destroying a little girl's life because you wanted to take her mother away from her? Because that's what will happen. Christopher's a good man, a great man, but even he won't let his own daughter go with Kitty if she chooses you. She'll go without her child. And then she'll regret it. Kitty will be miserable. You'll make every single one of them miserable. Is that the kind of man you are? I didn't get that impression when Kitty talked about you. You were kind, honourable. That's what she said. And this . . . this would be selfish destruction . . . and it would be neither kind nor honourable,' she finished.

Charlie was silent.

'Please, promise me, for Kitty, for Kitty's child, for all of them, you won't . . . you won't do anything. I'm *begging* you.'

271

'I won't do anything,' Charlie said eventually. 'I won't destroy their family. I won't see her. I'll go.'

'Now?' she pleaded. 'You'll go right now?'

'Yes,' he said flatly. 'It's what's best. I'll leave now.' He climbed from the barstool, his beer untouched.

'Thank you,' he said to Janie.

'For what?'

'For looking out for her, for putting me straight, for being a good sister. I'm pleased she's happy. I'm pleased she has the chance to be a mother, I'm pleased he's a good man. and I'm pleased she has you.' Tears fell down his face and he wiped them with his sleeve before turning and leaving the pub one final time.

He went to the bench he'd sat on before with Kitty in happier times and sat down. He couldn't spend long here; if what Janie said was true, people would talk and word would get to Kitty and he'd have ruined everything for her without even having seen her. There was a small part of him that wondered if this was it. The end. What if Janie's story wasn't true? But why would she lie? He felt cold just thinking about never setting eyes on Kitty again. He couldn't do it. He couldn't come this far and not at least glimpse her. He just had to be sure Janie wasn't lying. He had to know for himself. He'd keep his promise not to destroy Kitty and her new family though. He wouldn't talk to her, he wouldn't go near her. He was just going to look, just going to look at the farmhouse, see if he could see her, see if he could torture himself by watching the woman he loved be happy with another man. Just once. He'd go and look just for a few minutes and then he'd leave and he'd never see her again.

He closed his eyes and counted to ten and then got up

slowly and walked purposefully in the direction of the farmhouse. He skirted the back edge of the field and stood by the oak tree and watched a picture of domestic happiness that cut him to his core.

CHAPTER 38

Kitty stood at the edge of the farmhouse gardens where the line of lush green grass blurred into the wheat field and looked out across at the oak tree where she'd known such happiness with Charlie. She was sure she could see someone, a figure by the tree. She shielded her eyes against the sun, stepped forward a pace and looked again, squinting through the light. But there was no movement and so she looked away, back to her family.

Christopher, sat in a deck chair, took her hand as she walked over to him and brought it to his lips. She looked down at him and smiled. She was learning to love him in a way she'd never had to try before. She'd never love him the same way she had Charlie – with a sheer intensity that had burned and made her feel alive. With Christopher it was different. He made her feel safe. And he loved her, passionately and completely. She only wished she could feel the same instead of just gentle affection.

When Christopher released her hand, she smiled warmly and stooped to pick up Alison from the picnic rug next to them. Alison put her arms around her mother's neck and Kitty kissed her head through her curly hair. Her little baby was growing so fast and wasn't so little anymore. Alison started laughing and Christopher stood up and took her, making a fuss of her and making her laugh louder still.

Kitty laughed. 'You have a magic touch when it comes to her. She loves you.'

He smiled at her. 'I love her. I love you both.'

She said it back automatically. Slowly and surely, day by day, it no longer felt as if a piece of her soul was being ripped from inside her when she said it.

With Alison settled with her toys, Christopher gently pulled Kitty towards him, encircling her waist with his arms. She looked up at him and for a fleeting moment she pictured Charlie's face. She blinked it away. The pain wounded her as Christopher's lips touched hers.

She kissed him back. It would never be the same but she had to try, she simply had to. She wanted to make him happy and she knew she would fail if she didn't try just that little bit harder. He'd done such a wonderful thing, marrying her, saving her, and in the end it had all been for nothing. Shortly after they'd married, she had lost the baby in its early stages. It had traumatised them both but it had bonded them together, and she had loved him just that little bit more when, afterwards, he'd been honest and told her if she wanted to leave him he would love her until the end of time but that he would let her go if it was what she wanted.

She didn't. She couldn't have done that to him. She'd had her great love. She didn't need to go in search of another. She had wrapped her arms around him, told him she loved him and swore that she would never ever hurt him. She had

275

sworn she'd be a good wife to him, and shortly after they'd made love for the first time and soon after, they made Alison.

From the side of the house, Kitty's father entered the garden, waving merrily. Kitty pulled away from Christopher and bent to pick Alison up. Kitty's father walked forward with a smile on his face, his arms already outstretched for the little girl. Kitty looked one last time across the wheat field, towards the oak tree. Was there someone there? She shook her head. She was imagining things.

CHAPTER 39

Charlie slumped against the oak tree and slid down the rough bark until he collapsed on the hard ground. He turned his head away. He couldn't watch anymore. He'd tortured himself long enough. Watching Kitty and the little girl with Christopher had hurt more than he could ever have imagined and now he wished he'd never done it. A part of him wished he'd been killed instead of taken prisoner. At least then he wouldn't have suffered this on his return.

He put his head in his hands and let the tears fall freely. By the time he stood up, Kitty and her family had gone inside, the picnic blanket, deck chairs and a collection of toys all that remained on the grass. She had looked happy, loved. She was a wife, a mother now. He wanted to run over there, grab Kitty, tell her he was here, that he was alive, beg her to leave Christopher and run away with him. But he couldn't do it. He couldn't be that kind of man. They were a family. He would never know happiness with Kitty; he only had the memories of those few precious weeks when he thought nothing could touch him because he was in love.

But now, with his heart shattered into a thousand pieces, he picked himself off the cold, shaded ground underneath the oak tree where he and Kitty had picnicked, talked and made love, and walked slowly back to the village. Once he set foot on that boneshaker of a bus it was all over. Soon he would be far away from here.

As the ship pulled away from the dock, Charlie knew he would never love another woman the way he'd loved Kitty. And as England faded in the distance he took one final, regretful look at the country that had given him such happiness and such sorrow and knew he would probably never see Kitty again. It ripped him to his core.

CHAPTER 40

Summer, 2011

On the drive back to the village Amy worried for Kitty. She worried for how Charlie's return would affect Kitty now, at her age. How would she take it all in – that he was alive, that he'd been alive the entire time, that he'd found her all those years ago, known she'd been happy, married, a mother and had then left . . . knowing his arrival would do more harm than good.

Jack's hand crept across the back seat and he took Amy's hand within his. He turned to her and gave her a questioning smile. His expression mirrored hers, concern. Charlie seemed hellbent on finding Kitty now he knew she was alive and nearby.

'You okay?' Jack whispered.

She looked at him, made a worried face.

'Is now a good time to tell you I'm really pleased you and I aren't cousins?' Jack said with a wicked grin.

Amy's other hand flew to her mouth as she tried not to laugh. 'Oh God, Jack. Don't.'

They both tried not to laugh. 'Maybe you should warn your mom,' he said in a more serious tone. 'See if she can beat us there, see if she can . . . I dunno, ready Kitty in some way,' he whispered.

Amy nodded. She could hardly call and express her worry with Charlie sitting in the car with her so she sent a text message to her mother and to Caroline and told them in no uncertain terms to kick any remaining customers out, close the tearoom and go to her gran's house.

When they arrived at the farmhouse, Caroline's car was parked on the gravel drive. She and Alison were already inside and Amy asked Emmett if he'd park by the side, a little way out of view of the house.

'Perhaps you could just give me a few minutes . . .?' Amy asked.

Charlie nodded. 'I've waited so long. I can wait a little longer.'

Amy jogged across the gravel and into the farmhouse. In the kitchen the three women looked as mystified as each other. Amy didn't know where to start.

It was Kitty who broke the ice. 'What's wrong, darling? Your mother and sister have just turned up out of the blue, ordered, apparently, by you to be here.'

Amy needed a glass of water and took a glass from the kitchen sink drainer, filled it from the tap and downed it in one go.

'What's going on?' Caroline chimed in. 'What's happened?' She had no idea where to begin.

'Gran, I've found Charlie,' Amy said.

Kitty blinked. 'What do you mean?' she asked.

Amy wasn't sure how much of the story from the cemetery Kitty needed to hear. Instead, she cut to the chase. It would all come out – in time. 'He's *alive*. He's still alive. And . . . he's here.'

'He's . . .?' Kitty trailed off as disbelief clouded her face.

'Alive, yes.' Amy clarified. 'And here. He came back here for the Heritage Day. And he's . . .' Amy glanced out of the window where the men, unnoticed by the women in the farmhouse, were standing outside the car in deep discussion. 'He's still here.' She said the next bit gently, warily. 'He's outside.'

Kitty inhaled sharply and sat down suddenly in a dining chair. 'He can't be.'

'He is, Gran. He's here.'

'Who's Charlie?' Caroline questioned.

'Someone Gran used to know,' Amy said vaguely. She looked at Kitty for permission to give away more . . .

Kitty looked forlorn, but Amy had summoned her family here for moral support and to help Kitty if she needed it and they were in this conversation blind. 'Charlie is someone Gran used to be in love with. He died. Or so she thought and . . .'

Kitty cried.

'Oh, Gran,' Amy said and embraced Kitty. 'Gran, it's okay.'

'Are you sure?' Kitty asked through falling tears. 'Are you sure it's him?'

'Yes. I didn't believe it but . . . it's a long story. All of it's a long story and he can tell you himself. But, Gran . . . outside is a man who loved you, who . . . I think still loves you and he would like nothing more than to see you. If that's okay? Can I go and get him?' Amy asked. 'Can I get Charlie for you?'

'Oh God,' Kitty cried. 'I . . . It's been so long. It's been over sixty years. How do I . . . what do I do, what do I say?'

'Why don't you let him do the talking, Gran,' Amy replied. 'He's got so many things he wants to tell you about where he went and . . .' Amy paused. Charlie's return to the village, the fact he'd seen Kitty, seen her content with her new family and then still chosen to do the right thing and leave – this wasn't Amy's story to tell.

Kitty didn't want an audience. She retreated into the relative safety of the sitting room, asking Amy to fetch Charlie and bring him to her there. Amy paused nervously, glancing back at her gran as she stood in the bay window, waiting for the man she'd loved, the man she'd not seen in almost seven decades, the man she'd thought up until a few minutes ago, had died. 'You okay, Gran?' she asked a quivering Kitty.

'No,' Kitty replied. 'Not really.'

Amy turned back. 'It's okay to be scared. It's okay to not want to do this. It's okay if you want me to send him away, I will. Gran, I don't . . .'

'Don't be ridiculous,' Kitty said with a half-hearted smile. 'Go and get the poor man.'

Amy walked back through the kitchen, finding Jack standing awkwardly in the doorway, his hands on either side of the door frame, talking in hushed tones with Caroline and Alison.

'Hey,' Jack said. 'Is Kitty okay?'

'I'm not sure. I really don't want this to give her a heart attack or something but I think I've led her into the situation as best I know how. Do you want to go and get your grandad?'

'Sure,' Jack said.

'This is mad,' Alison said. 'This man meant a lot to Mum, didn't he?'

Amy nodded. 'He meant everything to her. And she to him, I think, before Grandad.'

Charlie walked into view of the kitchen door and Caroline muttered, 'I guess we're about to find out how much they meant to each other.'

Emmet and Jack followed him as Charlie greeted the women in the kitchen but his eyes scanned the room for Kitty.

'She's in the sitting room. She's waiting for you. I'll take you through if you're ready?' Amy spoke with encouragingly wide eyes, waiting for him to decide if he wanted to do this or not.

'I've been ready since forever,' he replied.

Charlie stood behind her as she pulled open the door to the sitting room. Kitty was standing, her eyes fixed firmly on the doorway as they entered.

Charlie cleared his throat politely and Amy stood aside so they could see each other, finally.

Charlie was the first to speak. The emotion in his voice made Amy's heart hurt as he said her grandmother's name, 'Kitty.'

On seeing him, Kitty burst into tears again. Charlie moved forward, leaning on his stick and moved towards her.

'Charlie,' she said, between tears, her smile reaching her eyes. 'It's really you.'

'I'm afraid so,' he said with a chuckle.

'I'd know that laugh anywhere. And that smile,' Kitty replied, looking at him properly.

'You haven't changed,' Charlie said.

'It's been so long,' Kitty said. 'Of course I've changed.'

'You don't look a day older to me,' he said, his eyes crinkling at the sides as he smiled.

'I can't believe you're here. I can't believe it's *you*,' Kitty said.

'It's me,' Charlie said softly. He stepped forward, lifted his hand slowly and touched her face. 'Only I'm older now.'

'Oh, Charlie,' Kitty said.

'I know,' Charlie replied with a sigh. 'I know.'

A lump formed in Amy's throat and she left the room, giving them privacy and closing the door gently behind her. She stood there for a few seconds trying to compose herself. The muffled voices from behind the door were full of disbelief, laughter, joy and tears.

Kitty looked into Charlie's eyes. The young man she'd loved was here. His dark eyes were the same, as was his smile. She wondered how he saw her now she was elderly.

As if he read her mind he said, 'You're still the most beautiful woman I've ever met. I never stopped loving you. Never,' he said.

Kitty nodded as tears rolled down her face. 'You left me,' she cried. 'Why did you leave me? Why didn't you come back for me?' He moved forward, held her in his arms, and to Kitty it was as if the years suddenly fell away and it was she and Charlie, young again.

'I didn't mean to leave you, I promise you. You have to believe me.' He told her about getting shot down, crashing into France and his ensuing time in prison hospitals recuperating, losing his mind, his memories before being moved from prison to prison further into Europe as the advancing Allied troops pushed through.

He told her about his mother passing away while he was a prisoner, about how he went back to the US to put things

284

straight, how he came back to the village to find Kitty. Kitty's mouth fell open at this.

'You came back?' she whispered. 'Oh Charlie. I had no idea. Why . . . why didn't I know this? Why didn't you find me?'

'I did,' he said. 'I did come back. I went to find you at the pub and then . . . even when your sister begged me not to, I came to find you. She'd told me you were happy, that you were a mother and that you were married. She told me that even though I'd been away for two years it wouldn't have mattered because you'd been married about a month after I got taken prisoner. And I didn't know why but . . . today your granddaughter told me why, and I think . . . I think I've worked out what happened and maybe it all makes sense. I'm so sorry, Kitty. I'm so sorry about everything.'

Kitty looked at Charlie sadly. 'She isn't yours,' she started. 'Alison . . . she isn't yours.'

He nodded and after a beat said, 'I know.'

'I was pregnant with your baby,' she confirmed. 'I lost it. Only a short while after Christopher and I married.'

His expression matched hers, sad and wistful for a life they never had together, for a family they never had together.

'I'm so sorry you lost our baby by yourself.'

Kitty tried not to let more tears fall. She'd dealt with the emotions years ago but the pain had never left. 'I wasn't alone. There was Christopher.'

Charlie nodded sadly. 'I saw you with him. I knew I had to see you. And I did,' he continued. 'I did see you. I saw you with Christopher, I saw you happy, I saw you with a little girl – Alison?'

Kitty nodded. 'But . . . my sister saw you?'

Charlie nodded. 'I saw her before I saw you. If I'd found you first I'm not sure if things would have turned out the same or not. But I guess, for the sake of your marriage and for the sake of your daughter, it's best they didn't turn out any other way. It's best you didn't see me when I saw you.'

'When, where?'

'One day in the summer of '46. I stood by our initials at the oak tree. I watched you be happy. I won't lie, it hurt, it hurt like hell. And then I turned and I left.'

Kitty cried. 'Oh, Charlie.' Emotions stirred inside and she felt the loss of him all over again, the pain of losing him cutting through her afresh.

'Can we sit?' Charlie asked, wiping Kitty's tears from her face. 'I like to think I'm still twenty-six but my body reminds me I'm ninety-three.'

He reached out and held her hand within his. Their hands looked so different, so much older. So much time had passed and it shouldn't hurt in the way it still did but it all felt so fresh, so raw.

'I never stopped loving you. And I'm so sorry,' Kitty said.

'Why are *you* sorry?' he asked, his dark eyes lifting to meet hers.

'Because I didn't do anything right back then. I didn't know I was having a baby until it was too late. And I'd thought you and I were going to be forever. And you didn't come back. And I was told you'd died. And then I found out I was pregnant and I . . . I ran away.'

'You ran away? Oh, Kitty.'

'But Christopher found me and when I told him what had happened to me, he was so kind . . .'

'You don't have to justify what happened, Kitty. Honestly, we've had lives since then.'

286

'I want to,' Kitty replied quickly. 'I want you to know that I loved you, that I never stopped loving you but then Christopher . . .'

'He'd always loved you?' Charlie cut in. 'I could see it in his eyes whenever he saw us together. He never looked the jealous type but when he looked at you, there was love there.'

'He did love me,' Kitty replied. 'He loved me and he said he'd look after me, and even though I was having your baby he said if I would try to make it work with him, if I'd marry him, he'd look after me, and the baby and he'd love it as his own forever.'

'Oh, Kitty,' he said sadly. 'I don't know what to say. And then . . . then you lost the baby,' he said gently.

'Yes,' she continued softly. 'And Christopher didn't get the chance to prove how much he could love another man's baby. But I knew he would have done because that's just the kind of man he was. We married ever so quickly, even by wartime standards.' Kitty managed a smile. 'And he never expected anything of me. And when I lost the baby . . .'

Charlie squeezed Kitty's hand tighter.

'When I lost the baby,' she continued, 'he held me so tightly, stroking my hair, and when I looked up at him, his face was streaked with tears and he'd been crying too. And I told myself then, that even though you were gone, he was such a good man and I had to make the most of it all because it was the right thing for everyone.'

'I'm happy for you,' Charlie said eventually. 'Does that sound crazy? I'm so . . . happy to know that even though all of that happened, you were safe and you were loved and you were cared for by a man as solid and as *good* as he was.'

Both Charlie and Kitty had tears in their eyes and Kitty nodded. 'Yes, he was good. And I'd always loved him as a friend. I worried I'd never love him properly but I did. Not with that fierce, burning intensity with which I'd loved you. But eventually, love came and it healed me, in a way from the loss of you, from the loss of our baby. I grew up, practically overnight, and became the kind of wife Christopher deserved. And I counted my lucky stars that he'd been there when you'd gone. And then we had Alison and . . .' Kitty trailed off.

'And you had a good life?' Charlie asked.

'Yes,' Kitty agreed. 'I had a wonderful life. Please tell me you had the same?'

'I did,' Charlie said with a smile. 'Eventually. It took me a while to get over you though.'

'You married?'

'A long time after. A local gal I hired to help with bookkeeping. Barbara. And Barbara and I had Emmett.' Charlie gestured towards the kitchen where his son was with the others. 'When she passed away he was in his twenties and we became a team, because we kinda had to be. He helped on the farm and grew up and got married himself, and stayed nearby, and now he runs the farm. And they had Jack, who's kinda sweet on your Amy from what I gather.'

Kitty inhaled. 'Jack? Jack is your grandson?'

'He is.'

After a pause when she took this in, she said, 'Well he's a fine young man. And I did rather think he might be *sweet,* as you say, on Amy in order to clamber around in the attics for me, an old woman that he'd never met.'

'You're not old, Kitty.'

'I'm not young,' she countered.

They looked at each other, hands entwined, the missing years stretching out behind them.

'I have something of yours,' Kitty said quietly, untangling her hand from his and reaching to undo the St Christopher hanging round her neck. She held it out to him and his eyes widened in disbelief.

'Is this . . .?'

'It's yours. I found it underneath the tree . . . after you'd gone.'

Charlie stared at it for a long time and then he leaned forward and put it back around Kitty's neck. 'Maybe I didn't need it. It's kept you safe all these years. You should keep it.'

She smiled, touching the necklace.

'I'm so sorry I left you,' Charlie said quietly.

'You didn't leave me, not really,' Kitty said in return. 'War tore us apart.'

'And now we've been brought back together again,' Charlie said into her hair as they moved forward to embrace each other. 'And if you want me, all these years later, I promise I'll never let you go again.'

They held each other tightly, neither one of them quite able to believe they were in each other's arms after all these years, after everything that had happened to them, after the lives they had led so far apart from each other, but knowing each of them had never been far from the other's thoughts.

CHAPTER 41

In the kitchen there was a scene of quiet excitement. Caroline, Jack, Emmett and Alison were deep in conversation as Amy filled them in. With Charlie in the other room letting Kitty understand what had happened to the man she'd loved, Amy decided there'd been enough revelations for one day. She leaned against the sink, listening to the excited chatter and staring exhaustedly into the middle distance of the field until Jack came over.

'How do you think they're doing in there?' he asked.

Amy sighed and looked at Jack. 'No idea. It's unfathomable isn't it, that someone can be gone for so long and return into your life.'

'I think it's amazing,' Jack said.

'So do I, but what happens now? Now they've found each other.'

'What do you mean?'

'Do they say goodbye again or . . . what?'

'Oh,' Jack said, 'I've got no idea.'

'I don't suppose they know what to do either,' Amy mused.

'Why don't we make some tea for them,' Jack said. 'All that talking.'

Caroline moved over to them. 'They're going to need more than a cup of tea to get them through the rest of this day.' She reached for Kitty's favourite Christmas brandy and began pouring everyone healthy measures. She disappeared with a glass each for Kitty and Charlie while everyone sat quietly at the kitchen table, contemplating what Kitty and Charlie's reunion meant for them both.

'There's a flood of tears going on in there. From both of them,' Caroline said, joining them at the table. And then, 'It's always the quiet ones, isn't it?' Caroline gestured to the sitting room, which gathered a smile from everyone. 'I'd never thought of Gran as a wartime heartbreaker.'

'I never knew there was anyone before Dad. It never occurred to me Gran had a whole other life before your grandad,' Alison mused.

Jack looked at his watch and his face formed into a startled expression. 'I need to get some fresh air. Amy, do you want to walk with me?'

Together, the two of them walked across the field towards the oak tree.

They walked side by side, Jack's hand finding its way inside hers. She liked him so much but he was leaving. His grandfather was inside telling *her* grandmother the story of how the two of them were parted, how he'd come back to find her. She had no idea what was going on in that room. Were Charlie and Kitty putting their lost years to rights, were they saying their goodbyes all over again? And then there was Jack. Jack who she'd thought she might be falling for; Jack who she thought might have been falling for her. Compared to Kitty and Charlie's wartime love, she and Jack

291

were living in a simpler time, but he was leaving and it all still felt so complicated. Even more so with today's revelations.

They stood silently by the tree, Jack staring up at the names and initials carved into it. 'I guess we know what this is really all about now?' He pointed up to the heart, carved into the wood of the tree, *C&K 1944*.

Amy touched the carvings and Jack's fingers met hers. 'I'm really gonna miss you,' he said.

Amy smiled. 'Likewise.

There was nothing more to be said. She didn't wait for his cue, didn't wait for her brain to tell her that she was really going to regret kissing him again because the memory of him would hurt all the more. Instead, she pulled him towards her and kissed him.

He leaned into the kiss, putting his arms around her and holding her as they kissed under the shade of the oak tree. When they pulled apart, it was bittersweet. He planted delicate, final kisses on her lips and then murmured, 'I have to go.'

Amy nodded reluctantly. 'I'll walk back with you.' They held hands as they returned to the house, their final few moments alone together.

Emmett looked up as Jack laid his hand on his shoulder. 'Dad, I need to leave now. I've got to catch my flight. I don't want to interrupt them so can you say bye to Grandpa for me? I'll call you when I land.'

'Bye,' he said to the room and the women waved. 'It was nice to see you all again, even under these strange circumstances. Goodbye, Amy,' he said with a rueful smile. 'See y'around I guess?'

She nodded, raised her hand to wave goodbye. And with that Jack was gone and her insides felt hollow.

Eventually Charlie and Kitty entered the sitting room. They were hand in hand. There was silence but Amy, Alison, Caroline and Emmett watched them with interest.

It was Emmett who broke the silence. 'Jack had to leave. He has to catch his flight. He said to say goodbye. He'll call later.'

Charlie nodded. 'He's a good boy.'

Emmett laughed. 'He's nearly thirty-five, Dad. Hardly a boy.'

It was as if everyone was avoiding the elephant in the room until Alison spoke. 'Mum? Is there something you want to tell us?' she asked with a wide smile. She was almost laughing at how extraordinary all of this was.

Kitty and Charlie sat next to each other at the table. They were still holding hands.

'Oh, my darling,' Kitty started. 'Where do I begin? It all feels like a lifetime ago.'

Charlie gave Kitty's hand a squeeze and she took a deep breath and told them all everything she'd never told them.

'There's something else we need to tell you,' Charlie said when the story had ended and hopes for the future were now in their minds. He looked at Kitty. She nodded and gave him an encouraging smile. 'It involves all of you, but particularly you.' Charlie looked at Emmett.

'Me?' Emmett said in surprise.

'Kitty and I have missed out on a lifetime together. We've spent the last hour or so catching up on what went wrong, what took us apart from each other, but we have a lot of time to make up for. I'm no spring chicken—'

'Neither of us are.' Kitty laughed.

'And so that's why I want to spend some time here, in England, with Kitty,' Charlie finished.

Amy gasped happily, her smile wide.

'You're staying here?' Caroline asked Charlie.

Charlie looked at Kitty and they exchanged a loving smile.

'We have a whole lifetime to catch up on,' Kitty said.

'We do,' Charlie agreed. 'Is that okay with you girls?'

Kitty shot them a warning look. Amy laughed at the look. 'It's nothing to do with me. I want you to be happy, both of you.'

Caroline and Alison agreed. Emmett sat back in the chair and folded his arms. 'Well, this is . . . unexpected. But then, this whole day has been unexpected. I guess I'm *really* running the farm now then?' he said.

'You already have been, son.'

'Okay then,' Emmett said, 'if you want to stay here, we'll talk often and I'll fly over every now and again. And when you're ready to come home, I'll come back and get you.'

Charlie looked at Kitty and they exchanged a knowing smile. Emmett took the hint. 'Okay, so maybe I'll just fly over every now and again and bring some of your things over with me so you have them here.'

Charlie squeezed Kitty's hand as the chatter continued between them all.

Amy thought of Jack, getting ready to board his flight, leaving England. It was a good thing he was leaving, she reasoned. Especially now. What if she and Jack had got together? What if they'd fallen in love, what if they'd fallen out, broken up down the line? It would make family Christmases complicated to say the least now both their grandparents were with each other after all this time. She

294

was trying to convince herself that maybe this way, she and Jack could just be friends – *should* just be friends. In the long run it might be better for the sake of their grandparents. And besides, he didn't even live here. He lived thousands of miles away. How would they have made that work? Long-distance relationships between two very busy people who loved their work . . . that wasn't ideal. This way, they'd remain as friends, they'd see each other, what, twice, maybe three times a year at most for family occasions? And it wouldn't be awkward.

And that was only if Charlie was planning on staying in the long-term. If not, she'd probably never see him again.

That thought was even worse.

CHAPTER 42

Over the next few months Amy saw her grandmother blossom with Charlie. Kitty was genuinely happy whenever the family gathered for their usual Sunday roast at hers. He was hands-on in the garden when the two of them worked side by side on the vegetable beds, harvesting produce for their suppers, giving each other loving glances and moving in harmony with each other. He helped around the house, they shared news stories from the paper with each other and he was adept at folding laundry. The two of them appeared very much in love and completely at ease, as if they'd never been apart, as if he'd always been here, as if they should have been together the entire time. Only the universe hadn't planned it that way.

As the weeks drifted on there was quiet speculation about Amy and Jack between Kitty and Charlie and *loud* speculation between Caroline and Alison, but Amy didn't want to talk about it. Perhaps Jack's return to New York had been a good thing. Kitty thought they needed time.

'Young people are often so quick to rush in,' Kitty said as she washed up at the Belfast sink one afternoon.

'Like we were?' Charlie asked. He stood by the draining board, tea towel in hand, ready to dry the dishes.

'That was different,' Kitty replied softly.

'Was it? How?'

'It was a different time,' she said.

'Love is love regardless of time or place,' Charlie countered. 'I saw the way Jack and Amy looked at each other. I'd recognise that tell-tale look of love anywhere. It's the same one we had for each other.'

'Is it now,' Kitty said knowingly. 'They've not known each other that long.'

'Neither did we. But I knew. I knew I loved you.'

'I still have that look,' Kitty said. 'Do you?'

'Of course. You were the love of my life.' Charlie put the tea towel down after drying the final mug. 'You still are.'

Kitty dried her hands and softly touched Charlie's face. 'We've lost so much time. How do we get it back?'

He shook his head. 'We can't. But we can make every day count from now until we grow very old.'

'We are very old,' Kitty teased.

'I mean older. Much older.'

Kitty laughed and then Charlie put his hand in his pocket and pulled out a small box.

Kitty looked at the box as Charlie lifted the lid. Inside was a delicate diamond ring. She inhaled sharply. 'Oh, Charlie.'

'I never asked you back then. Not properly.'

Kitty's heart filled with overwhelming love but she was lost for words.

'But if I ask you now,' Charlie took the ring from the box and placed it on Kitty's ring finger, 'will you say yes?'

She smiled as her eyes met his. 'Ask me,' she said, 'and I'll tell you.'

'Gran and Charlie get their happy ending after all,' Amy cried in the farmhouse kitchen that evening as they toasted the news with Champagne, all of them invited round for an impromptu celebration.

'I can't say I'm surprised,' Caroline chimed in. 'It was meant to be. Do you think either of us will find a love like that?' Caroline said as an aside to Amy.

'I'm not sure I want one quite like that,' Amy replied. 'To be in love with someone and they leave, and in their place is only heartbreak and pain?' She shook her head.

'I think that's sort of what happened with you and Jack, isn't it?'

Amy baulked, giving her sister a look that said *be quiet*.

'Do you have any idea of wedding plans?' Alison asked.

'We did have some idea,' Kitty said. 'Nothing too flashy. Just a simple wedding. We've both been married before so we don't want to overegg the pudding. And we are aware we are slightly over the hill for a big white wedding. Neither of us wants anything like that. We just want our nearest and dearest to join us for a simple ceremony at the local church followed by a small gathering here.'

'That sounds perfect. Can I make the wedding cake?' Amy volunteered.

'Yes, I would love that. But only if you call it a wedding present. We don't want gifts so don't go spending all your hard-earned money on trinkets.'

'Caroline told us that you were thinking of ramping up

the catering side of your business,' Charlie said. 'If you're up to it, we wondered if the two of you would like to cater for the wedding. We'll pay you girls, of course. Only if you feel you can manage it. And if you want to. It's not a sit-down dinner. We don't want anything like that. Picky things on trays. Buffet food, that kind of thing. Hopefully very simple.'

Amy smiled. 'We can do picky things on trays and buffet food.' Her mind buzzed with excitement at the sort of thing she might be able to plan. 'Do you have a date?' she asked casually.

'We thought in three weeks,' Charlie said.

'Three weeks?' Amy sat up straight. 'Three weeks?' She struggled to keep the shock from her voice.

Kitty laughed. 'It gives us enough time for the banns to be read in church. If it's too much like hard work for you girls, just say.'

'No, it's fine,' Amy said, throwing her sister a desperate look. Caroline looked back at her just as desperately.

Kitty smiled. 'Are you sure? We can just get Waitrose platters?'

Amy jumped in. 'No you won't. We can manage the catering. And the cake,' she said.

'Only if you're sure. We're not as young as we once were,' Charlie said. 'We don't need a year to plan a service and a party, like all the young folk seem to these days.'

'The only problem *might* be in finding bridesmaid dresses in that sort of time,' Kitty said. 'I was thinking something elegant, simple, off the peg, perhaps a cocktail dress that could be worn again.'

'Who needs bridesmaid dresses?' Amy asked.

'I thought both of my granddaughters, if you'd like to be?'

Amy and Caroline both whooped.

'Really? I've never been a bridesmaid before,' Caroline said jubilantly. 'Thanks, Gran.'

'Me neither,' Amy confessed. 'I would love that. It would be such a privilege.'

'And you, Alison, would you be my maid of honour?'

'Oh, Mum,' Alison said with a tear in her eye. 'I would love to.'

'Now, what time is it in Iowa?' Charlie asked when the women had finished discussing wedding cake ideas. 'I'm off to make a phone call if you'll all excuse me. I need to tell Jack and Emmett they've got a wedding to attend in three weeks.'

'Is Jack in Iowa?' Amy asked far too casually. 'I thought he was in New York.'

'He went home for a bit to be with Emmett,' Charlie said, moving towards the telephone in the study.

Amy could feel the women's eyes on her. She knew they were all itching to ask her about Jack. And every time his name was mentioned they looked directly at her, utterly hopeful that she would confess her feelings for him aloud. But all she could think about was that in three weeks' time Jack would return and she had no idea what that was going to do to her.

The days flew by in the lead-up to the wedding. Alison took Kitty shopping in Ipswich for a suitable outfit for the bride but Kitty didn't like anything. Amy and Caroline went shopping in shifts for matching bridesmaids' outfits. Neither of them liked what the other chose and having been given carte blanche by Kitty to choose something they loved, in the end they compromised on a black cocktail dress with a pale pink silk bow round the middle. And then Amy glimpsed a beautiful pale yellow skirt suit. She thought how wonderful her gran would look wearing it and took a chance. It was a risk but, as yet, Kitty hadn't chosen anything and the big day loomed.

Amy drove straight to Kitty's to show her all the outfits. Her gran looked at the black satin dresses and made an uncertain face. 'Black?'

When Amy tried it on with a pair of glossy nude heels and tied the sash round the middle, Kitty smiled. 'Oh that's perfect, very elegant. And you can wear it again.'

Amy turned, pulling out the pale yellow skirt suit from its carrier. 'If you hate it, I can get a refund. But try it on and see what you think. They'll also take it in or up or let it out for you if you need, so if it's not quite right we can sort it. If you like it, that is.'

Kitty went off to change and emerged looking a bit nervous, smoothing the outfit down. 'What do you think?' Kitty asked.

'Oh, Gran,' Amy said breathlessly. 'You look marvellous. So pretty. Do you like it?'

'I love it,' Kitty replied. You clever thing. Do you know, I had a dress this colour when I was young.' Kitty moved to the full-length mirror standing next to her dresser and turned herself slowly, taking in her reflection. 'I went to a dance in it, with Charlie, at the airbase. We danced to Glenn Miller,' she reminisced. 'I'd never heard him before. He was wonderful.'

In Amy's mind, she heard the melodic beat of swing music, remembered dancing to Glenn Miller with Jack at the Heritage Day. She remembered the warm feel of his hands on her as they danced, being on the grass with him drinking and watching the world go by, the kiss under the tree before he left.

301

Kitty smiled at Amy before turning back to the mirror. 'It's a beautiful outfit, Amy. This is it. This is the one. Thank you.'

CHAPTER 43

The wedding came round quicker than Amy could believe. Being both a bridesmaid and one half of a catering team was proving trickier than she had imagined as they unloaded cakes, sandwiches, various cold cuts and other tray-food covered in cling film into the little van before going back and loading up again.

The crockery, cutlery, glasses and drinks had already gone over to the farmhouse and Caroline was locking up behind them as they made the final run. They'd gone over the timings for the wedding day multiple times and had hired in some silver service students from the local catering college to serve Champagne and keep the food moving between the guests.

Kitty and Charlie had invited more guests over the past two weeks. Kitty's bridge club, gardening club and book club friends were now coming as was her old friend Susan, who was making the trip back from her home in Wales especially. Great-Aunty Janie wasn't well enough to fly over from South Carolina but had sent a large bunch of flowers and had promised to catch up over the phone with Kitty this week. Charlie was chuffed that some of his friends from Iowa were making the trip over from the States to see him get married. His friend Ray, who had accompanied Charlie over from the States originally, had been ecstatic to discover the wonderful reunion that had taken place the day he'd been visiting his granddaughter. He would be at the wedding too.

Amy pushed some items back to keep them secure and went to close the van door as she loaded up more items from the tearoom kitchen.

Behind her, a courier van pulled up. 'Can you take this before you go?' the driver asked.

She looked at the size of the parcel – it wasn't huge. 'Put it in the back, I'll take it with me.' Was it something she'd ordered for today? She couldn't remember.

'Right,' Amy said to the catering college team – who were unloading the van with her and Caroline – when she arrived back on site at her gran's house. 'We'll be back from the church by half past one and then it's drinks first and canapés—'

'They know, Amy,' Caroline said. 'They know. We all know. We've gone through this five times.'

'Okay. I know. Sorry. I just want it to be perfect.'

'It will be,' Caroline said. 'Everything's sorted. Don't worry.'

Kitty, Amy, Caroline and Alison stood outside the church, waiting. There was a faint chill in the air, the summer having long since left, heralding the start of autumn when there was as much chance of cloud as there was of sun. Amy was grateful for the matching baby-pink cashmere shawls Kitty had purchased for them. Soon autumn would make way for winter and then Christmas would be here and the village would look so different. But as the sunshine slowly slid from behind a cloud, crowning Kitty in a halo of light, the vicar came out to tell them he was struggling to get some of Charlie's friends to sit down so they were delayed by a few minutes. Having not spoken to Charlie since he set off for England months ago, his friends were trying to glean as many details from him about how he'd found his lost wartime love after all these years.

'I've had to get Charlie's grandson to start gently manhandling them in the direction of the pews,' the vicar said. 'Won't be long now. I'll pop back out and give you the nod when we're ready.'

'Jack's arrived just in time then,' Caroline said pointedly to Amy.

'His flight was delayed,' Kitty replied, brushing down her pale yellow skirt. 'I'm pleased he made it in time. Charlie would have been devastated if not.'

Amy breathed in, breathed out. In all the frenzy about the wedding and the catering arrangements, she'd tried but failed to put the impending arrival of Jack completely out of her mind.

It had been months and she and Jack hadn't messaged, hadn't spoken at all. She'd deemed it for the best and clearly so had he, but now he was here, and Amy didn't know how to behave. Would it be awkward? Were they friends, were they not? Were they going to pick up where they left off and then she'd be confused all over again, just like last time?

Alison turned to her daughters. 'Oh, my lovely girls, look at you both.'

The girls reciprocated compliments to Alison and then

turned to their gran. Kitty was fumbling with the petals of her bouquet.

'Stop it, Gran,' Amy said gently. 'Everything is exactly as it's supposed to be.'

'Sorry,' Kitty said. 'I don't know why I'm so nervous.'

'It's going to be wonderful,' Caroline said.

'It already is,' Kitty replied happily.

'You look phenomenal,' Amy chipped in.

'Thank you,' Kitty said absently, looking up at the church spire. 'I'm reminded of your grandfather, today. I married Christopher here.'

Amy and Caroline exchanged glances.

'It's happy memories,' Kitty clarified. 'Nothing sad.'

'He'd approve,' Alison said. 'He'd never have wanted you to be unhappy in later life.'

Kitty smiled sadly. 'I know. And I am so happy again with Charlie. I only hope Christopher is looking down on me and giving us his blessing.'

'I know he is,' Alison replied.

The door opened and the vicar appeared. He gave them a big thumbs-up.

'Oh my word,' Kitty said as she moved forward. 'Everyone's going to be looking at me.'

'That's the idea, Gran,' Amy said.

Kitty turned to her granddaughters and gave a huge smile that made her eyes twinkle. 'Here we go then.'

Amy had been expecting the wedding march but instead the organist was playing a lovely, slow melodic classical piece that seemed to calm the church and the trio of women as they made their way one by one down the aisle.

Kitty led, looking resplendent in her pale yellow outfit as she walked past the smiling congregation. Alison

306

followed, with Caroline after her and then Amy. And at the front of the church Charlie stood waiting. His face lit up with a smile so wide it made Amy's heart lift. Next to him stood his best man, Emmett, and in the front pew stood Jack, looking directly at Kitty with an expression of happiness that matched the rest of the small congregation. And then Jack glanced at Amy and smiled. Amy's stomach knotted. He still looked as handsome as ever, clean-shaven, perfectly groomed and dazzling in a dark blue suit and white shirt.

They took their seats in the front pews and Amy tried her hardest not to look at Jack across the aisle. Seeing him again stirred up emotions she didn't know she'd been hiding from herself. She could hear his deep voice as he sang during the hymns; out of the corner of her eye she saw him turn the pages of his hymn sheets and adjust his tie. He turned slowly and looked at her and she looked directly at him and Amy felt her breath leave her body.

Her grandmother looked radiant and Charlie looked handsome in his suit. Amy couldn't hold the tears in as, nearly seventy years after meeting each other, Charlie and Kitty finally said, 'I do.'

As the girls exited the row, Jack and Amy fell into step alongside each other. His presence was suddenly intoxicating. She could smell his aftershave, clean and lightly citrusy.

'Hi,' he said.

Every part of her tingled in his proximity. 'Hi,' she said back, glancing up at him,

'How've you been?' he asked as they fell into the throng and walked towards the church doors, towards the sunshine.

'Good,' she said, hating how awkward she'd become. 'You?'

He laughed. He knew it was awkward too, Amy could tell. 'I've been good too,' he said.

The ice was broken.

She could do this. They could be friends.

He smiled down at her. She had no idea what to say next, or what he was going to say.

'Would you excuse me?' he asked suddenly, surprising her. 'I was so late getting here there are some people I've got to say hi to.'

'Right, yes, of course,' Amy replied and watched him as he went over to shake hands with some of Charlie's friends in the churchyard.

'How was that?' Caroline whispered as they waited for a moment to get near their gran and Charlie to say their congratulations.

Amy thought. 'Awful, actually. I feel tongue-tied. I just don't know what to say to him.'

'Then don't,' Caroline suggested. 'Talk to other people instead. There's plenty of them. You can probably spend the whole day avoiding him if you want.'

Amy glanced over at Jack. Was that what she wanted? Did she want to avoid him? No. Quite the opposite. But he seemed to be quite happy avoiding her. He was still laughing along with a group of Charlie's friends. Amy was torn. She told herself that as they'd spoken to each other, even though it was only a few words, it would be easy. But now it felt anything but easy. He'd go home after the celebrations and then it would all go back to normal. For now she would enjoy the party, keep an eye on the catering staff, make sure everything was exactly as it should be. She could focus her energies on that. This was her second big catering event and being hands-off wasn't really an option, although with the addition of the staff from the catering college, Amy thought that if today went without a hitch she was going to start looking at expanding properly. It was time. She'd been putting it off for too long. On Monday, after a rest, she'd start looking for a commercial kitchen.

'Everything okay? Anything I can do?' she asked one of the catering staff as she encountered him carrying a box of wine back from the van once they were back at the house.

He gestured towards the vehicle. 'There's one box left in the van. You could grab it if you don't mind?

Amy nodded, heading for the van, happy for the distraction. The remaining box was the one the courier had dropped off earlier. She started opening it and began pulling out bubble wrap. She had no idea what this was. She looked inside and saw something large, wrapped tightly in protective wrapping. A note was stuck to the wrapping. Amy opened the envelope.

> *Amy,*
> *Call it a late birthday present,*
> *See you at the wedding of the year.*
> *Jack*
> *x*

Amy's heart beat loudly in her chest as she re-read the short missive. There was no opportunity for hidden subtext in a note that short. She traced the letters with her finger. He had nice handwriting. She held on to the item for a few seconds before opening it. She wasn't sure what she was going to find under the bubble wrap. She wasn't sure how she felt. He had obviously liked her, and she had really liked him.

She moved the bubble wrap aside and put it next to her in the back of the van, turning the frame round so she could see the front. She smiled when she saw it. It was the picture Jack had taken of her, in the field by her grandmother's house. His signature, Jack Young, was on the mount.

In the photo the wheat was high in the field – unlike now when the harvest had long since been and gone – and Amy's hair whipped out behind her as if a gust of wind had just taken it, or as if she'd turned round quickly to look at Jack behind the camera.

She moved away from the van and looked at the field and out towards the oak tree. She could picture Jack's smiling face that day, her laughter and embarrassment at having been photographed unawares, images on a camera screen being shown to her.

She heard the crunch of shoes on the gravel and looked up to see two of Kitty's younger book club friends sneaking round the side of the house for a cigarette. They waved at her and she waved back but Amy didn't want company. She just needed a few minutes by herself. She held on to the picture tightly, trying to work out where she could go. If she went to hide anywhere in the house she'd have to get past wedding guests and so she looked to the field and towards the oak tree, walking purposefully towards it, still clutching the picture. She just wanted to look at it in private. Amy reached the safety of the tree and put it down, resting it against the trunk and looking at it thoughtfully.

From the house the slight sound of music drifted across. She recognised the tune. A breeze picked up and carried the music away but the rest of the bars sounded in her head. 'Moonlight Serenade' by Glenn Miller. It came to her suddenly and she smiled. She and Kitty had talked about

310

this tune the other day. Amy had danced to it with Jack. She remembered being close to him while they'd danced. He'd smelled lovely, just like he had today in the church. She remembered the way she had felt, her head resting on his chest, his hand on her back, the other holding hers. Her heart had raced then, the way it was racing now. Seeing him again now, only a few short weeks after she'd been telling herself they should just be friends, it was too much. And the gift, what did that mean? Was she reading too much into it? If he did still care about her, why hadn't he messaged her? Although she hadn't messaged him either.

She thought it would all just go away. As she looked at the picture, and at the note he'd written, she knew she didn't want it to all go away. She remembered the kiss they had shared on her doorstep and right here by this tree before he'd left. Oh God, she liked him, she knew she liked him. It was all such a mess.

And then she heard someone behind her and she stopped still as she saw Jack walking towards her. He was over halfway through the field. In the autumn sunshine he'd removed his dark blue jacket and had thrown it over his shoulder, holding it up with a finger. His tie had been discarded and he'd opened the top button of his shirt to cool down. She could barely cope with that. He was coming to find her, wasn't he? That had to mean something. Oh please let it mean something.

He stopped a short distance from her. Amy's heart thudded.

He looked past her, towards the picture positioned against the tree, smiled at what he saw. 'You got it then?'

It was now or never. She had to be brave. She had to tell him how she felt or she was going to lose him and she'd never know what it would be like to be loved by and to love Jack Young. Because he had left such an impression on her heart, she knew it had to be love. What else could it be? She opened her mouth to speak, to dare to put her heart on the line, but he got there first.

'Amy, I've missed you so much,' he said. Amy's heart lifted and she smiled widely.

'Really?' she whispered.

He looked pained and couldn't meet her eye. 'I can't even explain how happy I am when I'm with you. And how awful I've felt these past few months since I left. But if you don't feel the same way, then . . .'

'I do,' she said. 'I do feel the same way.'

He looked directly at her. 'Shit, really?' he said in surprise, making her laugh and then he laughed in return.

'You didn't message me?' she said.

'Neither did you,' he said, stepping forward.

She closed the distance between them. 'It's so complicated. You live there and I live here and as if that wasn't mad enough, your grandad just married my gran.'

'Yeah, it's all kinds of crazy,' Jack agreed, his smile widening as he stepped close to her.

She took in every part of his face. The feeling of love hit her so unexpectedly hard now he was here, standing in front of her, that she couldn't keep it to herself.

'I think I love you,' she said helplessly. An even wider smile spread over Jack's face and she returned it before her face fell again as she realised something. 'But how is this going to work?' She gestured towards the farmhouse. 'With them?' She didn't care what he said to this, not really. She wasn't letting him go again.

He smiled, cupping her face in his hands. 'I wouldn't worry about them. They're rooting for us so hard I can

312

practically hear them cheering from all the way over there.'

'But you live so far away,' she pleaded as the real obstacle presented itself.

He looked around as if assessing his surroundings. He shrugged. 'England's not so bad. I know a certain tearoom owner who manages to sell a lot of my photos and who I happen to have fallen in love with. And I'm sure, with a little encouragement from her I could happily spend a lot more time here. If she wanted me to stay.'

Amy's elation was palpable. She'd never been this happy. 'Oh,' she said, leaning in to kiss him again. 'She *definitely* wants that.'

AUTHOR'S NOTE

The medieval Suffolk village of Lavenham changed geographically so much in my novel that it didn't feel fair to call it Lavenham. But those familiar with the village will recognise it. The Duck pub, where Kitty lived in her youth, is obviously The Swan Hotel, and if you're lucky enough to visit, do look in the Airman's Bar where American wartime servicemen signed their names on the wall.

Although I originally wrote *The Lost Memories* in 2019, I went back to it in 2023 when I decided I wanted it to be my sixth published historical novel. In the ensuing time I was so pleased to see that in 2022 a memorial weekend actually occurred at Lavenham Airfield, including the unveiling of a memorial dedicated to over two hundred personnel from the United States Army Air Force 487th Bomb Group who were based at Lavenham and who gave their lives. The memorial is a replica of the station identifier – a large panel on the ground showing the letters LV for Lavenham on a black background, which would have been visible to returning aircrews, confirming to them which airfield they were approaching. There is also a memorial plaque in Lavenham's Market Place, which is what sparked the original idea.

RESEARCH & BIBLIOGRAPHY

The Cambridge American Cemetery
https://www.abmc.gov/Cambridge

Rougham Control Tower Aviation Museum
https://rctam94th.co.uk/

Land Girl: A Manual for Volunteers in the Women's Land Army 1941
Wilfred Edward Shewell-Cooper, Amberley Publishing, 2011

Women at War 1939-1945: The Home Front
Carol Harris, Sutton Publishing Ltd, 2010

With Wings as Eagles, The Eighth Air Force in World War II
Philip Kaplan, Skyhorse, 2017

The American Bomber Boys, The US 8th Air Force at War
Martin Bowman, Amberley Books, 2012

Suffolk Airfields in the Second World War
Graham Smith, Countryside Books, 1997

ACKNOWLEDGEMENTS

Thanks to my lovely editor Rachel Hart for helping to make this book stronger. And to all the team at Avon for bringing it into the world.

Thanks to my fabulous agent Becky Ritchie, as always. And to Oli Munson who's been diligently holding my hand this past year while Becky's been on maternity leave. And to all at A.M. Heath's foreign rights department for continuing to bring my novels to readers across the world. Thanks also to Jack Sargeant, as usual, for guiding me through the joy of foreign rights contracts and tax forms.

Thanks to Steve, Emily and Alice for putting up with me when I disappear for months on end upstairs to my office, emerging in the kitchen for dinner and a glass of wine before I scurry away again. Likewise to Dad for your love and encouragement and all your plane and war knowledge! It's very handy having someone in the family as obsessed with WWII as I am and who also happens to be a pilot. It made writing this book a bit of a breeze!

To Mum, special thanks for being so wonderful in general and for all the school pick ups. (And for always recommending my books to anyone who'll listen.) To Luke, Cassie, Natalie, Nicky and Sarah – thanks for all the love and fun!

Super thanks to Mandy Robotham, Jenny Ashcroft, Iona Grey, Amanda Geard and Nikola Scott for immense encouragement and support. Likewise to the Romantic Novelists' Association Chelmsford Chapter and to our offshoot Write Club. Peter, Snoops, Tracy, Sue, Nic, Karen . . . big, big thanks for forensic analysis of each other's chapters. And thanks to Savvy Writers on Facebook for always being a great sounding board.

But, as ever, the biggest thanks goes to you the reader for purchasing this novel or borrowing it from the library. I so love being tagged in photos of readers holding a copy or locating one of my novels in a bookshop. It makes my day. Thanks to those of you that do this and super thanks to those of you that take the time to review on Amazon or Goodreads or both. Reviews (and pre-orders of the next book, hint hint) mean the absolute world to authors.

Join my newsletter via my website, where every now and again I remember to actually send a newsletter and host various bookish giveaways. Or come and say hi to me on social media. I'll always say hi back!

Lorna xx

www.lornacookauthor.com

 /LornaCookWriter
 /LornaCookAuthor
 /LornaCookAuthor
 /LornaCookAuthor

On the eve of a world war, a forbidden love will blossom in the garden of a stately home, where one young woman will make a choice that will change her life forever . . .

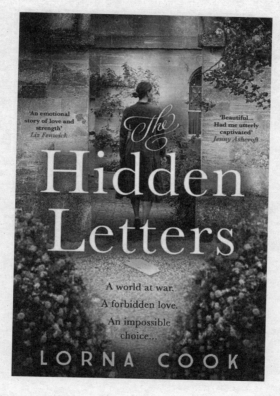

If you loved *The Lost Memories*, then don't miss this epic tale of love, war and the strength of the human spirit.

Available now.

1941, Nazi-occupied Paris: In the glamorous
Ritz hotel there is a woman with a
dangerous secret . . .

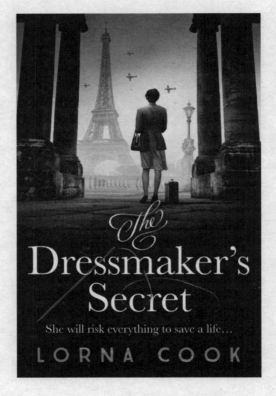

A sweeping, romantic and heart-breaking tale set
in WWII Paris.

Available now.

1943: The world is at war, and the villagers of Tyneham must leave their homes behind . . .

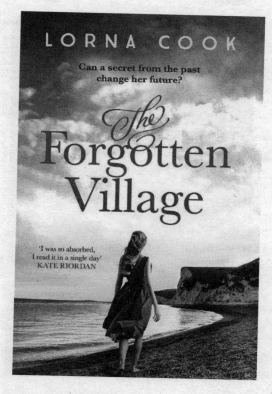

Don't miss Lorna Cook's #1 bestselling debut novel.

Available now.

Can one promise change the fate of two women decades apart?

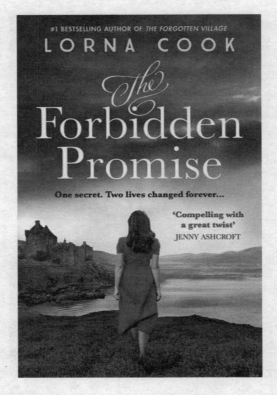

A sweeping wartime tale of love and secrets that will have you hooked from the very first page.

Available now.

A world at war. One woman will risk everything.
Another will uncover her story.

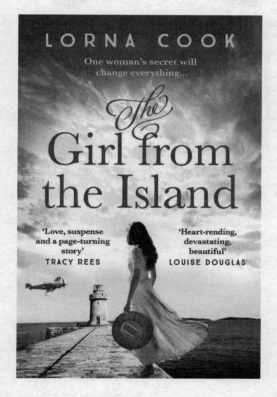

A timeless wartime story of love, loss and survival
that will stay with you long after you have
turned the final page.

Available now.